At Water's End

A Evan Mason Adventure

By **J**ames **M**aureen

James Maureen

This is a work of fiction. Names, characters, businesses, places, events, locales, and incidents are either the product of the author's imagination or used in a fictitlous manner. Any resemblance to actual persons, living or dead, or actual events is purely coincidental.

Copyright © 2019, James Maureen

Treasure **B**asement **P**ublishing
Post Office Box 3043
Issaquah, WA 98027

All Rights Reserved

ISBN: 978-1-6924-0736-0

At Water's End

Dedication

To my wife and two sons for putting up with my odd behavior while creating this book, and for also providing the encouragement to keep going.

Thank You so much!

And to Wayne Stinnett for the courage to dare to dream of being a successful published author, and then telling others how he did it. Thank you for the inspiration.

James Maureen

Table of Contents

Nautical Terminology . . .   1
Puget Sound Map   2
Prologue   3
Chapter 1   16
Chapter 2   25
Chapter 3   31
Chapter 4   35
Chapter 5   39
Chapter 6   47
Chapter 7   55
Chapter 8   61
Chapter 9   67
Chapter 10   74
Chapter 11   79
Chapter 12   86
Chapter 13   95
Chapter 14 104
Chapter 15 118
Chapter 16 126
Chapter 17 139
Chapter 18 151
Chapter 19 157
Chapter 20 163
Chapter 21 173
Chapter 22 183
Chapter 23 193
Chapter 24 200
Chapter 25 206
Chapter 26 215

At Water's End

Table of Contents

(continued)

Chapter 27 224
Chapter 28 233
Chapter 29 242
Chapter 30 246
Chapter 31 254
Chapter 32 263
Chapter 33 272
Chapter 34 282
Chapter 35 286
Chapter 36 295
Chapter 37 306
Chapter 38 317
Chapter 39 326
Chapter 40 335
Chapter 41 342
Epilogue 345

James Maureen

At Water's End

Nautical Terminology

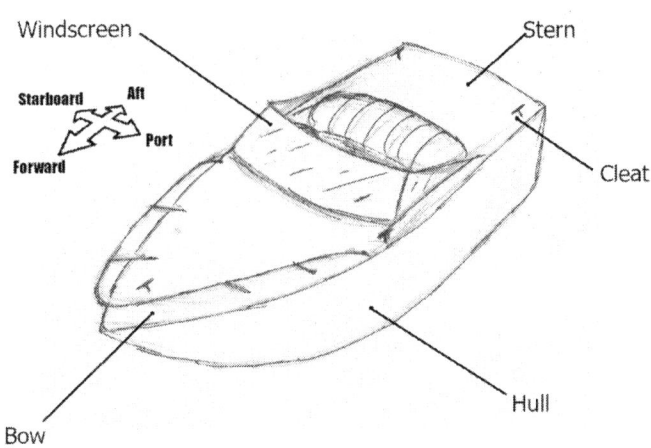

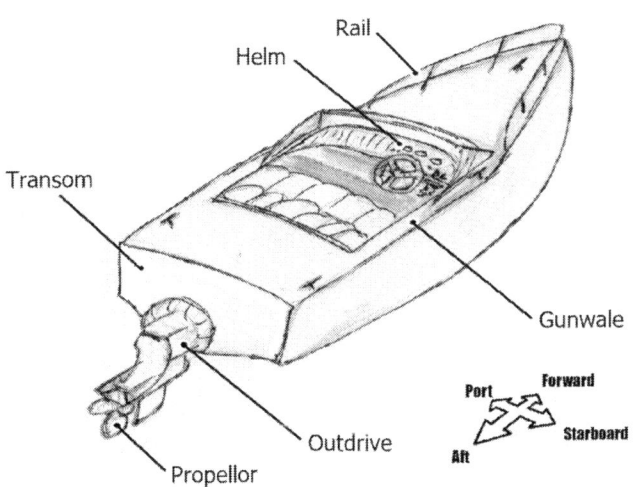

James Maureen

Puget Sound Regional Map

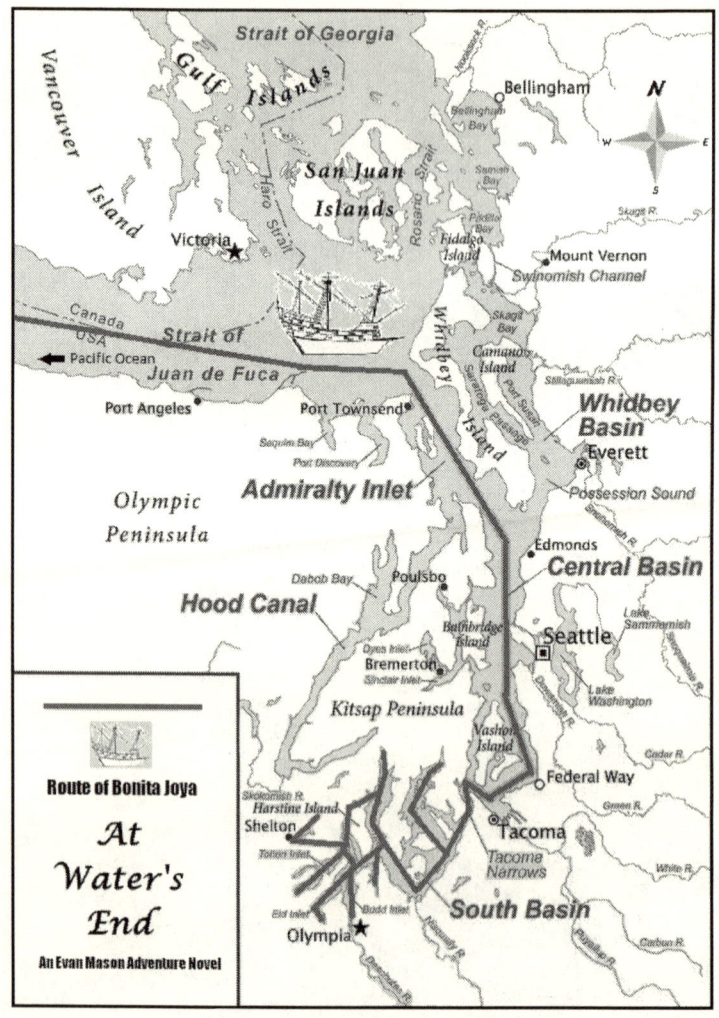

Prologue

Pacific Northwest coastline

Modern day Washington State, USA

(1791)

The Captain stood on the bridge of the one hundred and ten foot Spanish Treasure Frigate named Bonita Joya, or Pretty Jewel, looking south and aft over the stern rail into the twenty knot wind. The blowing wind was filling the ship's sails and slowly they moved ahead on an almost due north heading. The briny smell of the sea was all around him as a fine seawater mist exploded into the air as the hull pounded the waves cresting at nearly six feet. Looking to his left, he briefly locked eyes with the helmsman struggling with the four foot wooden ship's wheel. It was clear the helmsman's eyes were saying "I need help". The Captain turned to his left and stepped forward to grab ahold of two open hand grips to help steady the rudder against the swirling current. Captain Anthony Ramirez yelled for a crewman to replace him at the wheel. On the deck below the bridge, crewman Harry Garcia heard the Captain's order and was waiting for just such a chance to be at the helm of Bonita Joya. Since boarding for the first time in Spain, Harry had hoped to learn more about ships and take on more responsibility. Harry loved sailing. Doing it for his country and getting the adventure of a lifetime was more than he could ask for. Setting aside the work at hand, Harry made his way to the bridge to take over for the Captain. It was not easy with the ship pitching and rolling in both directions at once, and he stumbled numerous times, but never lost his balance.

Less than twenty seconds after Captain Ramirez called for help, Harry was at his side ready for orders. The Captain instructed Harry to take the ship's wheel and hold fast. He told him to take his instructions from the helmsman, patted him on the shoulder, gave him a look that said "you can do this", and then quickly disappeared down the five steps to the main deck of the ship. Harry took his position on the left of the helmsman, Roberto Alvars, and they both gripped the wheel and held on. The swirling current was due to a flood tide, which was exactly opposite of Bonita Joya's heading. Maintaining course was a challenging assignment in the conditions, but the determination on the faces of both Harry and Roberto was resolute.

On the aft deck, anything not lashed down was moving. The fore deck was in better shape, but with the sails flying a broad reach in strong gusty winds to make the run through the passage, there was a danger of being slammed by a flapping sail, or whipped by a loose line. Captain Ramirez surveyed the state of his ship and took pause to consider the situation.

After a very long voyage south, the direction turned north after rounding the southernmost point and they followed a course along the western coast of the New World. In their present location, they could be considered in violation of the Nootka Sound Treaty since just last year, the treaty had awarded England claim to these waters. Not one to normally abide by imagery lines sketched by a cartographer miles away, he had carefully sailed his desired course. As the summer season in their current location provided long days, they took advantage and explored a large inland waterway. It had taken many days for them to sail east, downwind along the waterway that eventually provided essentially a "tee" requiring a Captain's course decision. He had chosen south, and they continued to sail with the wind. Navigation south proved to be a formidable challenge as the waters were sprinkled with both large and small islands and many rocky outcroppings. He had wanted to be able to navigate a return route should it be required, and as such, followed the shoreline off the port side of the ship. For the return trip, if needed, he would simply put that same shoreline off the starboard side.

That was a good plan in theory. Unknown to him at the time was that the winds that had carried them south so easily a few months ago would not really change direction. And now the wind, plus an incredible current in the only passage back north, now has them trapped. The waterway he'd taken had tapered narrower and narrower until finally coming to a series of dead ends. The crew had been disappointed with the discovery, but that's what exploring is all about. So they had enjoyed the long days, made repairs and tried to provision the ship with local wildlife consisting of fish and venison they were able to smoke and cure.

As the days started growing shorter, the weather turned more cloudy, rainy and grey. Following a period of over two weeks without seeing the sun, he had declared that it was time to secure the ship for the voyage back to the ocean and to southern waters for the winter ahead. Sailing against the wind started out fine. Tack back and forth and try to hold close into the wind. The procedure worked for a time, but thinking back now, there had been a passage on the way south where the ship had seemed to be going faster, but not really appearing so relative to the water. At the time, it had been a curious sensation and he wrote it off to an optical illusion caused by the towering cliffs on either side of him. Now, he knew that they had ridden a flood tide on a downwind sail through the only gateway back to his home and his family.

Recently, the wind had finally made a shift in direction in their favor, and after numerous attempts to try and run the passage into the wind, even sailing with an ebb tide, this seemed like his best chance to get through the passage before winter set in. Right now, the sailing was rough, but manageable. They had seen worse on the open seas, but here in the narrow passage they had little room to maneuver. Maintaining their course was very important and he was glad he had two crewmen at the wheel. With that small comfort in mind, he steadied himself and moved through the buffeting wind toward his cabin.

On the bridge, Roberto and Harry were holding on for their lives. With the wind pushing the ship around, and the current swirling around the hull, the ship's rudder was under tremendous pressure. The crewman at the wheel knew the outcome if they could not hold course and get through this passage while they had favorable wind. A strong wind to be sure, but it was in the right direction. So they looked at each other, gritted their teeth, and gripped the wheel's hand holds even harder. The wind was howling around the masts of the ship, through the railings and across the deck. Standing at the wheel with their backs to the wind, they were wet from the sea spray, but were glad there was no rain. A surge of water slammed the ship on the aft starboard quarter and the ship shuddered as it took the pounding.

Below the waterline, the rudder also experienced the pounding of the surge. At the wheel, Roberto gripped hard and readied himself as the first of the water hit the ship. Harry being new to the steering of the ship, was unprepared for the forces of the rudder back driving the wheel, and the wheel was ripped from his hands as it rotated to the left. Fortunately Roberto had been prepared, and was able to mostly hold the wheel and limit the wheel spin. Harry quickly regained his balance and lunged for the wheel. Grabbing ahold and getting a firm stance, he helped Roberto bring the wheel to the right and get the ship back on course. Just slightly aft and below them, near the top of the rudder post, a hairline fracture had started to develop. In the maelstrom of wind and waves, the telltale cracking sound of the rudder post went unnoticed by the men at the wheel.

Captain Ramirez had made the difficult traverse to his cabin for two reasons. Secure the ship's log, and secure the sample of precious cargo that the crew had found while enjoying the end of the summer, just south of where they now feared for their lives. Even with the wind blowing steady near twenty knots and gusting even higher, they were struggling to make headway against the strong current flowing through the passage. Most of the shoreline was inaccessible, particular here where steep rock cliffs lined both sides of the passage and towered over the ship. Once inside his cabin with the door closed, he pushed the bed mattress aside to reveal a hidden compartment that could only be accessed by breaking in, or pushing the hidden rod near the foot of the bed frame to release the access panel. He wasted no time and pushed the rod in until hearing the familiar click indicating the panel was free to be lifted from the recess. Reaching into the compartment, he found the log book and grabbing it firmly, lifted it from its storage spot. He then sat down at a small table and while the ship was being tossed by the waves and wind, he set about to try and inscribe an entry.

"The onset of winter in the northern most portion of our journey has left us in dire need of divine intervention. In eagerness to explore the region, we sailed east along a great waterway with the open ocean behind us. A fork in the waterway was encountered after three nights past, and I hence ordered the crew to steer a course south. Favorable conditions accompanied the trip south, unfortunately only a dead end did we discover there. Now finding ourselves trapped by unfavorable winds with strong opposing currents, this 20th day in September, in the year of our Lord, 1791, we attempt an escape from probable death by freezing or starvation. The seas are wrought with peril and sailing in the uncertain weather conditions would not normally be attempted. The wind direction is to the north for the first time in months, and the strong wind may be enough to make it through this very narrow passage where so far, overcoming the strength and speed of the south moving current has proved to be beyond our ability. Two men stand fast at the wheel to steady the rudder against the turbulent waters and to maintain our course north. A large oak chest has been lashed by chain to the mast base in the forward hold. The chest is filled with raw gold extracted from the river that empties into the bay at the far south end of the waterway we now sail. Heavy seas and gusting wind conditions warrant taking precautionary action."

Closing the log book, the Captain let his weary eyes droop shut, and he breathed deeply while thinking about his options. There were really only two. Choose to turn back and wait for both the wind and the tide to be favorable, or push on and hope that his crew can manage a straight downwind course in the strong gusts and swirling seas. Feeling the weight of being responsible for their predicament, Captain Anthony Ramirez opened his eyes and they fell upon the small, ornate music box he had received from his wife before leaving on the voyage. Even in the midst of the rough movement of the ship, opening the lid of the music box provided a sweet melody that allowed him to recall the beauty and fragrant scent of his wife Sofia, and the happy times they had with their children before he had departed for the New World.

With a stronger sense of commitment to escaping the insane situation than ever before, he hurriedly closed the music box lid and tucked the log book into his jacket pocket. Reaching back into the hidden compartment, he extracted a handful of yellowish stones that he had wrapped in a soft cloth and he added that to his pocket as well. Spending the time to ensure that his topcoat was properly fastened and secure, he opened his cabin door and confidently walked out on to the ship's main deck and into the gusting winds.

Before returning to the helm, Captain Ramirez made his way to the forward hold to check that the chest of unprocessed gold nuggets lashed to the mast was secure. While he watched the chest, he noticed that the ship's movements caused it to move slightly, even with the restraints tightly wrapped around it. The padlock on the chest appeared as he had left it, but the Captain was taking the "trust but verify" approach. He lifted a section of leather cord from around his neck that held the padlock key and then opened the padlock and lock clasp, and lifted the top of the chest to verify the contents. Even in the low light, he was able to see that the gold still filled the chest nearly to the top. Reaching his left hand into the chest, he felt some comfort in the touch of the cool precious metal, and extracted a handful to get a better look. After about a minute, the Captain reluctantly closed the lid of the chest and firmly snapped the lock clasp back in place. He relocked the padlock and without looking back, walked out of the hold and made his way up and aft toward the helm.

The ship continued to be tossed by the heavy seas created by the wind and all thirty of the crew were on deck to make sure everything was lashed down, or to tend to the navigation of the ship. They had started the attempt to make it through the passage with a grey overcast sky in mid-afternoon, now the sun was starting to set and dusk was nearly upon them. Visibility and depth perception would soon be difficult when the object definition provided by shadows created from the small amount of light they did have began to disappear. Over and over, the lines holding the sails went tight, then loose, and snapped loudly when the sails billowed in the gusts as they moved downwind. At the helm, the Captain had made his way back to the wheel and had taken over for Harry to give him a break, and to get a sense of the steerage of the ship in the rough seas.

At the stern of the ship, just below the waterline and slightly forward of the transom, the rudder continued to be pounded by the swirling current and windblown waves. While the massive seven foot tall oak rudder took the brunt of the pounding, the rudder post that was part of the ship's steering system had to hold against the forces of the water hitting the rudder. Over the last few minutes, the fracture in the rudder post had gotten bigger. The rudder now started to move out of position slightly as the weakened rudder post began to twist. The result was a slight change in course to port.

There was still enough filtered light available from the darkening sky that the Captain was able to notice the slight change in the direction of the ship. He was immediately confused as he and Roberto had stood at the wheel maintaining their course north since he had taken over for Harry. As he pondered the strange situation, he felt the ship begin to roll at a different angle as it shouldered its way through the waves. He realized then that the ship was actually turning to port. He ordered Roberto to steer to starboard, still not sure why they were changing course. As he and Roberto started to turn the wheel to the right, they realized something in the steering mechanism had failed. While they were able to turn the wheel, it was binding, and they could not rotate it as fast as they needed to. As the ship cut at more of an angle across the waves, the ship started to roll more wildly at it crested each wave.

On the bridge, Harry had stepped forward to allow the Captain to take over and now held on for his life to the rail of the stairs that led down to the main deck. Harry watched the Captain and Roberto engage in a very animated discussion. He wanted to hear what was going on and released his grip on the rail in order to get closer. His timing could not have been worse. As Harry went to take his first step, the ship tilted to port and rode down the backside of a large wave. For Harry, the deck dropped away from his feet, and for a moment he hung weightless in the air. Then gravity took over and he dropped quickly to catch up to the tilting deck. With nothing to hang on to, Harry slid across the deck, slammed his back hard against the ship's outside port rail, and flipped over the rail falling into the icy cold water rushing by twelve feet below. The Captain and Roberto saw Harry flip over the rail, and both silently said a prayer, but they knew there was no saving Harry. Instead, they refocused their efforts to try and turn the ship so they could save themselves.

With the wind blowing to the north, and the current running strong to the south, Bonita Joya's failed rudder continued to turn the ship to the west. The Captain ordered the sails down, but it was too late. As the bow moved to port, the ship came abeam to the current and the ship's rudder became ineffective and could no longer control the direction of the ship. The wind was now blowing across the deck from port to starboard, and with the sails still up, the ship heeled over sharply to the north. The south running current aided in the heel over as it pushed the hull in the opposite direction that the wind was pushing the masts and sails. The sea on the starboard side was now very close to breaching the gunwale of the ship as the rail moved down to meet the water. The deck was tilting very steeply when a large wave swept over the starboard side and the force of the wave hitting the deck caused the ship to tilt over a little more.

Now every wave was crashing over the railing. The Captain and crew were thrown about the deck, with some of the men catapulted into the roiling water. The ship had now rotated ninety degrees and the masts and sails had touched the water. The strong current immediately swept the wet sails under the surface and that rotated the ship's keel up and out of the water. Almost at once, the weight of the ship's hull and the power of the current together caused the three masts to snap like toothpicks. There were now three gaping holes in the deck where the masts previously stood and the turbulent water shot through the holes with incredible force and quickly overwhelmed the ship. Not even two minutes had passed from the moment the Captain had noticed they were slightly off course until the ship, and all aboard, disappeared below the surface of sea.

Just one hundred yards south, Harry had witnessed the Bonita Joya alter course to the west after he had flipped over the side of the ship. He had been elated to see them coming about in order to rescue him from an almost certain death in the icy waters. He bobbed up and down struggling to stay afloat, and swallowed a bit more seawater each time a wave crashed against him. In between the waves crashing over his head, he saw the ship turn faster than he thought possible. Then he saw it tilt over at a very odd angle, and the port side of the ship rose out of the water to expose the keel to the cold wind blowing to the north. Seconds after that, the entire ship was gone. As Harry drifted south with the current, his thoughts turned to his crewmates, and the loss of the ship, and he realized that he had been careless by falling overboard, and in their attempt to save him, all has been lost.

Chapter 1

Northwestern Washington State, USA

(present day)

Evan checked his pressure gauge to verify that he had used almost half of the air in his standard sized SCUBA tank. Evan's dive buddy Michael's available pressure was reading about the same on his tank gauge. They'd been making this dive for years and almost always got their catch of Ling Cod, but so far, the normally slow moving bottom dwellers were fast enough when they needed to be to elude them. Often called the poor man's Halibut, Lingcod is a flavorful main course when cooked right, and they were determined to not leave empty handed. Having started their dive by wading in from the western shore, they were now at a depth of one hundred and twenty feet. Their bottom time was getting limited and they needed to make good use of the air they had left if they were going to secure dinner. Both carried their own Hawaiian slings at the ready and were scanning back and forth looking for their prey. In this particular area of Puget Sound, staying focused on the hunt can be challenging as it is easy to get distracted with plenty of sea life and history to look at.

They were diving just under the bridge in the Tacoma Narrows Strait in the southern portion of Puget Sound. A beautiful stretch of water to look at that is about a half mile wide and approximately ten miles in the north-south direction. The high rocky cliffs on both sides of the strait were formed by glacial activity years ago and are connected by one of the world's longest suspension bridges. Looming nearly two hundred feet above the water, the bridge deck provides a way for Washington State Route 16 to move vehicle traffic between Tacoma and the Kitsap Peninsula. The bridge hanging over their heads now was not the first of its kind. The first attempt at a bridge to cross the strait in 1940 lasted less than six months. Then one day in November, high winds roaring through the strait at a bad angle caused the bridge deck to fly like an airplane wing. That set up rise and fall undulations in the bridge deck between the suspension towers, and after a morning of small waves that were considered "normal", a series of larger gyrations over the course of an hour caused the bridge deck to crumble and collapse into the cold churning water below. Now, pieces of the old bridge known as "Galloping Gertie" are still at the bottom of Puget Sound where the remains form one of the largest man-made reefs in the world.

Evan and Michael had gotten an early start this Saturday in late September, and with nearly half of their dive complete, they could tell it was right around 9:00AM since the flood tide was slowing and would soon reverse. Evan had mapped out the timing so that they would change direction back toward shore when the tide turned slack, with better than half full tanks of air. In this way, even though the current is strong, by reversing direction with the tide change, they will return to the same point on the western shoreline that they got in the water, or very nearly. No fighting the current during the dive trying to maintain a straight out and in course, just a relaxed drift with the current.

Both Evan and Michael were familiar with the beauty of the Tacoma Narrows deep and knew it can be mesmerizing and one can sometimes forgets about the danger that can lurk just beyond the artificial illumination of the dive lights. A Pacific Northwest dive generally provides excitement in one way or another and this one would be no different. Today's visibility in the water was about thirty feet, a relatively small view in a very large body of water. Off to Evan's right loomed a very large chunk of concrete from the old bridge. They had been moving through other pieces of the old bridge while gliding just a few feet from the seafloor and this block was the biggest they had come across yet. It's common to see lots of red, blue and green in Northwest waters, but Evan thought he glimpsed the light reddish brown color of the suction cups of an octopus. Taking his dive knife out of the calf sheath, he reached over his head with his right hand and tapped the knife handle on his tank.

Michael immediately heard the ringing sound of metal on metal that carried so well through water.

With it tougher to locate the direction of a sound underwater, Michael was unsure where the noise was coming from, but with Evan's dive light glowing in the distance, he promptly made his way toward the light. Evan was pointing in the direction of a large piece of concrete that over the years, had been nearly covered by sea life. Using one of his many inventions, Evan displayed the word "octopus" on the screen of his forearm mounted waterproof device. About the size of a large smartphone, the DiveCom system uses some preloaded vocabulary and commands, but also whatever the diver wants to add. With the touch screen interface, it is easy to tap or sketch out commands on the screen that are associated to words or phrases. It's fast, and the clear communications provided by the system helps make diving safer. Evan already had "octopus" in the vocabulary database and the pattern was a simple "O". When Michael read the word on the DiveCom device display, he smiled as best he could with the regulator in his mouth, but it was his eyes that gave away his excited state.

While a surprise to sight a Giant Pacific octopus, it was not totally unexpected. The icy cold deep waters of the Tacoma Narrows Strait are known for sightings over the years, and with an almost fifteen foot arm span considered average for adults, these are the big boys. Not quite sure what to do as neither had ever encountered an octopus on their own turf before, Evan did a double tap on the DiveCom unit and the words "little heavier" were displayed. Evan and Michael both secured their slings and adjusted their buoyancy compensators to get a little less buoyant. Dropping ever so slightly, they could now better control their movements by touching the seafloor a little easier. Evan pushed a large button on the side of his DiveCom unit and the system switched into DRAW mode. He quickly sketched an overhead view of the concrete block with a mark on the backside where he thought the octopus might be. Not sure if they were coming across a hunting octopus or a possible den site, they didn't know how the giant would react. A hunter will probably flee, but if they surprise a den site, fleeing might be Evan and Michael's best option. Evan indicated on the screen that they would approach from either side of the concrete and attempt to get photos. Evan respected the giant cephalopods and did not want to shoot this one with anything but a camera.

Michael gave the accepted "OK" sign by touching the tips of his right thumb and index finger to form an "O". They shielded their dive lights to avoid flooding the area with so much light and then let their eyes adjust to the dimmer environment. With their underwater cameras at the ready, they each started to move around their respective side of the concrete block. As Evan moved closer to turning the corner of the concrete, he could indeed see that they had found a Giant Pacific octopus.

In the dim light, he could make out two large arms slowly moving through the water. Evan could also see the faint glow of Michael's light as he made his way around the other side of the concrete turned reef structure. It gave the silhouette of the arms an eerie gray green look, and sent tingles down Evan's spine. He advanced further to the corner and dared to take a peek around the edge. With a shot of adrenaline to his system, he gazed in sheer delight at the first Giant Pacific octopus he'd seen in the wild. After a few moments of enjoying the spectacle of the octopus graze the reef for food, he got his camera going and starting taking video and pictures. Michael had gone through the same series of emotions that Evan had, and was now getting his own camera going from a different angle. Together they managed to get roughly ten seconds of calm time before the giant beast of the deep decided to take notice.

Even in the dim glow of their muted dive lights, they could see the octopus was large and starting to get a deeper shade of red. This is a good indicator to any possible predators that, "Hey you there, I'm getting angry!" Along with the color change, all eight arms became more animated and began swirling about. Four of the arms grabbed ahold of the reef and the octopus lifted up from its cozy position among the bridge rubble and the swaying coral fans. Moving very quickly, the octopus rotated up and over the concrete with a slight turn to the right as it navigated back down toward the seafloor. Evan and Michael were both amazed with the swift action of the giant. That feeling of amazement turned to panic when Evan realized the giant octopus was coming right at him fast from behind, in a head on position that looked a lot like a bright red freight train.

Thinking quickly, he realized with the buoyancy compensator on he couldn't just duck out of the way. His only real option, and he took it, was to purge the buoyancy compensator and hope he would sink fast enough to get out of the way. Air bubbles swirled around his head as the air escaped from the purge valve. He couldn't see the octopus any more, but that didn't really matter. He was either going to get low enough or not. His fins touched hard and his knees followed quickly, stinging a bit when they landed on the rough surface of the concrete rubble reef. He felt very heavy now with no help from the compensator, but was glad to be able to crouch down and essentially hug the reef. Right then, a tremendous pressure wave shoved him even closer to the seafloor. The octopus was passing just over him and he wondered if he would survive the day. The pressure downward eased some and then he was pulled into the slipstream of the octopus's body. As the octopus went speeding by, Evan was clubbed in the back of his left leg by one of the arms.

He found out the hard way that being hit by the arm of a speeding Giant Pacific octopus is painful, and he reached down to massage the back part of his upper left calf. He was stunned at first, but quickly recovered and was able to look up as the octopus continued its furious maneuver toward Michael's position. Evan no longer saw any light from Michael's direction and was hoping it was because he had gone dark and was attempting to lay low. The octopus maneuvered around the edge of the concrete reef at an incredible speed with its arms flailing behind. The last Evan saw of the giant was the tips of the arms as they disappeared from his view.

Taking a few long slow breaths to calm himself, he pondered the encounter. He was damn lucky. Evan hoped Michael had fared as well and brought his DiveCom unit to life with a double tap of the side button. Michael wore an identical unit and Evan's technology provides interconnectivity over a limited range of about seventy-five feet. Evan drew the letter "U" on the screen and his device displayed "Are You OK?". On the other side of the concrete reef, Michael's DiveCom unit sprang to life with the same message displayed. An icon in the corner of the top right of the screen showed Evan's smiling face in a small white circle. Getting the message told Michael that Evan was probably OK. He quickly responded by sketching out the letter "Y" and his screen displayed "Yes". On Evan's device, he saw his screen change to display the word "Yes" and saw Michael's smiling face in a white circle in the upper right corner.

Glad they had both survived the encounter apparently unharmed, they retraced their respective routes to meet up at the same place that they had separated from. Once back together, having checked the air pressure in their tanks and seeing the needles lower than desired, they wasted no time getting a bearing on the course back to shore. Evan took special note of the time of day displayed on his Omega brand dive watch as they made the turn. This was key info for his thinking that if he knows travel time, distance from shore and the speed of the current, he might be able to calculate the location where they are right now. Considering the behavior of the octopus, Evan was starting to believe they had found an octopus den and was thinking about a trip back in the near future.

Although the current had taken them south a considerable distance, they were making their turn at slack tide and now the tide will begin to carry them north. With all the exertion of the octopus sighting and the subsequent attack, they had both used up more air than they had anticipated at this point in their dive. So now there would be no lazy drift with the current back to shore. Their limited air demanded a more rigorous swim. There were really no worries with nitrogen bubbles releasing into the blood stream since they were ascending gradually with the rise of the seafloor. However, running out of air and having to surface early will mean being swept away by the fast current at the surface. So Evan and Michael looked at each other, adjusted their buoyancy to stay just above the seafloor, and with determination on their faces, pushed off from the bottom and pumped strongly with their legs to propel themselves toward the western shore.

Chapter 2

Evan was starting to feel the increased effort required to take a breath, and he knew without even looking at his gauge that the air in both their tanks was getting really low. He was keeping a close watch on Michael as he had less air when they started the trip back to shore, and Michael was not in quite as good of physical shape as Evan so he would be using his air quicker. Based on their depth at the moment, and limited air, being able to wade out of the water breathing with the SCUBA gear was looking like it was not going to happen.

Evan got Michael's attention with a metal on metal tap of his knife handle to his tank. Michael stopped his forward progress and the two came together to communicate. Their depth was forty feet at the moment and the light from the sun above was starting to filter through the dark water. The current was running in the northerly direction at around one knot and they held to the rocks on the seafloor to avoid from being swept away. Forty feet above their heads, the speed of the current at the surface was approaching four knots. Using his DiveCom unit, Michael sketched out an "XX" and the words "Low Air, Time to Surface" appeared. Evan nodded in agreement. At this point, they had done the best they could to get back to shore. Now they would surface roughly thirty-five yards from shore in the surface current.

Together they added air to the buoyancy compensators. There was very little air left, but both were able to inflate the bladders and they started slowly ascending to the surface. As they rose from the depths, the effects of the current started to become pronounced. Evan could feel the pull of the water as he moved up, and with every few feet of rise, the pull of the current got a little stronger. The sun was getter brighter through the water as they neared the surface and they prepared to make the transfer from regulator to snorkel. Evan broke the surface first, and with the snorkel mouthpiece in his right hand, he pushed the regulator out of his mouth with his tongue and quickly replaced it with the snorkel. Just as Evan got his snorkel secure, Michael broke the surface and did the same thing. They had ascended together, but once separated at the surface, the current started moving them apart. Evan could make out their point of entry for the dive on the shoreline. Unfortunately, it was right in front of him about forty yards away and he quickly floated past it to the north as he moved with the water. With nothing left to do but swim to shore, they positioned their snorkels to minimize seawater coming down the breathing tubes and kicked hard toward the rocky shoreline just in front of them.

Evan only attempted to fight the current a little bit to get back south to their ingress location on the shoreline. He figured it would be best to just get to dry ground as soon as possible and then deal with the walk back to their site. The shoreline is hazardous with sharp slippery rocks, and dive booties are not the best shoes for walking, but with careful stepping, he thought it should be OK. Once he was within six feet of the shoreline, Evan was able to sufficiently standup in the current to be able to walk the last few yards out of the water. Michael had yet to make it to shore, but was very close. Evan watched Michael struggle to stand up in the current and nearly fall backwards with the weight of the SCUBA gear. Fortunately he was able to regain his balance and made it to shore about one hundred feet north of Evan's position, and Evan's position happened to be about two hundred feet north of their destination. Evan was anxious to get back to their site and their dry gear. Although the sun was shining, they had just come out of fifty degree water and it was cold. Their quarter inch thick neoprene wetsuits would help keep them warm, but Evan wanted to get back to their site quickly. Evan yelled out to Michael, "Hey Michael, hurry up, but don't fall on the rocks!" Michael looked Evan's way and gave him a wave. He was exhausted from the swim and not looking forward to lugging his gear across the rocky shoreline. He hooked his dive fins together and carried them in his left hand at his side while supporting the regulator in his right. He leaned slightly forward to better balance the heavy dive gear and then made his way south toward Evan.

Waiting for Michael, Evan considered the encounter with the Giant Pacific octopus. Size can be deceptive when looking through the glass of a dive mask, but Evan felt sure the arm span was at least twenty feet and the giant must have weighed one hundred pounds. That would be an above average size for a Giant Pacific octopus, but not close to the record numbers of thirty foot arm spans and weights near three hundred pounds that had been recorded. Still, Evan wanted to have another look. He had noted the time when they started heading toward shore from the one hundred and twenty foot depth, and now it was thirty eight minutes later. The bulk of the return to shore had been near the sea floor in slower current, so he figured with the surface swim included, they had moved north at maybe an average speed of two knots. Evan used his dive camera to take a series of pictures to capture this particular spot on shore knowing he could later identify the GPS coordinates using one of the many mapping applications available with satellite imagery. With all the speed, time and distance info available to him, he was hoping to calculate exact GPS coordinates so they could return later and find the same spot where they had encountered the octopus.

Michael was close now and called out, "Hey Evan, how'd you manage to get to shore so far south of me?"

Evan replied in a matter of fact way, "I was swimming hard, not out for a day of floating."

That got a "screw you" out of Michael, and they both laughed a bit. The excitement and discussion of the dive would have to wait though, since they were still soaking wet and needed to get to their dry gear. Keeping the talk to a minimum, they made their way south the few hundred feet to the access trail that would take them back to where they had parked over three hours ago. As they were making the turn from the shore up to the trail, they noticed two divers carrying their gear and slowly walking toward them. Evan gave them a wave and they returned in kind. They were close enough that Evan was able to ask where they were headed. As it turns out, they had already walked almost a quarter of a mile and still a quarter of a mile from where they needed to go. Amateur divers wanting to dive the Narrows, but not wanting to fight strong current getting in, they chose to start at near slack tide. The result was that they swam out and back, all the while being moved south by the current, and they got out a half of a mile from where they got in. Evan smiled to himself feeling good that he felt he understood the hazards and challenges of diving in Northwest waters, particularly the Tacoma Narrows where the current changes direction four times a day and can reach speeds over ten knots. As the wayward divers moved past, Evan and Michael wished them better luck next time and turned to head toward their parking spot.

Once back at Evan's bright orange and white restored 1972 Chevrolet Blazer, they quickly dropped their dive fins and slid the buoyancy compensators off their backs. Evan unlocked the truck and opened the Blazer's liftgate to remove his dive bag. From the bag he withdrew a smaller waterproof bag and opened it to take out one of the two towels that he carries for dives like today. Pulling off his wetsuit hood, he tossed it into the large dive bag and dried his face, neck and thick wavy dark brown hair with the towel. They had found a pretty remote access point, and with no one around, Evan and Michael peeled themselves out of their wetsuits, quickly dried off with the towels they had brought with them, and dressed in dry clothes. Tossing the wet gear in the dive bags, they zipped them up and loaded them in the back of the Blazer. Evan started the truck and let the 400 cubic inch motor warm up briefly and then shifted into Drive using the column mounted gearshift while keeping his right foot firmly planted on the brake. The transmission shifted solidly into gear with a reassuring lean forward by the Blazer as it tested the grab of the brakes. Hearing the smooth sound of the gears engaging, he moved his right foot to the accelerator pedal and goosed the throttle a bit. The truck's engine rumbled with a sound that hinted of much more power available, and both rear BFG All Terrain tires broke free of the dirt and threw two streams of gravel twenty feet behind them. He spun the steering wheel to the left a bit and fishtailed out of parking spot to get the big truck heading down the service road and toward the main highway. Like they were never there, in the rear view mirror Evan saw the small dust cloud they had left in their wake dissipate quickly as it was carried away on the wind blowing through the strait.

Chapter 3

The offices of Herkel & Grayson Attorneys at Law were situated on the top floor of the fifteen story Seafirst Bank building in downtown Tacoma Washington. A Partner in the firm for five years, Brenda Charling's office had a commanding view of Commencement Bay just to the northwest. She was just starting her day punctually at 8:00AM when the VOIP phone on her computer rang. Brenda was a very deliberate person. While sitting with the "answer call" button right at her fingertips, she chose to sip a bit of her Starbuck's Vente latte, looked out the window at the shimmering blue water of Puget Sound, and then picked up the call just before the fourth ring started.

"Good morning, this is Brenda Charling" she said. She listened carefully to the person on other end of the line and furrowed her brow at what the caller was saying. She asked one question about the circumstances of the subpoena that was to be served, listened intently, and then with just a simple "thanks", disconnected the call. It turns out that a case she has been working on very hard looks to be having a backwards step. The caller provided that the intended recipient of the subpoena has disappeared, and the subpoena delivery service contracted to serve the legal document has lost track of them. Silently she was screaming, "How could they have been so incompetent!" Outwardly, her facial expressions barely changed. She found it important to the image she wanted to project that she convey a sense of calm confidence. She didn't know exactly why, but this setback really rattled her and she took another sip of latte to distract herself from this unexpected loss of mental control. She breathed deeply three times and then opened the Calendar application on her computer. The firm had decided to be more accommodating to the weekly 9-5 workers in the local community and had recently changed office hours to include Saturday.

This Saturday, her day showed four meetings, all but one with people she has existing relationships with. She double clicked the notice for the meeting with the name of the person she didn't know. The particulars of this meeting involved the sale of a business entity known as Dungeness Technologies. Herkel & Grayson's client had contracted them to assess the potential liabilities that might be incurred with the purchase of a company named "Dungeness Technologies" located near Port Townsend. A principal of the company, CEO Evan Mason, is scheduled to arrive at her office at 3:00PM for an hour long meeting. Still thinking about the trouble with the subpoena earlier, she opened the file folder named "Business Sale_Dungeness Technologies". She had previously reviewed the business aspects of this case and had prepared herself for the meeting, but she did not know who she would be meeting today and wanted to become familiar with the man she would be interviewing. She went straight for the file named "Bio_Evan Mason". The file didn't contain very much information, but she carefully scanned the contents for what she could gain from what was there.

Evan Steven Mason
2161 W. Sequim Bay Road
Sequim, WA

Occupation: Chief Executive Officer
              Dungeness Technologies

Education: Bachelor's in Maritime Engineering
           Master's in Computer Science
           Master's in Business Administration

(21) United States patents, (3) International patents.

Credited with the development and production of the following commercially available products; waterproof wrist mounted SCUBA diver communications system, surface vehicle wake tracking and imaging system, dynamic auto trim system for high speed operations, deep water submersible drone with tactile feedback.

Work experience:

7 years:	Business/Product Development Dungeness Technologies President & CEO
4 years:	Research & Development Lockheed Martin - Submarine Division Chief Technologist
4 years:	Product Development & Implementation Cascade Marine Chief Engineer
2 years:	Deep Water Salvage & Welding Mason Enterprises Lead Diver

Age – 42
Marital Status – Single (divorced)
Children – none
Father: Peter – alive, Mother: Janine – alive

   After looking over Evan's short bio, Brenda was intrigued. Granted, all she really had was basic facts about the man, but considering the accomplishments and the apparent success as evidenced by the sale of a company that he has been running for a number of years, this should be an interesting afternoon. After the stressful phone call earlier, the thought of the coming meeting lifted her mood, and with the hint of a smile on her face, she set about preparing for her 10:00AM client.

Chapter 4

Davis sat looking at the ledger of the HG Enterprises quarterly accounting report with a blank stare. He had noted that the recent sale of large amounts of gold on the open market has resulted in an uncomfortable reduction in the overall value of his personal net worth. Normally not a problem, but Davis had been operating with a singular objective in mind over the last several years. In short, he was trying to acquire as much of the physical asset commonly referred to as gold, in the shortest amount of time possible. As a student of history, Davis found lessons to be learned by studying the actions and consequences of others. He recognized that while circumstances may have changed over the last several thousand years, a common thread is that the individual or group that acquires and controls the world's natural resources, also seems to have the power to dictate some of the rules. In his mind's eye, Davis tried to keep a vision of himself surrounded by a significant portion of the world's finite gold supply.

HGE had been in business for years and now operated as a parent company to many thriving businesses, most involved in segments of the commercial gold business. As the Director of Business Development for the privately held company for the last six years, Davis had helped to initiate an expansion into the refined ore distribution business with much success. While it is good business for HGE, it is primarily helping Davis's wholly owned company buy gold at rock bottom prices. While most would consider the practice unethical and ripe with conflict of interest issues, Davis had made his peace with it and slept well at night.

The drop in the price of gold was troubling from a valuation standpoint, but also represented a buying opportunity. Davis lifted himself out of his leather desk chair with some haste and it was enough that the chair rolled across the solid wood floor and slammed into the wall behind him with a loud clunk. He moved quickly around the desk and stepped out of his luxurious office located on the top floor of the twelve story HGE building. Too busy thinking, Davis passed by the spectacular view that was available outside his windows. The HGE building sat high on Queen Anne Hill. To the southwest, the view included Seattle's Elliot Bay with the iconic Space Needle built for the 1962 World's Fair in the foreground. To the southeast, a commanding view of Lake Union and the entire north side of downtown Seattle. The morning sun had cleared the Cascade Mountains to the east and now cast its brilliant rays on the shimmering water of Elliot Bay. The waters of the bay then reflected the light west to brighten the lush green landscape of Bainbridge Island and the Kitsap Peninsula beyond. Completely oblivious to it all, Davis walked briskly to the area of the top floor where the company analysts were located, and proceeded to walk right to the desk of the first person he saw.

Deena Ardosio was that person, and she looked up as her boss approached her desk. She knew he was coming even before she saw him, although she didn't know he would be coming to talk to her. That faint crashing noise that was heard from his office was a pretty good indicator that something was up. As he drew closer, his cologne preceded him. Not really unpleasant, the fragrance had a sweetness about it, but it was also pungent at the same time. The cologne he wore almost never changed in the nine months she had worked for him, and she still could not place the brand or product. And asking her second level boss what cologne he wears just seems out of the question, so she would keep on with her cologne guessing game for now.

Taking a quick deep breath, Deena turned up the corners of her mouth to produce a pleasant smile and greeted her boss with a, "Good morning Mr. G. Looks like there might be something urgent I can help you with. I'm on it!"

"That's good", said Davis, "because there is some urgency to what I need done. Oh, and good morning to you, too. I've been made aware that one of our clients requires significant gold to maintain their production process. I need a short list of suppliers that have the available physical resources right now so we can begin transporting immediately."

With that, Davis turned to leave without saying another word. Deena, reeling a little from the out of the blue request, gathered her wits about her and blurted out, "How much gold do they need?"

Davis slowed briefly as he moved back toward his office. Turning his head to the right while continuing to walk and making sure that he made eye contact with Deena, he said very clearly, "Just find out what they can ship right now and get a quote on their pricing. I'll worry about the client."

Deena thought it odd that he was taking such an active interest in a customer, but this Davis person appears to have some odd quirks. So she considered that this might just be the first time she would be helping her boss work with a customer. Since Deena had always prided herself on providing outstanding customer service in everything she did, she wrote down exactly what she had heard Mr. G say in the conversation. After jotting it down and rereading it several times, it dawned on her that the money involved with the inventory she was looking for is likely valued in the millions of dollars. That thought made her tremble a bit and she reread her notes again. No matter what, she was convinced she had it right, and Mr. G had said, "find out what they can ship right now." Knowing this was urgent info for her boss, she pushed aside the Seattle's Best Coffee cup that was almost empty anyway, and brought up the company's Dashboard application. Moving quickly through the menus, she started with a tab titled "Supply Chain".

Chapter 5

They'd been driving for about forty-five minutes and Evan and Michael were nearly halfway back to where Evan made his home in Sequim Washington. Turning off of State Route 3, the Blazer clattered over some highway expansion joints and then headed west on to the Hood Canal Bridge. They were now on State Route 104, and it spanned Hood Canal using one of the world's longest floating bridges. Evan considered how amazing it was that he was driving just a few feet above the surface of the water, at sixty miles an hour, for over one and a quarter miles! Throw in the fact that the bridge is over saltwater in Puget Sound, where tides can cause the bridge to rise and fall fifteen feet or more, and he was impressed with the engineering.

His thoughts wandered briefly while he recounted the bridge rubble in the Narrows this morning. That was from a suspension bridge done in by the wind. He got a chill down his spine when it occurred to him that he was now driving on the same bridge design as the ill-fated I-90 interstate highway bridge across Lake Washington. That disaster was the result of a careless act of leaving an above water maintenance hatch open to make pontoon ingress and egress easier. On a calm evening, a maintenance hatch was left open and when the wind whipped up the water that night, the waves started crashing against the building sized bridge pontoons. On the single pontoon with the open hatch, water was breaching the threshold and it was beginning to fill. With the interior safety doors between chambers not secured, the entire interior of the pontoon flooded. In the morning, a large portion of the bridge was below the surface of the water. A few hours after that, the weight of the filled pontoon pulled the bridge deck underwater and started a cascade effect that rapidly took large portions of the bridge down to the bottom of the lake. Evan thought about the Hood Canal Bridge, and not wanting to spend too much more time thinking about it, hoped that all the doors were securely closed.

Evan and Michael had been friends for a long time. They had met at the University of San Luis Obispo north of Los Angeles in the late 1990's when Evan was pursuing his Bachelors of Science degree in Maritime Engineering. With the familiarity of time together came the comfort of not having to force the conversations. This was such an occasion. After the dive and the excitement of telling each other their perspective of the octopus sighting, they fell into driving silently for nearly half of an hour.

Michael finally broke the silence and said, "Now that I've calmed down some, I want to circle back to talking about the octopus."

Evan snapped out of his distraction and said, "Sorry, what was that?"

Michael repeated, "Now that I've calmed down, I want to circle back to the octopus sighting. I got to tell you, that frickin' thing scared the bejeezus out of me when it took off straight up."

Evan agreed that Michael was not the only one scared. "I would have to agree. I don't know what my camera was doing when it came at me, but I know what I was doing. Trying not to shit my wetsuit!", Evan said with a slight quiver in his voice.

That got a laugh out of Michael, but for Evan, the statement was all too real. That was a harrowing experience. It was also incredibly exciting, and the adrenaline rush that he had felt then was a strong feeling still, and he liked it. Somehow that excitement clouded the parts about almost being crushed by an octopus freight train, running out of air early and the long walk on the beach in dive gear. He blurted out, "I want to go back." There was no immediate response from Michael, so Evan tried again, "Did you hear what I said? I want to go back."

Michael looked at Evan with bewilderment in his eyes and after a few seconds, Michael replied, "Did I hear you right? I just told you that I was totally spooked by that encounter and you tell me you want to go back?"

Evan explained, "You heard me right. I've been thinking more and more that from the behavior we observed, I would bet that there's a den close by. I noted the time that it took for me to get back to shore, and the location where I surfaced. With that, and the speed of the current that I can estimate by the time of day, I believe I can get us the GPS numbers."

"What then?" Michael asked. "We'll be in the same situation as we were today with no air left for any bottom time at the target location."

"So sounds like you're in then?" Evan noted with a wink.

"Whoa. Not yet. I'm just pointing out the fallacy with your plan." Michael protested.

Evan ignored the protest and explained further. "I never said anything about wading in from the shore the next time. Once we have the coordinates, I'm thinking we take a boat to the location instead. We time it so we get there right around slack tide, and then drop right down on top of that sucker."

Michael wrinkled his nose briefly and then his mouth broke into a smile. "You know, that could work actually. The wildcard is the accuracy of your calculations for the GPS numbers. Visibility won't be any better than today, maybe worse, so it could be a waste of time if your numbers aren't close."

"I agree. So I suggest we need to review all the video footage and pictures more closely. This time we'll take note of the surroundings so we can identify some landmarks, or maybe it should be watermarks in this case." Evan joked.

"Alright," Michael replied, "but let's use the drysuits next time so we don't have go through the polar bear freeze."

"I'm with you there. So let's both go over our pictures and footage, make note of any unique features or reef formations that we can easily identify and then get back together and map out a plan for a return trip." Evan suggested.

Michael noted that he was still apprehensive about getting that close to a large octopus again, but like Evan, the excitement of the sighting and interaction tended to cloud the memory of the danger. With a basic plan in place, they went on to discuss more mundane topics like last week's stock market rally, recent collector car auction results and what to eat for dinner since they had come up empty on the Ling Cod hunting trip.

The rest of the drive was uneventful and they neared Michael's property south of Port Townsend about thirty minutes later. Seven years ago, Michael and his wife Katie purchased a large piece of acreage just west of State Highway 19 near Anderson Lake State Park. At the time, the twenty acres was unused pasture and the house rundown. Anticipating that the state of Washington would legalize marijuana in the future, they took a chance and prepared to enter the marketplace as a producer and wholesale distributor. Their risk paid off and the enterprise has been successful, including developing a number of their own proprietary strains that have received high praise from the local critics. With the success of the business, Michael and Katie remodeled the house and added to their family. Now with two children, ages seven and four, they keep themselves very busy.

Slowing to pull the Blazer into the long driveway that led to the house on the property, Evan asked

Michael, "So with no catch coming home, what are you guys going to do for dinner?"

"Good question. I haven't let Katie know that I'm coming home empty handed yet. It's Saturday night, so we might just take the kids and head into Port Townsend for a family dinner," Michael said.

"Sounds like you might have a plan. As for me, I'm not sure how this meeting I've got in a few hours is going to go, but there shouldn't be any problems. Almost a formality as I understand it. I'll probably get a bite to eat on my way back from Tacoma," Evan said.

"Alright then. Well, thanks for the dive. It was incredible!" exclaimed Michael.

"Agreed," agreed Evan.

As the conversation ended, they pulled up to Michael's front door and Evan brought the Blazer to a stop. Michael jumped out and after closing the passenger door, quickly proceeded to the rear of the vehicle. Opening the liftgate, he took his gear out and tossed it on the sidewalk that led up to his house on a meandering route through the front lawn. He called to Evan through the liftgate opening to "drive carefully" and then he shut the liftgate with a firm slam. Waving goodbye, he picked up his gear and walked toward his house.

Evan shifted into drive and accelerated away down the driveway. Reaching the end, he turned right onto State Highway 19 and quickly got the truck up to highway speed. Glancing at the time displayed on the screen of the Pioneer sound system, he calculated that by the time he got home, he would have about an hour to get himself ready before he had to leave for the 3:00PM meeting at Herkel & Grayson's in Tacoma. Nudging the accelerator pedal down a bit, Evan pushed his speed up by five miles an hour and hoped he wouldn't be late.

Evan Mason's House on Sequim Bay

Chapter 6

The sun was in the sky all by itself without a cloud to be seen just after Noon on Saturday when Evan picked the ride he was going to take to one of the most important meetings of his life. On such a nice Fall day, he had been tempted to take his classic Honda Shadow 1000 motorcycle, but instead chose his blue velvet metallic 2016 Chevrolet Camaro SS. Considering that he needed to bring more than just himself to the meeting today, the Camaro was the prudent choice, and still a blast to drive.

As Evan backed out of the attached four car garage, the Camaro rumbled in anticipation of the drive to Tacoma. He could smell the tiniest bit of unburned fuel in the air as the big 6.2 liter engine warmed up. He already had a general sense of where the offices of Herkel & Grayson were located, but he dialed it in on the car's GPS mapping system for a door to door guide. The display highlighted the route and the application waited for an input to proceed with route guidance. Evan stared at the screen and noted that the destination icon was close to the water's edge just near the Tacoma waterways at the southeast portion of Commencement Bay. Having boated the Puget Sound region most of his life, he knew that the Tacoma waterways held a number of marinas and almost all had transient moorage. At this time of the year, he expected that there would be plenty of slip vacancies.

On an impulse, he changed his mind and parked the car back in the garage, turned the engine off, and closed the eight foot tall by eight foot wide insulated garage door behind him. Having noted the estimated time to the destination displayed by the car's mapping application, he had run a rough calculation in his head and arrived at an even better way to get to Tacoma, and it would be quicker. Grabbing his briefcase and his overstuffed backpack filled with product development documentation, Evan headed out the rear garage door and took a stone paver pathway across a small, well-manicured lawn. At the rear of the yard, he stepped into a six foot by six feet steel basket trimmed out with cedar wood that would carry him down the side of the steep bluff to his boathouse.

Pressing the Down button on the control pad started the electric motor and the tram shifted slightly as the safety locks were disengaged with a solid clunk. Once free to move, the motor quickly transported him and his bags down the one hundred and twenty foot drop to the shoreline. The braking mechanism provided a smooth deceleration of the basket and it came to an easy stop right at a wooden platform that was flush with a six foot wide deck that ran the length of the boathouse on the south side. Stepping off the tram with his bags, he set them aside while he secured the tram gate and after keying in the access code at the boathouse control station, pressed the Up button to send the tram back up the rail. Unlocking the boathouse access door and stepping through, the light sensors detected Evan's movement and automatically came on. The brilliant white light from the six HID fixtures flooded the interior space of the boathouse and lit up his two boats with their gelcoat sparkling in the artificial light. Evan took note that the ramp to the floating dock had dropped down another twelve feet right now since it was nearing low tide in the waters of Sequim Bay. He glanced at the forty-two foot Hatteras convertible yacht moored in the left-hand slip. Secured with a four point tie setup and spring lines for rougher seas, he gave the reliable old girl a wave and a shout out, and then turned his attention to the thirty-three foot Chaparral sitting high in the air on a boat lift.

He kept the Chaparral high and dry to keep the bottom and drive system from fouling, especially during the limited winter use in the Northwest. The Hatteras on the other hand was used all year and provided comfortable accommodations rain or shine, hot or cold. It had been refitted about five years ago, and while the yacht retained most of the original interior layout, the forward berth had been gutted and rebuilt from scratch to provide a large space for a combination bedroom and office. The new space also included a luxurious private head with a large stand up shower. The new design had shifted the forward berth bulkhead aft about two feet and forced a galley dining area lay out that took advantage of the height in the salon at amidships. Aft of the port side situated galley, three steps led up to the main portion of the interior where two recliners and a long couch were positioned in a fashion that made the space very inviting. To starboard, the interior helm had all the necessary buttons, levers, gauges, equipment and screens for boat navigation and control in just about any weather and lighting conditions. An antique eighteen inch diameter ship's wheel provided old controls for a new drive and steering system. While the engine bay dimensions of the Hatteras remained the same, the two Volvo/Penta diesels were replaced with two clean burning Caterpillar power houses equipped with twin turbos. Each engine developed in excess of nine hundred horsepower and with the efficient V-drives specified by Evan himself, the large nostalgic motor yacht cruised easily at twenty five knots and reached speeds near forty knots at Wide Open Throttle. The Hatteras brand yachts are ocean capable ships, and Evan's 1985 convertible model named "Molly Blue" was no different.

Today however, Evan was taking the Chaparral, and it was a different kind of boat. Much newer and still mostly all original, the boat's deep-V hull design with reverse chines to bite into the water for stability, allowed it to achieve a well-controlled top speed across the water of nearly sixty knots. The handling of the boat was supreme and Evan had found it performed exceptional in all the weather and sea conditions that he'd encountered so far. A fairly new Captain to the boat that he had named "Crab got Legs", Evan had taken possession of the almost new

2017 Chaparral 330 Signature just six months prior. It replaced a well-used twenty-seven foot Sea Ray Sundancer that had performed great for him over the years.

Making sure the space below the lift was clear, Evan engaged the switch to lower the boat. Slowly the shiny white and blue Chaparral inched toward the cold water of the bay lazily slapping against the base of the pilings that were supporting the boathouse. With three, twelve inch diameter navy blue bumpers already hanging in place on the port side, once the boat was floating and the lift had stopped in the full down position, Evan tied off the aft port line to the dock cleat just two feet away. Moving forward relative to the boat, he secured the amidships cleat to a dock cleat and prepared to board.

With his briefcase in one hand and his backpack in the other, he leaned over the gunwale and set them down in the corner of the cockpit. He stepped on the swimstep and then through the transom door moving quickly to the helm, taking a seat in the comfortable Captain's chair. Reaching below the Icom VHF radio that was located in front of his right knee, he reached in and retrieved a magnetic key box from the top of the small cubby beneath the radio. He opened a small metallic box, withdrew the set of keys and returned the key box to its hidden location.

Evan loved being on the water, so both boats saw plenty of use. That meant there was little effort required to get the Chaparral underway today and he looked over the bridge and cockpit areas to verify all was in order. He unlocked the salon door and then put the ignition key in its place in preparation for starting the engines. He opened the salon door and with his bags in hand, took the three steps down to the sole of the boat and made sure all was ready inside as well. He stored his bags and moved to the boat's shorepower panel and verified none of the circuit breakers had tripped while in storage. None had, and then he turned off the active circuits that were on. With that, he flipped off the main breaker and the boat was fully on battery power.

Moving back outside to the bridge, for safety he flipped the engine bay blower on to clear any gasoline vapors that might be lingering in the bilge. The blower was powerful, but Evan barely heard it tucked away in the well-insulated engine bay. Waiting patiently to come to life at the flip of a their respective switch, the two Mercruiser 5.0 liter V-8 engines that together provided seven hundred horsepower sat quietly beneath Evan in the engine bay. While the blower was running, he used a garage door style opener to open two large out swinging vertical panels behind the boat that separated at the center. The electrically powered gear systems at the top of each door opened them quickly and he was greeted with the afternoon sunshine filling the boathouse. While waiting a few minutes for the air to clear in the bilge, Evan disconnected the shorepower cable from the boat and coiled it neatly on the dock. He made one last check of the dock area and the boathouse and then stepped back on the boat. Evan turned the key for the starboard engine to the On position and heard the electric pump pressurize the fuel injection system. No worries with fuel Evan thought, as he made a point of keeping the tanks on both of the boats full when not in use. The Mercruiser Bravo 3 outdrives were already fully down and he pushed the Start button for the starboard engine. It jumped right to life and the throaty rumble of the engine could be heard as the exhaust bubbled up through the water just aft of the props. Evan followed the same procedure for the port engine, and with the same results as the starboard one, soon both engines were idling smoothly.

Exiting the boat, he released the forward port line from the dock cleat and secured it to the boat. Wasting no time, he removed the three bumpers and laid them in the cockpit. Evan used the swimstep to get back on board, secured all three bumpers in their rack at the transom, and then leaning over the gunwale, he released the aft line from the fixed cleat on the dock. Stepping to the helm and with the boat floating free, he shifted both drives into Reverse and when the props bit into the water, they pulled the large cruiser out of the boathouse and into the sunshine.

Turning the wheel to port once clear of the boathouse doors and then shifting both drives to Neutral, the Chaparral spun slowly to a bearing of due north. Evan closed the boathouse doors, slipped his Maui Jim sunglasses on, and brought the wheel to starboard to center the drives. Shifting both drives into Forward gear, the boat quickly stopped its drift and idled north toward the entrance to Sequim Bay. Evan checked all the gauges, verified both trim tabs were full up, turned on the VHF radio, the Furuno radar and chart plotter system, and with engine temperatures just approaching normal, he pushed the throttles forward and raised the engine RPMs. The boat climbed the wall of water in front of it in just a few seconds and was up on plane doing twenty-five knots just a few seconds later. Evan checked his RPMs and made a slight adjustment to increase to twenty-seven knots. Leaving the throttle alone, he then adjusted the trim tabs to lift the stern and provide a slight bow down attitude and the boat picked up almost another knot of speed. Nudging the throttles forward to maintain 3,250 RPM, the boat settled right at twenty eight knots. Then he relaxed in the comfortable Captain's chair in preparation for a beautiful two plus hour cruise to Commencement Bay just outside of Tacoma.

Chapter 7

The sun had continued its traverse of the sky all day with no interruption by clouds. Now mid-afternoon, the sun was shining brightly on the western side of the Seafirst building and the rays made their way directly through the windows of Brenda Charling's office. The sun reflected off the top of her polished wooden desk and at just such an angle that the edge of her computer monitor was bathed in bright light. While sunglasses are not always needed in the Pacific Northwest, Brenda did want hers now as the glare on her computer screen from the reflection was making it difficult to see. Looking at the time, she noted she had about twenty minutes until her 3:00PM meeting.

Leaning back in her modern desk chair with breathable fabric and all kinds of ergonomic adjustments, Brenda looked across her office to the far wall and raised her arms above her head stretching to the ceiling. Still stretching her arms high, she leaned at first to the left and held the position, then did the same thing to the right. The stretch felt good, but also made her realize that her body was a bit stiff and she'd been working almost nonstop all day. With that realization, she pushed her chair back slightly and stood up.

Stepping to the right around the edge of her desk, she made for the western window that was allowing the sun to cast the glare on her screen.

Looking out the window before adjusting the blind to block the sun, she fixed her gaze to the northwest. With the sun to the southwest, the northwest view was lit up like a jewel. The sparkling blue waters of Commencement Bay and Puget Sound beyond took her immediately away from the work of lawyering that had kept her occupied all day. In the distance, the clear air afforded a view of the southern tip of Vashon Island. Just to the west, not visible to the naked eye due to the distance of roughly fifteen miles, she knew that her house on the water in Gig Harbor was in her line of sight.

Now fully diverted from the work of Herkel & Grayson, she opened the top right drawer of the credenza in front of her. Taking out a pair of Bushnell marine grade 10 x 50 binoculars, she brushed her hair clear of her face and brought them to her eyes. Zooming in and training the binoculars on the southernmost point of Vashon Island, she closed her right eye and adjusted the binoculars for the best clarity at that distance. Then she closed her left eye and used the fine adjustment to dial in the best clarity for her right eye. She opened both eyes and squeezed the body of the binoculars together to line up the respective lenses with each eye. Now with excellent clarity and significant magnification, she panned to the left across the water until her eyes fell upon the well hidden entrance to the bay of Gig Harbor. Located on the Kitsap Peninsula, the city of Gig Harbor was one of the eastern most towns of the peninsula. Brenda's house was located along the shoreline of the small finger of land that jutted south into Puget Sound where the tip of the finger helped form the bay entrance. At the very end of the finger of land sat the Gig Harbor Lighthouse. Brenda now had the lighthouse fixed in her sights. Finding the shoreline in front of the lighthouse, she panned to the right slowly, looking for landmarks that she could identify. Approximately one half mile from the lighthouse, Brenda panned across her waterfront cottage. The bright orange of the hull of her ocean kayak as it sat in the rack she had built stopped her from panning any further north.

Relaxing her stance and getting comfortable, she focused the binoculars on her property. She owned the waterfront property free and clear and was proud that she had managed to pay off a fifteen year mortgage in eight years. It wasn't easy, and she had not eaten well some months, but in the end she felt so much better without the burden of the debt and the worry of a payment every month. While observing her one hundred feet of waterfront, she wasn't looking for anything in particular, just enjoying the look, and she smiled a little. Seeing the kayak did put an idea in her head, and she made a promise to herself that after the meeting coming up, she would pack up quickly and head home for a few hours of kayaking on the Sound.

While continuing to look through the binoculars, Brenda zoomed out to widen the field of view. For a late Fall Saturday afternoon with excellent weather, there were surprisingly few boats on the water. She did note one that was seemingly coming right at her. Reducing the field of view down and training her sights on the boat, she followed it as it moved into Commencement Bay. A large sunbridge style cruiser, it appeared to traveling at a very brisk speed. It quickly overtook on the port side, a smaller center console style boat that appeared to be running full out. Brenda continued to follow the blue and white cruiser as its southeast bearing took it right at her. As the boat neared the numerous waterways at the southeast corner of the bay, it steered a more easterly course toward the Hylebos Waterway. She watched the boat come off of plane and based on the size of the wake, probably violated the NO WAKE rule all the way to its destination in the Hylebos Marina. As the boat entered the marina, she did see that it had dropped its speed to idle and watched as it was expertly maneuvered past the small breakwater. While not able to see who was piloting the boat, she could see that it was a beautiful sunbridge style with a navy blue hull and a gleaming white topside. The forward rake of the radar arch made the boat look fast even just idling by. As the boat turned down one of the many rows in the marina, she lost sight of it and she dropped the binoculars away from her face. The nice diversion of boat watching reminded her of how much she loved the water, and she recommitted herself to the kayak trip after work.

Closing the window blind and setting the binoculars down on the credenza, she returned to her desk and realized she had lost ten minutes staring out the window. She shuffled the papers on her desk together in an organized fashion and placed them in the proper binders. Then she placed the binders neatly on the bookcase behind and to the left of her. Now that her computer screen was glare free, she could see fine and closed out of the applications no longer needed for the day. She opened the Dungeness Technologies folder and double clicked on the file named "Dungeness Tech_Interview_1" to bring up the Word document she had created in preparation for this meeting. The content included her thoughts on the business and the legal and social implications of her client acquiring said business. She scanned the information quickly to refresh herself on the details that she had compiled earlier. There was also a series of questions that she had already come up with, and she reread them as well.

Nearly 3:00PM, Brenda anticipated she would get a call from her secretary any moment telling her that her interviewee was here. Now ready for the meeting, she decided she needed a break and standing up from her desk, quickly walked the short distance down the hall to the restrooms. Taking just a few minutes, she exited the restroom and then headed directly back to her office. As she turned toward her office, down the hall she could she her secretary Amanda engaged in a conversation with a man at her desk. The man had striking features and was well put together from the brief glimpse she had gotten before striding into her office. The timing would suggest that the man at Amanda's desk was

Evan Mason and on que to confirm that, Amanda soon buzzed Brenda's line and said, "Excuse me Ms. Charling, just want to let you know that Evan Mason, your 3:00PM appointment is here."

Brenda replied, "Thank you Amanda, go ahead and send him in."

Knowing she was about to interview a prompt, handsome, successful man for an hour seemed to give her a little tingle, which she found odd. Brenda had been an all work, no play girl for many, many, years, so she simply considered Evan Mason's appearance a coincidence. She told herself to write the tingle off to the daydream out the window or maybe just a sign that since the goal of becoming a Partner in the Herkel & Grayson law firm had been accomplished, a new goal needed to be established.

Evan was quick to make it from Amanda's desk to Brenda's office and she was slightly surprised at his appearance even though she knew he was coming. Brenda was keen on judging a book by the cover and found it entertaining to try and guess a person's personality by their appearance. When she looked up from her desk at Evan flashing a muted smile with a glint in his eye that suggested a life of mystery, she felt that tingle again. Pushing through it, she stood up and strode around her desk with her right hand extended and said, "Hello, Mr. Mason. It's a pleasure to meet you. I'm Brenda Charling and I appreciate you coming in this afternoon to talk with me."

Chapter 8

With the meeting at Herkel & Grayson over, Evan headed out of the Seafirst building and started looking around for his ride. He had immediately after leaving Brenda Charling's office pulled up the Lyft app on his phone and scheduled a pick up right out front. As the app had predicted, his driver Kameron was pulling up in his Prius right on time, ready to shuttle another transportation deficient human around the city. The availability of the service was in Evan's favor today though. He was able to travel by boat to Tacoma and then a short car ride to the Seafirst building using Lyft worked out great.

What did not work out great was the meeting with that bitch lawyer from Herkel & Grayson. She seemed nice enough at first, but then turned apprehensive regarding the viability of the acquisition of Dungeness Technologies by her Client. As the meeting went on, she made it clear that she did not really see any synergies between the companies and that there existed numerous opportunities for possible EPA violations in the event of product failures. So the meeting left Evan a bit agitated and he responded rudely to the Lyft driver when Kameron welcomed him.

"I have to apologize for being rude to you just then. Had a surprise of a meeting and I should not have taken it out on you." Evan said with true sincerity.

"No problem," said Kameron. "I deal with people all day and nobody is ever in the same mood. I just roll with it. Pun intended."

That got a smile out of Evan and he thanked Kameron for his go with the flow attitude and promptness with the pickup.

"You're headed to the Hylebos Marina, is that right?" asked Kameron.

"That's right. You can drop me right at the entrance to the marina. No need for you to wind your way through the parking lot." replied Evan.

Sitting back in the right rear seat of the Prius with his backpack on the seat next to him, and his briefcase pinned between it and the seat back, Evan wondered what next step he was going to need to take in order to salvage the pending sale of the business he had worked so hard to create. Ultimately, if the sale did fall through, he would continue as the CEO and work through the projects he had been working on. It's just that the preliminary plans he has been making since signing to agree to sell the business appear to now be in jeopardy. With renewed frustration about the way the meeting had gone, he became annoyed by the smell of stinky diesel fumes and the noises of the loud cars and trucks. The pushy and erratic behavior of the other drivers was starting to irritate him, and he wasn't even driving.

Happy that the trip to the marina was short, he jumped out quickly and then reached back in to retrieve his bags. Thanking Kameron for his prompt service and fine driving, Evan walked through the entrance to the marina and toward the transient moorage slips. Moored in a side tie location, Crab got Legs rested calmly in the water secured to the dock on the starboard side, with just a slight bob as the water slowly rose and fell. Evan's boat had no neighbors at the moment, so casting off would be simple. He stepped across the gap between the dock and his boat's swimstep and then walked through the cockpit and bridge to the entrance to the salon. He unlocked the lock mechanism and moving the combination hatch/door forward, went below to secure his bags.

Once back in the cockpit, he flipped on the engine bay blower, and turned the ignition key to Start. With both engines still warm, he wasted no time and started the starboard engine and then right away, the port engine. Both engines were idling smoothly and Evan stepped off the boat to bring aboard the fenders. With the boat being held off the dock by a light breeze, he moved all three fenders to the rack on the transom. Ready to leave, Evan released the forward line from the dock cleat and quickly secured it. He stepped aboard using the swim step and walked through the transom door then turned around to release the aft line from inside the cockpit. The boat started to drift away from the dock at once, but the breeze was light and the little bit of drift actually helped to position the boat to leave the marina.

Sitting down in the Captain's chair at the helm, Evan checked his gauges and all looked good, including the fuel gauge that indicated almost three quarters of a tank. With the exit to the marina straight ahead, he engaged the drives in Forward gear and felt the comforting thrust from the props as the boat moved forward under power. Taking it slow at idle speed, Crab got Legs maneuvered through the rows of boats and around the breakwater. There was a short stretch of No Wake zone in the Hybelos Waterway directly in front of him before reaching Commencement Bay, and while idling along Evan thought again of the meeting he had just come from. This time however, his mind stuck on Brenda Charling, and he started to sense a wave of aggravation coming on.

Once clear of the speed and wake restrictions of the waterway, Evan wanted to forget about the meeting. He grinned broadly while at the same time pushing both throttles to their stops. The engines roared together and Evan could hear the power of them coming from the exhaust, and he felt the power in the seat of his pants. The twin outdrives, each with their own set of counter rotating stainless steel propellers, bit hard into the water and the stern settled lower. Seconds later, all six tons of Crab got Legs climbed the steep wall of water it had created and crested the top of the wave to get on plane. The attitude of the boat was now horizontal and the props were throwing huge amounts of water out the back. The boat continued to accelerate at a steady pace until the tachometer reached 5,200 RPMs. Crab got Legs was now running full out at Wild Open Throttle and making nearly sixty knots. Evan stood up and while holding tight to the wheel, leaned into the wind as it flowed over the windscreen and he became lost in the moment of exhilaration.

Following the meeting with Evan Mason, Brenda Charling sat in her office wondering how a meeting that she had prepared so well for had gone so unexpectedly bad. She had gotten somewhat frustrated during the meeting and felt she might have lost her temper. Recognizing that she wanted, and needed to be professional, she took a few minutes to take some deep breaths to calm herself. The water always helps and she stood up and walked to one of the windows that was not covered by a closed blind. Looking out, see tried to relax and started thinking about kayaking. That helped and she decided to let it go, close up her office and head home.

As she turned to leave the window, movement below in the Hylebos Waterway caught her eye. Looking closer, she thought she saw the same boat she had seen about an hour ago. Curious about the coincidence, she reached over and picked up her binoculars and trained them on the boat below. It sure looked like the same blue and white boat, but it was hard to tell. The boat was just clearing the waterway and she saw an explosion of water at the stern below the swimstep. The props dug in and the boat started to accelerate away from her on a northwest course. In a matter of moments, the boat was up on plane and moving away at an incredible speed, leaving a wake that could not have been straighter. Thinking about the boat and the water of Puget Sound again, Brenda finished her work, grabbed her briefcase, locked her office door and headed out anticipating a very arduous row in her kayak.

Chapter 9

Evan was cleaning up in his kitchen after a late light dinner and was thinking about why his mind had been elsewhere all day. Suspecting it might be the lack of follow up over the three days since the meeting he had had with Brenda "The Lawyer" Charling about the sale of his business, he simply shrugged his shoulders knowing there was little he could do at this point. Considering the way the meeting went, his expectations of a "rubber stamp" regarding his company presenting a small risk to the prospective Buyer seemed a distant dream. Brenda, the tough, well prepared person that she was, had pulled no punches. The primary concern and risk is that which is associated with Evan's designs and the Intellectual Property that he is selling. He understood the Buyer's need for performing their due diligence, and that was OK. With Brenda though, he felt her diligence was too much, and certainly not due. She was very thorough, almost mean he thought, in her questioning of the Dungeness Technology products, their design methods, and the processes and tools used to produce them.

Everything Evan knew about Brenda changed when he responded as one normally would to a doorbell, and he opened his front door. He found her standing on the other side, and not just standing, but rather posing, in a sultry kind of way. At least that's what Evan saw. Transported back in time three days, he clearly recalled her physical appearance at the meeting. She was tall at around 5'10" and he had thought she was well toned physically, and tonight she looked every bit of that. Her shoulder length brown hair looked more casual though and her well-proportioned facial features were accented by just a touch of makeup that he didn't recall seeing before. In his frustration with her questioning, he had forgotten just how striking she was. There was a hot blast to his libido and he felt his body get warmer in a very targeted way. He caught his breath for a second and sucked in some fresh air. His nose picked up her tantalizing scent however, and it disrupted the breath of fresh air he was trying to get. Her scent was much better than the fresh air he thought to himself. He could feel his face flush slightly and recognizing that his proper reaction should be surprise, he stammered out "Hello? Um, I thought our business has been concluded. Did I forget to sign a release or something?"

Brenda let her smile turn to a pout and her lips drooped slightly at the corners. In a voice that sounded like Evan had wounded her somehow, she said, "Why do you have to be so mean? I'm here as a favor."

"Really? A favor for who?" asked Evan suspiciously.

"Why you of course." she said while putting a smile back on her face.

Evan cocked his head slightly being taken by surprise at that statement. In fact, he was surprised that she was standing on his front porch. Not one to receive a lot of visitors, Evan led a fairly solitary home life. The action and adventure are out, away from his home port so to speak. So here's this beautiful woman, standing on Evan's front porch, and telling him she's there to do him a favor.

He switched gears to match Brenda's approach and said, "I think I should be afraid of a favor from you. It might be something like a First Class ticket on a train bound for Hell."

"Wow Evan, you must really think highly of me." Brenda said with a straight face.

"OK. That was maybe a little too harsh." he said to take away some of the sting.

"Anyway," Brenda said with some exasperation in her voice, "I just wanted to tell you in person that the Buyer is likely to accept my findings, and that they will probably agree with me that Dungeness Technologies, and the products that they design and produce, are not considered a significant financial or corporate citizenship risk going forward. In short, I expect they'll agree to the terms of the sale and within the next week or so, all should be complete. From a paperwork standpoint that is. As you know, the terms of the agreement require you to stay on to transition leadership and control of the company."

Feeling a little awkward for being rude to Brenda, holding the doorknob in his left hand, Evan took a step back into his house and with a sweep of his right arm, he welcomed her to his home and said, "I apologize for my rude behavior before. Welcome. You've brought me great news and I had jumped to the wrong conclusion. I do have to say that tonight though, it seems like you're a different Brenda." With that, Brenda stepped across the threshold and moved closer to him and explained.

"Well, I was working. I take my job very seriously, and when the clock is running, I'm working." she said unapologetically, but with a smile.

Evan wondered out loud, "I should probably check my phones and emails. Having you make the trip here must mean that my communications are out."

"Don't bother." Brenda said, "I'm here because you intrigued me at our meeting. I wasn't trying to break you down, just impressed with your eloquent impromptu answers and explanations. So I kept ramping it up, and you stayed right with me. As I said, I was impressed. So now I'm here trying to learn more about you."

Evan smiled a bit and replied, "Thank you for that complement, and the explanation. I must admit that it's a relief to know your interrogation was deliberately over the top. Well maybe not quite an interrogation, but like I said, it's nice to know that there's a softer side to you."

Now it was Brenda's turn to blush, and she walked past Evan quickly on her way to the living room just to right of the door. Looking around the large space, she found luxurious looking furniture. A series of sectional pieces were strung together to create and eight foot long by seven foot wide couch. A large ottoman was upholstered in the same rich gray-rust colored fabric and sat on the left side of the couch assembly. In what appeared to Evan as a very seductive manner, Brenda walked to the far right seating position of the couch and sat down. Evan stopped short of the couch and sat down on the edge of the ottoman right about the same time that Brenda sat down. She crossed her legs and revealed the upper part of her right thigh through a slit in her black leather skirt that Evan had failed to notice until now.

Looking at each other, there was a brief awkwardness as it seemed that both might be wondering the same thing. Namely, "what the heck is going on here?" The moment passed as they apparently were on a similar line of thinking and acknowledged each other with their eyes. The temperature in the room hadn't changed, but Evan felt some heat. Brenda must also have felt some heat as she slipped off her coat and let it fall on the floor to her left. Evan watched her as she repositioned herself for what looked to be shaping up as a very engaging, if not crazy, conversation.

Brenda leaned slightly to her left and propped her left arm on the couch armrest. The low armrest caused her to lean over in a pronounced way, and that accentuated her breasts as they settled nicely in her bra. From Evan's perspective, it wasn't much of a bra. When Brenda leaned over, her silky smooth blouse had slipped over her left shoulder and exposed the bra strap. The strap looked very thin and dainty, and at risk of breaking any second. Not that Evan would have minded. The whole scene was becoming very surreal, from Brenda at his front door, to her pronouncement that the sale of his business is happening, to her obvious advances now as they sat across from one another in his living room.

When Brenda tilted her head up and then swept back her auburn brown hair to expose her face, her blue-gray eyes were staring right at Evan's. Looking right back at her, he felt a bump to his libido again. This time however, he stood up from the ottoman and quickly took the two steps needed to cover the distance to the couch and sat down on Brenda's right side. In nearly the same motion, he wrapped his left arm around her shoulders and pulled her in toward him. With Evan's advance, Brenda turned toward him and reached around his neck as she eagerly moved closer to him. Evan let his right hand rest on Brenda's slender left hip and he found her waiting lips just inches from his. As tender as he could in the heat of passion, he pressed his lips to hers.

They both felt the sparks as their lips touched, and as they embraced the kiss became more passionate. Brenda's strong pressing of her chest to his was too much for her bra to take, and Evan felt the thin material slip away beneath her blouse. Brenda pulled back and in a flash extracted her failed bra from inside her shirt. Shifting her position, she reclined against the low armrest and whispered, "Not sure where this is going, but I'm liking where it's starting."

Evan did not respond verbally. Instead, he looked in her eyes and moved on top of her, slowly lowing himself down to maximize the body contact. He could feel her press her hips up and into his, and they both felt a wave of sexual excitement wash over them. Brenda pressed harder then, before relaxing in order to reach down and slide her left hand between them. After a brief period of exploration, she slowly withdrew her hand, teasing Evan with her light touch.

Looking coyly at Evan, she said softly. "I am so horny right now. I thought I could come over here and tease you a little bit, but it seems I may have teased myself. In just a matter of minutes, this has gone way beyond what I had planned." She rose up and kissed him hard on the lips, with her tongue moving to explore his mouth. They pulled together and kissed hungrily until they separated out of breath, but still pressing their bodies tightly together. Evan and Brenda stared hard at each other for a few moments until Evan suggested, "It's probably a long drive home for you, so you might want to consider spending the night."

Not breaking eye contact, Brenda promptly replied, "You read my mind".

Chapter 10

Evan woke with a start as the sun was just starting to brighten the mildly overcast skies. The early morning rays made their way through the almost opaque drapes that were closed tight over both of the large windows that looked toward Sequim Bay. Normally the drapes were left open, and Evan would allow his bedroom to light naturally, but last night was different. It was late when he came to bed and knew he was going to want more hours of sleep in the morning. It had worked, and he was able to sleep until almost 7:00AM before the faint sound of a boat on the water was sufficient to rouse him.

Different than he had originally thought things would go last night, Evan had woken up alone. At first he thought he had been dreaming about Brenda and an evening of passion. Then his brain began to clear the fogginess away that comes from a bit too much alcohol and he realized it was no dream. Brenda had not stayed the night. Instead, he recalled that she had left sometime before 11:00PM after a few hours of heavy teasing on his couch. They had agreed to stay in touch regarding the business transaction, and made no plan for anything else. Evan smiled to himself as he considered that the scenario that played out last night was exactly how a dream might have gone. Even though the only article of clothing that came off was Brenda's skimpy bra, they both had been taken to the edge, but not over, a number of times last night. He savored the memory of the spontaneous evening and relaxed into his comfortable pillow while closing his eyes. He grabbed ahold of the covers and pulled them up around his shoulders with every intention of getting another hour or so of sleep.

For a few minutes, he lay there calmly. Then his mind wandered to Brenda again and he found himself wide awake. She had clearly left an impression on him last night, and from the reaction below his waist at the moment, the impression was both mental and physical. She had tapped into a range of emotions that included; anger, surprise, intrigue, curiosity, and something erotic that he didn't recall feeling since a young man. His head was swimming with thoughts and further sleep was now out of the question. Instead, Evan whisked the covers off and made to stand up. Feeling a little light headed from the shots of whiskey that he'd had after Brenda had left, he sat on the edge of his bed until the dizziness subsided. After a bit, he stood up and pulled on a pair of sweat pants that were tossed across the arm of a Dansk brand reclining chair tucked in the corner of his room. Padding across the hardwood floor in his bare feet, he was soon standing on the soft throw rug in the bathroom and took care of the first business of the day.

In a very relaxed mood, Evan made his way to the kitchen thinking about breakfast. As he walked past the living room, he heard a buzzing noise that he couldn't quite place. Stopping to better isolate the noise, he tracked it close to the ottoman and then the noise stopped. Realizing what it was, he dropped down to the floor and started searching around the base of the ottoman. Sure enough, he found his phone just under the front edge. Looking at the display, he saw he had three missed calls with the last one being the one he just missed. Reviewing the recent calls list, he saw that they were all from the same person, Michael.

    Not one to make repeated attempts to contact people, Michael rarely displayed this kind of urgency. Evan got up from the floor and hurried to the kitchen, still thinking about breakfast. Before calling Michael back, Evan sliced one of the Everything bagels from the half dozen he had gotten yesterday at the Blazing Bagels shop in Port Townsend. "Sorry Michael," Evan thought to himself, "a man's gotta eat." Evan popped the bagel halves in the wide slot toaster on his counter and firmly pushed down the spring mechanism until the lever clicked in. Pulling his phone from his pocket, he found his recent calls screen and pressed the phone icon next to Michael's name to start a call. The phone was just starting the second ring when Michael picked up and poured out a stream of words that Evan could not understand. He elevated his voice and said, "Michael! Michael! I can't understand what you're saying! Slow down buddy, tell me what's going on."

Michael stopped to take a breath, and catching on that Evan didn't understand what he had just said, started over speaking slower, but still clearly excited.

"Last night I finally got to looking at our pictures and video from the Narrows dive. Like you said, I ignored the crazy octopus show and just focused on the surroundings. I've been calling because I found something that I think shouldn't be there. Granted, it could be trash, so I'm hoping your pictures and video will show a different angle and give us a better image. Did you see anything out of place or odd when you looked at the pictures?"

Evan admitted that he had yet to perform a careful review of the video footage or pictures. With that, Michael suggested, "Well, pack it up and bring it over! Let's have a look at it. Plus you can give me an opinion of what I found."

"OK," Evan replied. "Give me an hour to take care of some work and I'll be over. But how about a hint first. What do you think it is that you've found?"

Michael paused while trying to collect his thoughts and finally said, "I just don't know, but it looks old and manmade, and it might be worth a dive to get a closer look."

"An intriguing hint indeed. Well, tell Katie to start brewing a pot of her famous coffee and I'll be there shortly," Evan said.

"Sounds good," said Michael. "And what's with your phone going to voicemail?"

That brought a smile to Evan's face and he simply said, "No worries, just misplaced it for a little while. I'll see you soon."

Hanging up the call and slipping the phone back in his pocket, he stepped across the room and pulled the cream cheese from the refrigerator. He could tell his bagel was done as the air was now filled with the smell of toasted sesame seeds and French onions. He quickly spread the creamy white cheese on both halves so he could eat the bagel open face, and carrying the bagel on a plate in his left hand, and a small glass of V-8 juice in his right hand, moved to the eating nook near the sliding glass door. Located adjacent to the house's rear deck, the nook had a view out the windows to the sparkling waters of Sequim Bay one hundred and twenty feet below. Evan contemplated the conversation that he had just had with Michael, and while gazing out the window and wondering what it might be that Michael had found, he enjoyed his bagel and juice. Dropping the plate in the sink when he finished, Evan headed for his bathroom for a quick shower before he would handle some Dungeness Technologies work, and then he would make the drive to Michael's place near Port Townsend.

Chapter 11

Almost to Michael's house right after he turned northbound onto State Highway 19, Evan started looking for the somewhat hidden driveway entrance on the left. With the house set back from the road over one thousand feet, looking for the actual house provided little help with locating the property. Spotting the landmark he liked to use, he caught sight of their black and bright green mailbox and decelerated rapidly. The Camaro protested some at having to slow down, but cornered tight and smooth into the driveway and accelerated briskly away under Evan's heavy right foot. Two gradual turns later and the house came into view. Evan pulled into a large area to the right of the large detached garage, parked his car and quickly stepped out. Michael was already at the front door and urging him to hurry up.

Michael held the door open and Evan stepped inside. They went straight through a short hallway and past the kitchen toward the large recreation room at the back of the house. Once a game/theater room, the space had slowly turned into Michael's and Katie's home office. Comfortable, casual furniture covered in soft to the touch micro-fiber fabric was positioned nearest the windows in a large, almost circular fashion. The setup encouraged group conservations and there was an octagon shaped coffee table sitting in the center. A six foot opening nearest the large picture windows allowed access to the seats of the inner circle. The balance of the room was filled with three large desks, all facing the same general direction in an easy arc with four feet of separation. Everything faced the windows. Today, even with only the filtered sunlight from the thin cloud cover, an amazing view of the Olympic Mountains and the Strait of Jun De Fuca was on display. The lightly snow-capped mountains went from nearly twelve thousand feet down to the glimmering waters of the strait at sea level. Evan appreciated the view every time he saw it and stopped himself briefly to take it all in.

Michael, who having seen the view many times before, hurried past Evan to the center desk. He directed Evan to the "guest" desk and suggested he get started loading his files. Evan instead took a step toward the kitchen. He had picked up the aroma of Katie's coffee and decided before he did anything else, he would get some of the delicious brew, and thank the coffee maker of course, that being Katie, not the machine. Katie was standing at the sink with her back to him and Evan's greeting made her jump slightly.

Katie exclaimed, "Evan, why are you scaring me! You don't want to be sneaking up on me. That might get your ration of my coffee cut in half!"

"No, no. Don't do that to me!" Evan replied in a voice that conveyed genuine fear.

"Well, I should after the start you just gave me. You know where the cups are," she said with slight scowl on her face.

Evan moved around the large granite island and gave Katie a hug. He didn't mean to scare her, but she was preoccupied and missed his initial greeting. He wasn't going to argue the point, and after thanking her for the hot brew, got his cup of coffee to go.

Once seated and few sips complete, Evan loaded an SD card into the desktop PC just to his right. His dive camera's SD card held all the pictures and videos from the Narrows dive last Saturday and he was ready to have a look. With a solid state drive, the PC came to life right away and Evan navigated using the file viewer to find his SD card, and then the "media" folder that held the actual .jpeg and .avi files. He started by viewing everything as extra-large icons. Before he could begin looking closer at the thumbnail images, Michael called him over to his desk.

On his screen, Michael had an image of Puget Sound, one hundred and twenty feet below the surface. His camera had picked up incredible detail and definitely enhanced the available light to improve the contrast. Wasting no time, Michael explained, "This is a full size view. If you ignore the octopus, which is totally cool by the way, off to the left there are a lot of coral fans. It looks to be mostly small bridge rubble mixed in with the fans, but near the lowest part of it, I think I'm seeing a color that doesn't seem to fit."

Evan leaned in and followed Michael finger as he pointed to an area in the lower left of the screen. It all looked blue with hints of green, and green with hints of blue. It was difficult to distinguish any patterns and it all looked random. Staring at the image, Evan said, "Not sure I see anything except a lot of the same. Maybe if you point it out to me, I'll see it."

"I'd rather not give you any more hints," Michael said. "If you can't see it with a general area hint, then I must be imagining things."

"OK, let me look again," Evan said.

Michael pushed his chair back and Evan moved to be in a more straight on position with the screen. He closed his eyes and relaxed for a few moments. Opening his eyes, he let his gaze take in the whole image. Trying to ignore the bright red octopus that was getting ready to move, he shifted his attention to the lower left. Staring blankly at the blue green pattern, Evan's eyes caught upon a shade of color that was off slightly. Narrowing his focus, he could see that the color could possibly have distinguishing features. Raising his left arm and moving his index finger close to the screen, Evan said, "Could this be the area you're looking at?"

When he turned to look at Michael, he could tell he'd pointed out the object of Michael's excitement. He was beaming ear to ear and simply exclaimed, "Yes, that's it!"

Michael moved back close to the desk and zoomed in closer on the area, but not too close to lose perspective and image resolution. Sitting back again, Michael said, "OK, so would you agree I zoomed in on what you pointed at in the center of the screen?"

Evan agreed in the affirmative with a head nod.

"Now," Michael said, "go ahead and describe what you see. I've already written my description down and then we'll compare notes."

Evan began to describe what he was looking at. "I see a relatively small patch of a darker blue that looks out of place with the other hues of blue. I perceive it to be a 3D object because it looks like there might be some shadows being cast. And finally, there's a straight line across the odd blue patch that seems impossibly straight, even though I think that patch might only be three or four inches across."

Michael pulled out a piece of paper that had been folded in half. Unfolding the paper, he looked over what he had written. He tossed the piece of paper on his desk and leaned back in his chair. Taking a long slow breath in, he breathed out and said, "Close enough for government work. You can read it yourself, but I'd say we zeroed in on the exact same spot. That's my best angle and view that I could find, and believe me, I looked."

Evan wasted no time now and moved back to the guest desk. All of his images had the extra-large icons visible and he looked at Michael's screen for reference. There appeared to be a distinguishable edge on one of the large concrete block from the old bridge. Scanning his images, he located a few images with what appeared to be that same edge in the pictures. It was tedious work, and both Evan and Michael kept up the hunt for better images for an hour with no real luck.

They both finally took a break and discussed what they had found, and didn't find. In the end, it was really nothing more than what they had after Evan's initial look at Michael's picture. They discussed the pictures for a few more minutes and then went looking for Katie. Michael's kids were in school and daycare at the moment, so Katie was likely working and as suspected, they found her in a smaller office closer to the master bedroom. It was not all business though, as she had an Amazon search results page for athletic shoes displayed on one of the two screens.

Seeing them come in, she stopped typing and said, "So, did you bust Michael's bubble and tell him he's been staring at a piece of garbage for two days?"

Evan thought it would be funny if that really was the case, but instead he said, "I have to admit, I can't tell one way or the other. And we do like a good dive."

With that, Katie snapped her head their way and focused her attention on Michael. "Am I picking up that you're going to go diving again?" she asked.

"I think we have to," he said.

Michael continued, "We were thinking about another dive anyway to see if we could find, carefully, the Giant Pacific octopus. Evan found nothing on his pics, but I have three that would appear to show "the object" let's call it. With all three of those, the images are slightly different because I was moving. That little bit of movement will help us better isolate the spot."

Evan added, "And although we'd like to see the octopus again, that's secondary. Our primary objective is to get an on-site look at what we think we see in the pictures."

"Sounds like it might be a wild goose chase," Katie commented.

"There is a fun side of this for you as well," Michael offered with a slight hint of intrigue.

"Really?" she replied with genuine interest.

"That's right, there's a terrific boat trip on Puget Sound in the plan. Plus, you would get a nice long look at the beauty of the Tacoma Narrows Strait while you hold our dive boat on station," he said with a big grin.

Chapter 12

Deena Ardosio had worked for two full days on trying to compile the best places for one of her company's important clients to acquire gold. She wasn't sure exactly who the client was, but her boss knew, and that was enough. At first, given that her education leaned toward mining and processing, the gold distribution side of the business was an unknown to her. Erroneously thinking about gold the way most people might, she imagined shiny yellow nuggets of the dense metal, all ready to be counted and weighed out as needed. What she discovered was surprising to her. Not only is gold used extensively in the jewelry industry, but the technology industry uses considerable amounts given the metal's high electrical conductivity and its excellent resistance to corrosion. Then there's the large percentage of gold that is destined for investors, nearly rivaling the amount of the precious metal that flows to the jewelry industry.

In her research, she found a recent report on the subject that stated that roughly one hundred and eighty seven thousand tons of gold have been mined from the earth. What Deena had surmised, and was validated by her research, was that all the gold that has been mined throughout history is still in existence in the above-ground stock. That means that if one has a gold watch, some of the gold in that watch could have been mined by the Romans two thousand years ago. However, the way gold is being used in the technology industry today is different. In this sector, where it is often used in very small quantities, in each individual product, it may no longer be economical to recycle it. In short, for the first time ever, gold may truly be being "consumed". The revelation that the world's gold supply was essentially shrinking was a bit of an eye opener for her. This being the morning of the third day on the project, and now thinking that she had a handle on the supply and demand aspects of gold, there were questions that she needed to ask her boss.

Davis seemed to always be busy and from what Deena had observed so far, he could only be found in the HGE Building about half of the time in any given work week. Opening the Calendar application on her computer, she found and displayed Davis's calendar. There were large blocks of time marked as unavailable with no details and that made finding a time to meet with him challenging. She was hoping to meet with him soon and so concentrated on small open windows of time in the next few days. Although she hadn't seen her boss yet today, it looked like this afternoon would work and she created a meeting notice for today at 2:30PM, half an hour in duration, located in Davis's office. For the subject line, she typed in "Special client gold purchase, progress update." Checking that all was in order, she clicked the Send button and hoped for a quick response.

Deena then straightened up her desk and considered that she should start getting prepared to meet with her boss. It was odd that she felt nervous since she was confident in her knowledge of geology. What she was less confident of was interaction with senior personnel at HG Enterprises since she was new to the company, and new to the type of work she was doing. The job she now has had seemed to have fallen in her lap. After years of field work as an "apprentice" geologist, she finally decided she needed to pursue at least a Bachelor's degree in Geology if she hoped to move beyond the grunt work. So she committed to the process, and at the age of thirty five, graduated with the degree that she had worked so hard for. Having the degree opened up many options for her. When one of her professor's suggested she look at the role of "analyst", she did, and found the various descriptions of the work interesting. With the analyst role in mind, she scoured want ads and job boards looking for something that would take advantage of her degree, and not take her away from the Northwest. While perusing the trade magazines for the precious metals industry, she had come across a help wanted ad for a Precious Metals Analyst at HG Enterprises. Doing a little research about the company, she found that it had a long history as it had been founded in the state of Washington in 1848. Now with a global presence, it has grown to a significant player in the gold industry. Along with the mining, on-site processing and off-site refining, HG Enterprises also operates as a

At Water's End 89

distributor of the refined ore to end users. The Statement of Work as described intrigued her and she submitted her resume, had two interviews, and two weeks later she was employed as a Precious Metals Analyst.

Deena now knew that the demand side of things could be generally grouped in four sectors; jewelry, technology, medical and investors. She had established that the four sectors needed their gold resources in slightly different ways and slightly didn't purities, so with her main questions determined, and expecting Davis to accept the meeting request, she started making some notes in anticipation.

Much later in the day with lunch now over, Deena wondered if she would actually be having a meeting with Davis today. At about the same time that she was wondering, she got an alert of a meeting acceptance. She clicked on it to find that Davis had replied to confirm today's 2:30PM time and day. He had cut it short though since it was now five minutes after 2:00PM. Deena then busied herself with minor tasks, not wanting to get too involved with anything before 2:30PM.

At 2:25PM, Davis breezed through the workplace and into his office wearing the familiar suit and tie with his salt and pepper hair perfectly in place. He left the door open and Deena heard the noise of a jacket being removed and hung up. Along with the smell of his cologne, he also brought in the outside smell of a rain shower. Together, they seemed to provide a nice mix and Davis smelled a little better today. Grinning to herself for being prepared and prompt, at 2:29PM she picked up her notes and research materials, and headed to her meeting.

Davis was already in his desk chair with the PC up and running and apparently didn't notice Deena walk in. She intentionally brought her footsteps down a little harder on the last few steps to his desk, and that did get his attention. He looked up at Deena, and seemingly without spending any time actually looking at her, looked past her to the clock. Apparently liking the fact that she was prompt, his mood lightened and he pushed back from his desk. Standing up, he eased himself around the desk and approached toward Deena. She was watching him wondering why she was being welcomed to his office in such a formal manner. Instead, he walked past her and closed his office door.

Turning around, he said, "Deena, I'm glad you have some progress for me. We can sit over here at the table."

Deena moved to a position at the table that afforded a view of the door and put her back to the wall. Something she'd always seemed to do naturally, and at one time her friends had suggested she had Doc Holiday syndrome. Apparently a reference to Mr. Holiday's tendency to want to keep an eye on the door in case he needed to shoot someone.

After sitting down in the same style leather office chair she had at her desk, she spread her notes loosely and opened her notebook to a new page. She wrote down the day and time of the meeting, the subject, and the attendees. Davis had returned to his desk and came to the table with only a half full bottle of Aquafina water.

Davis went right to the heart of the matter. "So you have a list of sources for me?"

"Not quite yet", Deena said with some trepidation. "However, I do have some good candidate sources, but will need some information about our client. Namely what business sector they operate in and what grade and form of gold are required?"

"Good questions," Davis replied. "As I said before, this is an important client for our company and I'm handling our interaction with their Buyer. However, I can see you've done your research and are starting to have an appreciation for what we do here."

"Thank you for acknowledging that. The research work did help with getting a better understanding of HG Enterprises." Deena offered.

"Well, to help move this along, work to locate gold that would be of investment quality." Davis said.

"Any particular forms desired. That is, coins, bars, ingots?" Deena asked.

With his expression changing slightly toward a frowny face, she could tell that for Davis, the meeting was starting to run long. Recovering from what she perceived as a misstep, she hurriedly said, "I guess that's probably not a concern. Let me narrow my list down and I'll send you what I have before the end of the day."

Davis looked at her for a few moments and then his serious, no messing around face returned. "You know Deena, time is money, and I think you're getting it. If I have any questions after I go over the list this afternoon, I will let you know," he said, emphasizing "this afternoon".

He then stood up from the table and returned to his desk chair. As he went to sit down he looked at her and said, "Thank you for your effort on this. I look forward to seeing your work this afternoon."

Feeling he had sent a pretty clear message of urgency, Davis sat down and pulled his chair in to his desk. He assumed the same position he was in when Deena had walked in and like a switch had been thrown, he gazed into the computer screen and began thinking of who knows what.

Deena did know that it was her time to leave. She gathered her notes and putting them inside her notebook, quickly stood up and walked out of Davis's office. She thought to herself that that might have been one of the oddest meetings of her life. It certainly did not change her opinion of Davis. Knowing that in a few hours he expected to be going over a list of sources that can immediately supply large quantities of investment quality gold, Deena stepped quickly across the office floor to her desk and got started on narrowing down the list.

Tacoma Narrows Bridge

Chapter 13

Hoping that the limited bit of "artifact" location knowledge gained from the picture and video reviews will help, Evan, Michael and Katie neared the Tacoma Narrows Bridge just before 10:30AM Saturday morning. They had taken Evan's Chaparral 330 Signature that had been mostly loaded for the trip the night before. All of the dive gear, an extended boarding ladder and a small portable winch system that Evan had designed were stowed aboard. Saturday morning packing only required what would normally go along with a picnic in the park. That is, lunch, snacks and drinks for the day. The well optioned Crab got Legs had a fully equipped galley, but the food stores were typically thin and a trip such as today's required that the boat be stocked. They had stocked it with deli sandwiches, a selection of flavors of Doritos tortilla chips, different cheeses, fresh fruit, crackers, trail mix made from dried fruit with an assortment of nuts, and plenty of water. The boat's galley was well stocked with libations and coffee, so that was already covered. Weather this Saturday morning had started with a thin marine layer of clouds sitting low over Puget Sound, but by 9:30AM that was mostly gone.

Near the beginning of the trip, after clearing Point Wilson at Port Townsend and adjusting to a southerly course toward Seattle, they had sighted a

Killer Whale pod that was moving north. The whales are an amazing and elusive sight to see, and Evan and his crew were excited that they had not missed the show on the port side as they cruised in the opposite direction. Other than the whales, the trip to the Narrows was uneventful. Now, as they looked south and up at the Tacoma Narrows Bridge looming in the distance being lit up by the mid-morning sun, the four massive towers holding up both directions of State Highway 16 for well over a mile made for quite a sight.

Today's relatively small eight foot high to low tide difference would put current speed near the low end, but still fast. They wanted to be in the water about twenty five minutes before slack tide and then surface an hour later. At that time, the ebb tide would just be starting and Evan and Michael would drift with it slowly to the north. Katie would be at the helm keeping the boat on station flying a bright red flag with a diagonal white stripe displayed prominently indicating that she had "divers down".

Still on plane, Evan turned to Katie who was riding comfortably in the large passenger seat adjacent to the Captain's chair and said, "OK Katie, we're almost there. We've already talked about your role and it's pretty simple. Are there any concerns or questions about the boat?"

Katie took hers eyes off the beautiful scene before her and replied, "I think I've got it. Once you guys go in the water, I just hang around at the GPS coordinates where you went in. That about it?"

"That's right," Evan said. "I've already set a Mark on the chart plotter so you know the spot. We'll get in the water while you're in Neutral and once we're clear of the swimstep and away from the boat, you're on your own."

"What happens if the boat dies?" Katie asked with clear worry in her eyes and voice.

Evan confidently told her that he had not had that happen to him so far in his ownership and also added, "If it does happen, just make sure you're in Neutral and follow the starting procedure I showed you before. It will all work out fine."

Katie seemed to calm some, but Evan could tell she was still a bit nervous taking over as Captain, and with no crew aboard.

Michael was just finishing pulling out the dive gear from the cockpit storage area and getting ready to transfer the tanks from the storage rack to the buoyancy compensators. He had heard Evan and Katie's conversation and offered, "Hey Katie. This boat almost drives itself. You can move around a bit and you don't have to stay right at the Mark. Just watch the time, stay close, and move to the Mark position about an hour after you drop us off."

"I know it should be easy," she said. "I'm just concerned since I've never piloted this large of a boat before, or one with two engines!"

"Well, since you're just going to be idling around and shifting in and out of gear occasionally, I really don't foresee any problems. If there are other boats in the area, stay close to our Mark so they can see the divers down flag." Evan told Katie, and at the same time gave her a look that said he had complete confidence in her.

"The simplest method is to just move north and south," Evan explained. "Head into the current a little past the Mark and then shift to Neutral. You'll drift back over the dive entry spot and when you're a little past, shift to Forward and do it again. You'll notice in about half an hour that the current will go slack and then change direction. You just keep doing the same thing, but now in the opposite direction."

Considering the conversation complete, Evan turned his attention to navigating the boat. Seeing he was just a few hundred yards off the Mark, Evan pulled both throttles back slowly and Crab got Legs slowed as well. As the boat speed dropped below twenty knots, the stern settled first and the bow wave created by the boat continued to roll forward as the boat came off of plane. Evan held the throttles at seventeen hundred RPMs just long enough for the following wake to crash against the transom below the swim step which avoided swamping the cockpit through the transom door. Once clear of the wave action created by his own boat, Evan pulled the throttles back to idle and made straight for the Mark shown on the chart plotter now fifty five yards away.

With the heading set toward his destination, he looked to his left at Katie and said, "It's time."

She pulled her legs up and to the left in order to make room for Evan to pass. Easing by her, he stepped away from the helm. Katie wasted no time and scooted over behind the wheel and her jeans caused a slight squeaking sound when hitting the marine grade vinyl upholstery of the Captain's chair. She noted that the gearshifts were in Forward and both throttles at idle. She scanned the helm station looking at the large OLED screen in the center displaying dual gauges for oil pressure, engine coolant temperature, outdrive oil temperature and alternator voltage. The high definition display included indicators for both trim tab positions, both outdrive tilt positions and also visually showed the currently selected outdrive gear and the respective engine's throttle position. She scanned one hundred and eighty degrees around her, looked down at the controls of the boat, and then reached out and grabbed ahold of the polished wood steering wheel. A broad grin appeared on her face as she nodded her head slowly up and down, and she turned to Evan and said confidently, "I got this."

Evan replied in kind with a broad smile. He put his hand on Katie's shoulder and squeezed lightly. She nodded at him and then turned to look down briefly at the Furonu chart plotter to confirm their course and distance. She then trained her eyes straight ahead to look for an invisible location on the surface of the water. With that, Evan stepped aft into the cockpit to help Michael finish preparing the gear for the one hour dive to the bottom.

Evan could see that Michael had nearly completed getting the gear ready, so he proceeded to assemble the polished stainless steel portable winch system he had built. He first slipped a two inch diameter by four foot long post into a receptor socket hidden by a small trim panel in the starboard side of the swimstep. He then secured the two post support arms with clevis pins to the sturdy receiving mounts already in place on the transom. The post was now fully supported and free to rotate. Evan spun the post so the large hook hanging at the end of the two foot horizontal bar at the top of the post was out over the water. He plugged the power cable into the 24V water resistant socket mounted high on the starboard side of the transom and tested the system for operation. Seeing that the winch was able to spool out the 3/16" diameter steel cable, stop, and then reverse and raise the hook to the full up position satisfied Evan that the system was ready for use. He turned toward Michael and said, "Looks like all that's left are the drysuits."

Before Michael could respond, Katie shifted both drives to Neutral, paused briefly, and continued into Reverse for a few seconds before shifting back to Neutral. The big boat came to a stop relative to the water and Katie called out, "OK guys, we're here!"

Michael complemented Katie on her skilled stopping of the boat and called out, "Nice job, Babe. Not sure Evan could have done any better."

"Thanks," she said. "You guys were right, the boat seemed really easy to handle."

"Most boats are," Evan said, "When the conditions are favorable. But when Mother Nature decides she wants to, she can be one nasty bitch and change moods really fast. Speaking of which, we've got great weather right now, but periodically switch the VHF radio off of channel 16 to the weather channels for any change in conditions. Just hit the button labeled WX."

Katie looked at both Michael and Evan with their gear all laid out and preparing to slip into their drysuits and said excitedly, "I can't believe we're actually doing this! I know we have no idea what dangers might be down there, with the exception of the giant octopus, but treasure or not, if feels like we're on a treasure hunt!"

The two men standing in the cockpit stopped what they were doing and looked at each other for a second and grinned. They both turned toward Katie and Michael said, "You're right Babe. This does feel like a treasure hunt! Let's hope that when we get back it didn't turn out to be a wild goose chase."

That lightened the mood and they all chuckled at Michael's comments. It all turned serious for them though when the drysuits were zipped shut and Evan and Michael took turns lifting each other's buoyancy compensators up to help each other get outfitted for the dive. Having checked their regulators and mouthpieces for airflow, verified the tank pressure levels were full, and with each having a DiveCom unit attached to a wrist, they felt they were ready to go. Evan was the first to shuffle through the transom door on the port side of the boat and then moved to starboard to make room for Michael. Michael just started to move and Katie jumped up from the helm and moved quickly to the edge of the step that dropped down to cockpit deck.

She leaned over and wrapped her arms around Michael's neck as best she could with the SCUBA tank on his back and said, "Be careful down there. I love you terribly, and would be lost if something happens to you."

"I love you, too Katie. Evan and I have done this dive many times and granted, the octopus find last time was a surprise, but now we know it might be there and we'll be cautious," Michael reassured her. He also added, "And keep your DiveCom unit on. If we're nearby we'll be able to communicate."

She hugged him tighter. Standing on the step of the bridge she was at Michael's eye level. Looking right in his eyes, she simply pulled him toward her and gave him a long kiss.

"OK guys, time to dive," decried Evan.

Katie released her hold on Michael and checked the boat's position. She then stepped to starboard and got up on the cockpit's bench seat and gave Evan a quick kiss on the small part of his right cheek that wasn't covered by the rubber drysuit material.

"I haven't forgotten about you Evan. I love you, too. Now go find some treasure!" Katie said with excitement in her voice.

Evan lifted his mask up and placing the faceplate to his face and stretched the strap around his head to a comfortable position. He reached around his back with his right arm and swept for the regulator. Finding it, he placed the mouthpiece in his mouth and that completed the suit up process. All that was left was to step off the boat.

Michael had now joined Evan on the swimstep and was just finishing his final steps of the process. Evan checked his always reliable Omega dive watch for the time that they were starting and made note of it in his head. Evan and Michael looked at each other and almost simultaneously gave each other the diver's "OK" sign. At 10:39AM, they both turned to look south out over the waters of the Tacoma Narrows Strait and with Evan going first, and Michael right behind him, they used the giant step method to enter the water creating two resounding splashes in the deceptively turbulent current.

Chapter 14

While on the boat standing in the sun, the late September temperature of sixty degrees Fahrenheit seemed warm. When Evan stepped into the fifty degree temperature of the water, it was a different story. The heat transfer efficiency of a fluid over a gas was immediately validated. The drysuit kept Evan's body from getting wet and thus dampened the immediate effects of the cold water, but the small portions of his face that were exposed to the water felt bitter cold right away as the water sucked the heat from his face. Following the initial shock of the entry, Evan soon breathed evenly. He looked around for Michael and found him ten feet away, also shaking off the effects of the initial exposure to the cold Puget Sound waters. Evan looked past Michael and found his boat slowly moving away from him under power, Katie waving her left hand high and looking back at them as they bobbed in the current running to the south. Both men waved back signaling to Katie that they were OK and she stopped waving and turned to focus on the task of piloting the boat.

Clear of the boat and adjusted to the water, Evan and Michael signaled to each other that they were ready to descend. They had discussed the game plan beforehand and so each knew what to do. The DiveCom units were on and while above the surface of the water used the world's GPS system to capture positional coordinates for latitude and longitude. Looking at his screen now, Evan saw that Katie had been very close to the Mark so they were within twenty feet of the desired position. Giving Michael the thumbs down to descend, they released air from their buoyancy compensators and as bubbles surrounded their heads, began to sink below the surface.

With the filtered sunlight shining through the water, the visibility near the surface appeared to be about fifty feet. Slowing at around twenty feet below, they made sure that the pressure on their ears was equalizing properly and then they moved on. Evan knew that darkness would soon envelope them as they made their way down and he grabbed the handle of the dive light that was hanging from his right wrist. Turning it on at about thirty feet provided only darkness with many small marine animals adrift in the current.

Suddenly his DiveCom unit flashed and he noted that Michael's did too. Looking at the screen, he saw a message that said "have a good dive" and Katie's face filled the icon at the upper right of the screen. Evan ignored the message and would let Michael respond if he wanted to. He apparently did as he saw Michael's movements and interaction with his DiveCom unit. On the surface and just at the range of the system, Katie's unit displayed the words, "thanks, drive carefully" and showed Michael's face in the icon at the top right. Katie smiled to herself and then returned to monitoring the waters for other boats and watching her position relative to the Mark on the chart plotter. Realizing she had another hour of the same thing, she relaxed and enjoyed just being on the water on a beautiful day in the Northwest.

Below the surface, Evan and Michael were approaching a depth of sixty feet. Descending at a constant rate helped ensure their ears had time to respond to the increased pressure and avoid the pain associated with being unable to equalize the pressure across their ear drums. So far so good and they continued the descent into the darkness. At eighty feet deep and with the aid of his dive light, Evan was able to make out the seafloor below them. Dropping the next twenty feet brought some definition and hints of color below. At the one hundred and twenty foot depth, they were about ten feet above the seafloor and the colorful world of Puget Sound marine life seemingly appeared out of nowhere.

Always fascinated with underwater life, Evan gazed in awe at the small rugged creatures clinging to the rocks and concrete rubble. Where there was only sediment, there were Orange Seapens standing tall and lightly swaying in the subdued current at the bottom of the strait. Patches of Purple Encrusting Hydrocoral and Red Gorgonian Coral were all around and at first, trying to figure out where to head next seemed impossible. Going with the first thing any adventurer would do, Evan checked the compass on his dive watch to establish the directions of East, West, North and South. Knowing which way was North didn't really help with navigating to the location that they thought they had pinpointed. However, by using specific details in both Evan's and Michael's pictures, they thought they had identified the same coral clusters in the photos. Having the images of the coral clusters from two perspectives afforded a more three dimensional view which they used to create a very detailed sort of roadmap to navigate with. The key to using the map as they had come to call it, was finding that very large concrete block from the collapsed bridge. That was really their starting point. Once they located the block and figured out which direction to take, the map would come into play as they slowly searched for the small "landmarks" that they had been able to identify with some degree of certainty, or so they thought.

It turns out that the waterscape of the seafloor that surrounded Evan and Michael in all directions looked very similar. Knowing that they would be confronted with this issue, Evan took a compass reading and faced north. Dropping to the seafloor, he retrieved one of the two foot tall bright orange flags he had secured to his weight belt and planted it in the bottom. He then used his DiveCom unit to let Michael know they were about ready to start going north for the first eighty feet of the search grid, where they would plant another flag. They would then turn west for ten feet before turning south for a return pass. They would continue in this fashion heading west with each turn for a total of six passes. That would cover roughly five hundred square feet of seafloor. If after that they have not located the desired concrete block, they will proceed east for seventy feet, ten feet past where they started the grid, and do it again, but making turns to the east. With almost one thousand square feet to search in the forty minutes they had allocated for searching, and essentially pitch black without their dive lights, Evan and Michael assumed comfortable horizontal neutrally buoyant positions. They kicked their legs to propel themselves over the various sized pieces of concrete rubble from the old bridge that were strewn randomly below them, and each scanned the seafloor looking for the biggest piece they could find.

After four passes, the view of the beautiful seascape through their dive masks was starting to look indistinguishable. Just beginning the fifth pass, a large dark mass flashed by them to Evan's left. Startled by the movement he halted his progress. Michael had also picked up on the movement and was floating stationary to Evan's right. Both had large eyes as they looked at each other wondering what they had just seen. While sharks are super rare, bull sharks have been seen to Puget Sound waters. Much more prevalent are the Killer Whales. As they floated there, turning their heads left and right, they pointed their dive lights out into the blackness around them, now aware that they had been discovered by something that calls the water home. Evan brought his DiveCom unit to life and sketched out, "what was that?" Michael read his own screen as Evan sketched, and he started moving his head back and forth to convey that he didn't know. Now fully alert, with their dive lights pointed out and apart to provide maximum coverage, they both caught the movement as it materialized out of the murky darkness surrounding them.

With no time to react, a large seal lion swam directly at Evan as if to ram him. At the last possible instant, the seal careened around him and without slowing down, looped behind them and appeared on the other side of Michael. With their heads spinning and their lights moving from the flurry of action, they just managed to catch a glimpse of the strong rear flippers of the seal powering its large body away from them. They looked at each and the worried faces were gone. The sea lions pose no real threat to humans, but they are hunted by the Killer Whales and one wouldn't want to be mistaken for a seal. With the excitement over, and no longer feeling like it was about lunch time, and not theirs, they resumed scanning the bottom looking for the concrete needle in a rock pile.

Near the end of the sixth pass, Evan was thinking he'd check his air consumption when they finished the pass and before heading east to begin the second half of the search grid. Being lost in his thoughts, he jerked slightly when surprised by a tug on his right dive fin. He quickly realized it was just Michael trying to get his attention, and he stopped kicking and drifted to stop. Michael was immediately next to him and sketching something on his DiveCom unit. That prompted Evan to look at his own unit and he read. "see large block to the right." Evan trained his dive light to the west and Michael did the same. They panned the lights slowly in the general direction Michael was pointing hoping to see what they were looking for, essentially a chunk of debris that looks the same as all the other chunks of debris, just bigger.

Evan stopped moving his light and immediately noted the direction displayed on his compass as NW. Michael added his light to Evan's for better visibility, but it did little to penetrate the darkness. On his DiveCom unit, Evan instructed Michael to remain in position in the search grid and he would venture out for a closer look. Evan then re-established his light on the fuzzy shapes in the distance and kicked his fins to follow his light beam. At forty feet away from Michael, Evan began to get a clearer view of the shape in front of him. It was indeed a piece of bridge debris, and was certainly the largest piece they had seen yet. Given all their research and calculating, the odds were good that this was the block of concrete they were looking for. Evan turned around and could just make out Michael's dive light in the distance. He waved his own light back and forth, and then used his DiveCom unit to let Michael know that he should make his way to toward his light. Michael dropped to the seafloor and using two bright orange flags together, marked the position where he exited the search grid.

On the surface and in the bright sun, Katie patiently idled into the current, shifted to Neutral, drifted downstream for a bit, shifted into Forward and then did it again. She had lost count of how many times she had performed the maneuver with Crab got Legs, but felt sure she could now be considered an expert at it. Looking at the time on her Apple iWatch told her that the dive was about half over, and she thought about how the guys were progressing. At the moment in the "drift" phase of the cycle, Katie took a chance and used her DiveCom unit to sketch out a note. She sent, "Hey guys, hope all goes well. All good here on the surface." A minute passed and there was no reply. She hadn't really expected one, so gave the lack of a response little concern. Setting the DiveCom unit aside, Katie shifted into Forward gear and resumed her mission to stay close to the Mark.

One hundred and twenty five feet below her, and just slightly to the west, Evan and Michael had convinced themselves that they had located the site of the octopus encounter just one week ago. With that came the realization that the same Giant Pacific octopus they had surprised might still be in the area. Using more caution than they had earlier on in the dive, they advanced toward the man made concrete block turned reef that easily blended in with the seascape.

The map they carried was a series of images from the dive last week. Many of the images were enlarged images of the coral and rock that they intended to use like "bread crumbs", except going backwards. That is, since they do not know where the object of their search is exactly, but do know the general vicinity, they will use the detailed images to essentially pattern match the seascape around them. An incredibly daunting task given they were underwater in drysuits, looking through the tiny windows of their dive masks and the only illumination available was coming from their dive lights. Since they were breathing compressed air from half full tanks, they would need to move quickly if they hoped to find the area where they believed the small patch of odd blue color was located. Plus once they found the coral formation closest to the spot, they would then need to do a detailed inspection to try and actually locate the blue color they had identified in the pictures. Evan considered the odds of finding the tiny spot in the dark cold waters of the Tacoma Narrows Strait with the limited amount of time they had left, and suspected that they would be needing some luck.

Evan and Michael looked at each other, and then out over the seafloor beyond the large concrete block. They had their DiveCom units turned on and in the "IMAGE" mode to display the series of pictures they had assembled. The pictures were annotated with numbers indicating the order that they expected to see the coral and rock formations on the way to their destination. The enlarged photos had the associated non-enlarged image number plus an alpha character. Since they had used the photos taken from Michael's perspective for the non-enlarged images, and they recalled his position was on the right of the block as they now looked at it, they leaned forward and kicked slowly with their fins to move lower and toward the right side of the block.

Once at the corner, Evan planted two bright orange flags signifying their starting point from the block. He checked his tank pressure gauge and noted fourteen hundred psi, just below the halfway point. Michael had done the same and they both showed each other the "OK" hand signal indicating their volume of air is fine to proceed. Each had the first image on their DiveCom screen and together they headed away from the block in the general direction they wanted to go. Once clear of the block by about fifteen feet, they stopped and turned completely around to study the concrete block. Shifting to the left, Evan lined up the corner they had just left with the first appearance of the flat section of the block just behind the corner. He now had a line of sight along the right side of the block. They had painstakingly used both Evan's and Michael's pictures to create a rudimentary three dimensional view. Using that information to guide them, they believed that image number one was a picture of the coral and rock formation looking along the line as defined by the right side of the block. Now equipped with a specific direction to proceed, precisely as he could, Evan turned one hundred and eighty degrees around. With Michael right next to him, they focused their eyes twenty feet straight ahead and kicked lightly to advance to the coral formation directly in front of them.

They reached the coral with just a few kicks since they were aided by a slight current in their direction. As they neared the coral, Evan could clearly see the strawberry anemones, the red gorgonian coral and the brown cup coral they had identified in what they referred to as image number one. Since to his left and his right the seascape appeared the same, he was hoping they had found the right spot. Using his DiveCom unit, he switched to "SKETCH" mode and communicated with Michael, "starting point here, try and match the enlarged images."

Michael nodded his head and brought his DiveCom unit closer to his face to study image number one, view "A". With the image visible and his dive light shining on the reef in front of him, he leaned closer trying to compare the shapes of the actual corals looking for the exact ones shown on the DiveCom unit's display. Before Evan commenced with the search, he placed firmly in the seafloor an orange flag boldly marked in black with the number "1". Back in IMAGE mode, Evan also had image number one, view "A" on his display and he started to carefully compare the picture to the reef. Staying mostly in the same place not wanting to venture too far away from the orange flag, Evan had now switched through all five of the enlarged images for Position One. Michael was being more patient and was just now switching to the "C" image for Position One. The angle of the dive light beam and Michael's perspective were perfect and he had to do a double take to check his vision. Almost like his DiveCom unit was a camera, the image on the display nearly matched exactly a small section of the reef directly in front of him. Evan was fully absorbed in his own search, but did catch the flashing light as Michael waved his dive light back and forth. Evan's DiveCom unit displayed a message from Michael, "maybe found it! Verify image 1C."

Evan switched to image 1C and moved close to Michael. Without Michael having to point it out, he could tell which section of the reef Michael thought it was. He had to agree that it appeared to be a match. Evan smiled and gave Michael a thumb's up. He then retrieved the orange flag and relocated it right next to Michael marking the position. They both then switched to the full view image of the next location, Position Two. From the three dimensional view they had created, an overhead perspective provided that they should take a bearing roughly forty degrees to the left of the imaginary line running from the concrete block to Position One. Evan looked at his compass and after sighting along the imaginary line from the block, rotated his body forty degrees to his left. With Michael right next to him again, they headed straight ahead to the reef illuminated by the penetrating beams of their dive lights.

Reaching the suspected location of Position Two, Evan planted an orange flag with the number "2" on it. Knowing what they needed to do, they both set about comparing DiveCom unit images with the actual reef in front of them. After what seemed like a long time looking, Evan thought he had a match. He had been looking at image "2D" and showed it to Michael when he arrived after Evan had alerted him. Michael switched his DiveCom unit to image "2D" and after a few minutes hunting, identified the same small portion of the reef that Evan had. Evan quickly relocated the orange flag to mark Position Two.

Michael got Evan's attention and pointed at his tank's pressure gauge. While certainly not panicking, Michael was being insistent that Evan check his gauge. Evan reached back and retrieved the gauge and rotating it around so he could see it, noting the needle was just touching the red zone that started at five hundred psi. Michael's gauge was a bit lower, and with a slow ascent ahead of them that includes a seven minute stop at a depth of twenty five feet for decompression, it was time to leave.

The search had taken longer than they had anticipated and with the current picking up now, they would be slowly drifting north as they rose to the surface. It was early in the ebb tide and since their search was ending prematurely, getting back to this spot to finish the effort would mean estimating the distance traveled north during their ascent. Once at the surface, Evan knew he could capture the GPS coordinates, so getting back to the flags he hoped would be relatively easy if his estimate for average current speed was right on. He considered that a way to improve their odds of locating the orange flag he was floating next to would be for one of them to attempt a vertical ascent while the other drifted with the current while ascending. In this way, with both

DiveCom units capturing GPS coordinates when reaching the surface, he'll have a distance to use as a check for his average current speed calculations.

Evan figured that it was worth attempting if they hoped to return another time and finish what they started. With a plan in his head, he used his DiveCom unit to sketch out what he had just envisioned and Michael acknowledged with the diver's "OK" hand signal. Before leaving, Evan took out his underwater camera and took a series of pictures and in particular the seascape surrounding the orange flag marking position number two. With that complete, Evan gave Michael the signal to ascend and they each added a bit of air to their buoyancy compensators. As the air bladders started to inflate, Evan and Michael started to rise from the depths. As they continued up, they began to separate as Michael drifted away to the north while Evan attempted to ascend straight up by kicking against the current.

Chapter 15

A stream of bubbles preceded Evan's return to the surface and he appeared in the midst of the bubbles a few moments later. He was the first to surface and still with sufficient air, left the regulator in his mouth to breathe easier. He also added some more air to the buoyancy compensator for better flotation to keep his head well out of the water. Checking his dive watch, Evan noted the time as 11:42AM and in his head calculated their dive time as one hour and three minutes. The DiveCom unit had already established Evan's GPS coordinates and he saved that information to the unit's memory. He was drifting north now and he looked in that direction expecting to see Michael surface very soon. Almost on cue, Evan could see a disturbance in the water maybe two hundred feet away and then Michael's head popped above the surface. Evan spun his head in both directions and caught sight of his boat to the southeast also about two hundred feet away. He saw the water churn at the stern of the boat and he knew Katie had seen them. To confirm that, Crab got Legs turned her bow toward him and the hull lifted slightly while parting the water and pushing a bow wave to both sides of the boat. He could barely make out Katie at the helm waving to him, but he didn't miss his DiveCom unit come to life and display a message from

Katie saying, "Welcome to the surface! Your ride is on the way."

In no time at all, Katie expertly maneuvered Evan's boat so he could grab the extra deep swimstep ladder that Katie had secured to the transom. Once he had a handhold on the ladder, he reached down and pulled his dive fins off and then stood up on the second to the bottom rung. He tossed his dive fins into the cockpit through the transom door and pulled the regulator from his mouth. He immediately took several deep breaths of fresh air and then greeted Katie with a "Hello there Katie! Thanks for the lift."

She responded with, "You got it. Glad you're back safe. Secure yourself and we'll be off to pick up Michael."

Evan felt super heavy now that he was out of the water and standing on the swimstep. The near weightless feeling of being buoyant in the water was completely gone and he fought the effects of gravity that wanted to rip the SCUBA tank off his back. He lifted his mask off his face and carefully made his way through the transom door. Once through, Katie shifted to Forward gear and gave the engines a bit more throttle. The boat covered the two hundred feet to Michael quickly and Katie demonstrated her piloting skills by bringing the port side of the swimstep close to Michael before shifting to Neutral. Michael followed nearly the exact procedure as Evan and was soon aboard the boat and placing his SCUBA tank in the rack.

As the current was running to the north in the direction they were headed, Katie simply let the boat idle along while the guys got themselves out of the drysuits and worked on getting the blood circulating in their faces and extremities again. The cabin heater was running full blast and Katie had kept the salon door closed to keep the space warm. Evan welcomed the wave of warm air that escaped when he opened the door and then stepped down the three stairs to the floor of the salon. He quickly removed the drysuit and hung it in the head. He then removed his thermal underwear and dressed in jeans and a light forest green sweater that he pulled on just as Michael was coming down the stairs. They switched places and Evan headed out to the bridge with Katie.

On the bridge, Katie was preparing to relinquish the helm to Evan and he stopped her with a compliment. With a grin he said, "Nice work with picking Michael and I up back there. Want to keep driving?"

She looked at him with a glint in her eye and she said, "Well, I don't know about drive, but I would definitely like to travel at a speed above idle."

"How about both," Evan said in a matter of fact way.

Katie's face lit up and she repositioned herself back in the Captain's chair with a swiftness that told Evan she was preparing to leave in a hurry. Evan reached over and put his right hand on her left shoulder and said with an empathetic look, "Hold on a second, let me stow the dive gear before you mash the throttles." Katie looked at Evan and pouted slightly, then relaxed into the comfort of the luxurious seat she was in.

Evan stepped to the cockpit and quickly removed and disassembled the unused winch system and stowed it away in a transom locker. He pulled the dive ladder aboard, folded it up and lashed it to the tank rack. The buoyancy compensators were still wet and he simply laid them out neatly on the cockpit deck along with the fins, dive masks, regulators and DiveCom units. As he reached for the transom shower sprayer, he heard the faint sound of a pump and knew that Michael was washing down the drysuits in the head shower. Pointing the hand sprayer at the equipment on deck, he washed everything down with fresh water on one side, then flipped things around and sprayed everything again. Leaving the hose out, he lifted the dive gear and tucked the buoyancy compensators in the forward starboard corner. The fins, masks, regulators and DiveCom units he laid in a tub he'd secured behind the bridge's passenger seat.

After spraying down the cockpit deck, Evan secured the shower hose in its compartment on the port side and as he stepped back to the bridge, called down below and suggested to Michael, "Better hurry up down there! Katie's got a plane to catch!" A few seconds later, Michael stepped through the salon door and made his way to the cockpit lounge area.

Evan sat down in the passenger seat next to Katie and looked at her while saying, "OK, let's go."

She didn't need to be asked twice. Already lined up on a bearing of almost due north, she pushed the throttles off of the idle position and brought the engines up to thirteen hundred RPMs. The boat responded to her touch and right away the speed doubled to seven knots. She looked over at Evan with a big smile on her face and Evan smiled back and nodded. As he intended, she took the nod to mean more throttle, and she firmly pushed both of the engine throttle controls to their stops. Crab got Legs did not hesitate and smoothly rose out of the water at the bow while the stern dug in. In just a matter of seconds the boat was up on plane and accelerating toward its Wide Open Throttle speed of sixty knots. Evan looked over at Katie who was staring straight ahead and smiling ear to ear as she gripped the steering wheel with her left hand, while still keeping pressure on the throttles with her right.

On the western shore about one hundred and fifty feet up from the water's surface, Billy Desary was watching the activity on the boat with interest from the driver's seat in the cab of his twenty year old white Ford F-150 pickup. He had arrived at his usual lunch spot right at 11:25AM, which was really no more than a large vehicle pullout overlooking the Tacoma Narrows Strait with the bridge looming just to the south. He had noticed the boat right away. Gleaming in the sun, the big sunbridge style cruiser was hard to miss just a few hundred feet off shore.

He had watched the boat go back and forth as he sat in his truck and ate the foot long deli sandwich he'd picked up from the Subway shop on his way to the overlook. Billy was a hard worker with a full time foundry worker job and also ran a fledging enterprise with three partners. It was his role as a fencer of boat parts that he was thinking about now.

Even before the divers surfaced, he had used his high power binoculars to survey the boat, which included noting the state registration number of WN8569CT that was clearly visible on both sides of the foredeck. Billy worked the supply side of the new venture and that meant having boat parts available to be sold. The nearly new looking Chaparral could be parted out for considerable money and that interested him. Years ago Billy had to finally admit that he was a thief, and in doing so, freed himself to become a very good thief. For his current venture, Billy obtains primarily boats in great working order that are then disassembled and the untraceable parts sold via the many distribution channels that the internet provides. The circumstances surrounding his acquisitions are always questionable, and many times downright dangerous. In this case, after surveying the boat and finding the single woman on board, he felt seizing the boat on the open water seemed like a good idea. He'd done it before a few times and he recalled with some satisfaction the way those events had played out.

Having found the lone boats with just a Captain aboard, like the Chaparral in front of him, he had posed as a person in trouble wearing a realistic looking full head mask. Once close enough to tie off, he managed to get aboard and subdue the Captains. Then he simply transferred them to the small, now non-functional stolen boat he'd been using, and set it adrift before piloting their vessel away to an obscure location just south of Bremerton. Having finished his sandwich, Billy used his binoculars again to study the boat. He lingered longer than needed on the tall, sultry looking blonde woman at the helm, and could feel in his groin that he liked what he saw. He wished he would have been ready with his plan today as he would have enjoyed some extra time with the Captain on this one.

Billy's daydream dissolved when the boat turned and accelerated toward the nearest diver that had surfaced and then quickly made its way to the other. Shortly after the second diver boarded, he saw the boat leap forward and a split second later heard the roar of the boat's engines. The boat was up on plane quickly heading north and was soon too far away to follow. He made a mental note of the blonde woman and added the boat's registration number to his phone using the Note app. He also added the name of the boat. With a wry smirk, he entered "Crab got Legs" and saved the record. With the handful of pictures he'd taken and the boat's information saved, Billy considered it a good lunch and set his phone aside. Later, his Department of Motor Vehicles contact would get him the boat's Hull Identification

Number and the owner's information for his consideration and possible use.

Chapter 16

    Sunday morning arrived before Evan knew it and he lay in his bed thinking about the same thing that he was thinking about when he went to bed, yesterday's dive in the Tacoma Narrows Strait. They were so close to what they thought they were looking for and it was frustrating that they had had to leave. On the boat trip home, Evan and Michael had made a plan for a third dive to the site having felt certain they had narrowed down the search area for the out of place blue color to just a small portion of the seafloor. While they started planning the next dive, Katie had stayed at the helm navigating around the many Washington State Ferries that ran mostly east and west all day long in and out of Seattle. She had done a good job of handling the boat through the deceptively strong wakes from the ferries since Evan's thirty three foot cruiser was still susceptible to the power of the water. Once clear of Elliot Bay and Seattle to the east, Evan had taken over the helm and thoroughly enjoyed the easy cruise home with his friends.

    Shaking off the thoughts of treasure, Evan made his way to the refrigerator in the kitchen by way of the bathroom. As he reached out for the refrigerator handle, a small postcard that had come in the mail a few weeks ago caught his attention. Normally one to throw unsolicited mail in the recycling bin, he had kept this one and used a guitar shaped magnet from

Seattle's Experience Music Project to hold it to the door. It was good timing for the card to catch his attention since it was marketing a local event that was happening today. The postcard advertised:

<u>5th Annual Port Townsend Classic Car Show</u>

All cars and trucks 1974 and earlier
   (pre-catalytic converter)
Prizes awarded for numerous classes
   (spectator voting)
Refreshments and food available
   (well stocked food court)
Vendor booths with new tech for your old ride
Register at the gate upon arrival

Sunday, September 23rd
10:00AM to 4:30PM

Jefferson County Fairgrounds
Port Townsend, WA

Evan had kept the card as a reminder because he thought he was going to go last year, but did not. So this year the card did help him remember, and since he had not made any plans as yet, and the weather looked to be free of rain today, he decided he would spend some of the day at the car show. His 1972 Blazer would qualify as a car show entry, but instead he decided he would take his Limelight Green 1970 Plymouth Road Runner. With his mind on the car show now and there being a few things he needed to look after on the Road Runner, Evan ate a light breakfast of fruit, cottage cheese, some toast and a glass of V-8 juice and then headed to the garage.

With the white walls and ceiling, the space lit up brightly when he turned on the overhead lights. He walked around the late model Camaro in the first bay and slid his right hand along the crisp lines of the Road Runner's left rear quarter. The survivor muscle car was all original where it mattered including the 426 Hemi engine that rested between the front tires and the four speed pistol grip transmission connected to factory gearing in the rear end. Evan looked across the roof at the third and fourth bays of his four car garage. Both those bays doubled as workspace and both were full. The Blazer had the fourth bay and was regularly used, but in the third bay sat a project. Nearly done, but still plenty to do, the very rare Pontiac had been covered and untouched for months.

On a whim he pulled off the cover to remind himself of what he had and tried to envision the completed car. The original Russet Metallic paint was in OK shape, so the car looked good just sitting still. The original drivetrain was another story. The Pontiac 455 V-8 with the Super Duty option needed to be rebuilt and the four speed transmission as well. While generally a purist, Evan did modify the twin snorkel hood to accept the functional Ram-Air system from earlier models so the big engine could really breathe when it needed to. And since Evan had a heavy right foot, he thought it a good idea. He smiled to himself recalling the lucky find of the car several years ago, and got excited thinking about driving the 1974 Pontiac Super Duty Formula Firebird when it was up and running. Then he slid the car cover back over the vehicle and returned to preparing the Road Runner for the car show in Port Townsend.

Evan anticipated he would spend maybe four hours at the show. He had left his place a few minutes before 10:00AM, and was at the entrance gate just over twenty minutes later. The Road Runner drove flawlessly, and with the exception of going a little too deep in to the throttle coming away from a stop sign and getting sideways, the driver did too. Having taken care of the registration at the gate, Evan found his designated class of "Muscles Cars – Unmolested" and backed into a space on the grass next to a white Mustang with black stripes. As he stepped out of his car, he noted the Mustang's sandwich board that declared it to be a 1971 Boss 351 Mustang. Evan gave his neighbor for the afternoon a nod in appreciation of the nice condition of the rare car and got a nod back for his Road Runner. He emptied the trunk of his car of its contents that consisted of two comfortable canvas lawn chairs, a small table, a medium size Yeti cooler and his own sandwich board. He quickly arranged a sitting area about eight feet behind the car. Then he picked up his own sandwich board and walked it to the front of the car to stand it up near the right front fender. As he was adjusting the board, a bright color caught his eye and he glanced to his left.

Opposite Evan and several spaces away, a Vitamin C Orange Dodge Challenger was backing into a spot. He stood up straight and watched as the car came to a stop. He could just make out the sound of the exhaust system rumbling smoothly at idle before the car went silent. He was about to turn away when the driver's door opened and a striking woman with flowing auburn hair dressed in tight blue jeans and a black leather jacket stepped out. She reached back in the car and when she stood back up, flipped her hair back by quickly spinning her head to the left. Evan had been watching her the whole time and when her head stopped, she was looking in Evan's direction. Taken by her looks, he just gave the standard head nod. She did not react so Evan figured she hadn't seen him staring at her. Then she did react, and gave a slow head nod and a wave of her right hand. Evan felt himself flush briefly and then raised his right arm and waved back. She flashed him a broad smile showing him her pearly white teeth and then turned on her heels. She walked to the rear of the car and was soon out of sight behind the open trunk lid of the Challenger.

Evan shook off the slight embarrassment and settled in for a few hours of chatting with people making their way through the hundred or so cars and trucks that the event had attracted. Although the events and circumstances of the barn find story of the survivor Plymouth were the same to Evan every time he told it, each new person seemed enthralled with how the low mileage Road Runner came into his possession. Having discussed his car, and theirs, enough for a while, he locked things up and strolled toward the food court while looking at the myriad of different cars and trucks. Some of the resto-mods looked incredible with the cleverly disguised technology. There were antiques as well with a handful of Model T's and a Model T truck. There was a mid-century display with some very nice examples of cars from the 1940's and 50's, and the Monster Truck class brought out about a dozen heavily modified 4x4 trucks and SUVs where Evan was eye level with the bumpers.

He enjoyed a lunch that started with a large slice of pepperoni pizza from Angelo's booth when the smell in the air was too much to take when he walked by. Then he finished with the delicious, buttery, sugar and cinnamon, fried dough treat that is an Elephant Ear. Glad that he had a long walk back to the car to burn off some of his lunch, he used the fairground's restrooms and then meandered back to his Road Runner.

Once back at his car, it was almost 2:00PM and Evan started thinking about leaving. Right then a young man in his mid-twenties stopped by and Evan relayed the survival story of his Road Runner. This young man owned a similar car to Evan's Road Runner, a Plymouth GTX, but it was in a project state. Evan only nodded and smiled when the man discussed his ambitious Do It Yourself plan. Just preparing to sit down in his lawn chair after the man had moved away, Evan heard a pleasant female voice behind him say, "Hey there, isn't that the exact same story you've been telling all day?"

The voice startled him, but he was too late to stop from sitting down and he ended up tipping sideways and nearly falling over when he had tried to look behind him at the same time. He heard the woman laugh under her breath as he steadied the chair and then quickly stood back up and turned around. Once he had, he was pleasantly surprised to put a voice with a face. Standing on the grass strip between the unmolested muscle cars and the resto-mod muscle cars, Miss Vitamin C Orange was looking at him from not more than ten feet away. While talking with the man about his GTX, she had snuck up behind him and given him a start. He said, "What's that you were saying about my story?" He paused briefly before giving her a hard look and saying, "And how is it that you would know if I've been telling the same story anyway?" He let his hard look dissolve into a small smile and she gave a little smile back.

The woman looked even better now than when he had seen her this morning from across thirty yards of grass. Evan guessed she was nearly six feet tall, and the curve hugging blue jeans and leather jacket showed her body to be in great shape. As she stood there with the jacket unzipped, he could now clearly see the snug black T-shirt with the large gold "MOPAR" logo that she was sporting underneath.

"Didn't mean to make you think you were being stalked," she said unapologetically. "It just sounded very similar to what I heard when I walked by earlier today."

"Well then, I would say you have a good memory, because it was nearly the exact same story that I've been telling all day," Evan replied as if he'd just told a giant secret.

She replied with, "I haven't heard all of it, but it is probably a good story, and as long you don't get bored telling it, who cares, right?"

Evan smiled and started to step toward her extending his right hand and said, "Hi, I'm Evan Mason."

"Hello yourself, my name's Deena," she said.

Evan noticed she had a sexy sway about her as she raised her right leg to step up and over a temporary rope barricade that had been put in to separate the cars. He could see she was a bit of a rule breaker as well as she moved past the crowd controls, and he liked her right away. Gripping her hand gently but firmly, she responded in kind to his offered right hand and after the requisite three pumps and you're out American style shake, they hung with the handshake longer then would normally be comfortable. He got a wisp of a scent that was sweet and tart, and while still holding her smooth but toned hand, he offered, "Would you care to rest and enjoy a refreshment at my campout oh weary event goer Deena?"

Evan then dropped her hand and presented her a lawn chair which she graciously accepted and then sat down. Evan proceeded to sit down as well, but first moved his chair out of the way for access to the cooler. After repositioning his chair to her right and sitting down, it was hard to miss that the lawn chairs somehow ended up noticeably closer together. Deena gave Evan a coy look, and then glanced around at the considerable space surrounding them. She looked at Evan again and said, "Seems like you might have a secret to tell me with how close we're sitting."

Evan laughed and said, "Well, no secrets, but I will admit that I did mean to move the chairs a little closer together. Was it that obvious?"

With the filtered afternoon sun through the trees hitting her face, Deena's smile was dazzling when she pulled her lips into a broad smile and said, "I'm going to go with yes. It is kind of close for somebody I don't know, but since you're a MOPAR man, and together with my gut instinct, that's good enough for right now."

"Thanks, I think," Evan said wondering if he should continue the dialogue.

The sun had been out on and off all day and they both had sunglasses on at the moment. Evan had been taking advantage of his dark shades and was covertly checking her out when she said, "Probably not too hard to tell I'm a fan myself of gold and MOPARs." Then she pulled her jacket open, thrust her ample chest out, and the sparkly gold "MOPAR" logo expanded in front of Evan's mostly concealed eyes.

"Yes, I can see that. Thanks for making it clear," he said with a big smile on his face.

Deena let her jacket drop back into position and she said playfully, "Hey, my eyes are up here." She couldn't really see Evan's eyes, so didn't know where he was actually looking, but after that display, she suspected she knew. She also considered why she would do that given that it was way out of character for her. Letting the thought go, she continued, "This is one of my favorite shirts."

Evan truthfully responded with, "What?"

"The gold MOPAR logo," she said. "It's one of my favorite shirts. I like gold, and MOPARs, and who can look away from gold," she offered.

"Right, right. I agree, it is hard to look away from gold," he said nodding his head, admitting that he did have to agree.

Changing the subject, Deena asked, "So I never did hear the full story of your classic Road Runner there," pointing at the Evan's car.

Evan looked at her and cocked his head slightly. Reaching up with his right hand, he lifted his sunglasses off of his face and commented, "Looks like we have the same great taste in sunglass manufacturers." He offered her his sunglasses and said, "See, Maui Jim's."

Deena smiled and raised her hands to the temples of her sunglasses and smoothly slipped them off her lightly tanned face. Evan was taken back with her beautiful penetrating almond shaped eyes that grabbed his attention as soon as Deena removed her sunglasses. With very little makeup, her deep soulful brown eyes appeared to hint at some Asian heritage and that caught him off guard so that he almost missed her response of "really?" He stumbled to say, "I think so. Isn't that your brand?"

The light banter went on for over an hour, but they had also talked and found out a few real things about each other. At almost 3:30PM, Deena suggested that she needed to get going and started to get up. Evan got up quicker and helped her out of the canvas chair. He offered, and she accepted, a bottle of water for the road trip to her home that Evan now knew was on Bainbridge Island. As he walked her back to her car, he commented again on how nice and original the car looked. He noted that he had heard the exhaust this morning and it sounded like a non-OEM camshaft or maybe a tuned exhaust. Deena stopped short of the car and turned to Evan. Looking at him seriously she said, "I might have led you to believe this vintage Challenger here is my car. It isn't really, technically. On paper it belongs to my ex-husband, and he lets me borrow it sometimes, like today."

Evan didn't react to that news right away, but processed it quickly and asked, "Ex-husband huh? How long has that been a thing?"

"Going on four years now, but we split as friends and we tried to work it out fairly. In the end, with no kids it was pretty much a clean split except we agreed to share custody of "Sunkissed", the 1970 Challenger," Deena replied.

Evan was rolling with the situation and suggesting she had a nice arrangement under the circumstances was about all he could offer. Deena took the last few steps to the Challenger and before opening the door, she turned and handed one of her business cards to Evan and volunteered that she might be up for another get together in the future if he was so inclined.

Evan casually accepted the card and replied with a smile, "I appreciate that. I have certainly enjoyed the car show today, especially the last few hours of it."

Deena smiled back and opened the car door. She elegantly eased herself down into the driver's seat and gripped the steering wheel with both hands. As she lifted her legs into the car, Evan felt aroused by the sensual look of her tight jeans and the supple movement of her shapely legs. She closed the door and blocked his view, and then quickly turned the key to bring the car to life. The power of the engine could be felt, heard and seen as it rumbled under the shaker style hood. Wasting little time, she secured her seatbelt and shifted into drive. Once her foot was off the brake, the car started to roll forward and Evan stepped back a little bit. Deena rolled the window down and waving her left hand said, "Bye Evan. Nice meeting you today, and hope to hear from you."

With that, Deena turned the car to the right and Evan could hear the engine RPMs come up slightly as she accelerated toward the gate. He looked down at the business card in his hand and suddenly all of Deena's talk of gold made sense. There on her HG Enterprises business card, in bold gold print for everyone to see, her job title read "Analyst – Precious Metals Division".

Chapter 17

Brenda Charling hesitated with her right hand hovering over the desk phone wondering if she wanted to call or email the news she had. It was Monday, the start of the normal work week for most people, but for Brenda, with the odd schedule of Sundays and Wednesdays off, sometimes it felt like she just worked all the time. This morning she had arrived at Herkel & Grayson's a bit late. Due to no fault of her own, she had been caught in a traffic backup caused by a truck that had stopped on the bridge. The careless driver failed to properly secure a large excavator on the equipment trailer he was pulling, and when it shifted, he stopped on the bridge to tighten the tie downs. That slowed the eastbound traffic coming over the Tacoma Narrows Bridge and made Brenda twenty-five minutes late.

Realizing her frustration with the traffic jam was clouding her thinking, she thought about Evan again and decided to just do it and picked up the phone's handset. Looking down at the info in front of her on the Dungeness Technologies file folder, she keyed in the mobile number she had for Evan Mason. The phone began ringing and after the third ring, the call was picked up.

"Hello", came a voice from the other end of the line.

"Hello. Is this Evan Mason?" Brenda asked the person that had picked up.

"It is," Evan said. "Who is it that's calling please?"

Brenda could recall his voice from last week and although it was just coming over the small phone speaker, it sounded good to her. She had tried to forget about their second meeting and had done well throughout the week. Hearing his voice now though, made her change her mind about how to deliver the news she had and decided an in person meeting would be best. Brenda answered Evan's question in a professional, but a sort of familiar kind of way and said, "Hi Evan. This is Brenda Charling calling on behalf of Herkel & Grayson. Do you have a minute?"

Evan had known it was Brenda right away as her voice was distinct and he picked up on it as soon as she started speaking. He said in casual way, "Hi Brenda. Good to hear from you. I do have a minute. What can I do for you?"

"I won't keep you as I know you're a busy guy, but I want to try and set up a time to meet with you. Mainly to let you know where things are at with the report my company has prepared," Brenda said in a matter of fact way. "If it makes it easier, I could meet you somewhere, too."

Evan replied, "Well, I am anxious to hear about the progress and I actually do have a few hours today. We can meet for lunch maybe if your schedule permits it."

At Water's End 141

Brenda was glad she was on the phone so Evan couldn't see her big smile when she heard his answer. Composing herself quickly, she volunteered, "How about Bremerton? I know a good café style place that makes great sandwiches. Have you ever heard of Hector's?"

Evan thought he had heard of the place and let her know, "I think I have heard of the place. Is it on Charleston Blvd?"

"That's the place," Brenda said a little more enthusiastically than she had intended. Dialing it back a bit, she asked, "Would 1:00PM work OK for you?"

Evan considered his schedule for the day and replied, "Yes 1:00PM will work fine. And by the way Brenda, I look forward to seeing you."

"And I look forward to seeing you too Evan. Until 1:00PM then. Goodbye," she said, and heard Evan reply with "goodbye" before she hung up the phone.

She leaned back in her chair and gazed out the window at Commencement Bay. Today's weather looked to be overcast all day and maybe rain toward the evening, but no matter the weather, Brenda always enjoyed the view. She was immediately having second thoughts about a face to face meeting with Evan though. The last time they had gotten together, things had moved very quickly to a sexually charged situation and she wondered if it was really a good idea to see him again. This was especially true since he would likely wonder why she had felt they needed to meet in person given the good news she had to deliver. Clearly, Brenda wanted to see Evan again. Resigning herself to the thought that she was maybe starting to feel something for him, she moved on to the next thing on her To Do List and let the thoughts of an interesting lunch in Bremerton today move to the back burner.

On the other end of the line, Evan hung up and looked curiously at the phone. Brenda had sounded a little odd on the call, but he could not put his finger on what it was exactly that bothered him. He really did look forward to seeing her. Although the night she showed up at his house had surprised him, and when the evening took a sexual charged turn almost immediately, he had not been prepared for that. Having heard nothing from her until the phone call a minute ago, he wondered what was in store for him at 1:00PM today.

The morning passed quickly and soon Brenda found herself rushing to leave her office by 12:30PM. According to the map app she used, the time from her office to Hector's was estimated at twenty eight minutes. Knowing she would be back to her office later, she quickly pulled her desk together and stacked three neat piles of file folders for the projects she had going. One of them was Evan's business sale. She grabbed that stack and slipped it into her shoulder bag along with her clutch. She looked around and with everything in order, stood up and walked out of her office toward the restrooms. She mainly wanted to check her appearance and freshen up, but would also avail herself of the convenient facilities before getting on the road.

The Seafirst building had a parking garage for tenants and Brenda's vehicle was just a few steps from the elevator once she got to the garage level. The silver Lexus RX450 SUV that she had purchased used with low miles beeped and lit up when she hit the unlock button on the key fob. Realizing she was pressed for time now, she quickly got in the driver's seat and laid her shoulder bag in the passenger seat. She started the SUV and while it warmed up, she retrieved her parking garage access card from the overhead storage console. Buckled in and ready to go, she backed out of the parking space, moved promptly to the exit gate, stopped briefly to scan the access card to lift the gate, and then turned left out of the garage. She gave the accelerator pedal a little more pressure and the Lexus picked up speed as she headed toward the Tacoma Narrows Bridge and the Kitsap Peninsula beyond.

The drive was without incident and before she knew it, the map app on her phone indicated she was just a few minutes from Hector's. On the drive from Tacoma she had used the time to ponder what she was doing. She felt slightly out of control. She knew there was absolutely no business reason why this meeting with Evan had to take place. All she really had to communicate was that her law office had completed the report and had submitted it to their Client as of three business days ago. This morning, she had received an email indicating that the report had been reviewed and with no further questions or issues, the Client agreed to the terms and conditions regarding the acquisition of Dungeness Technologies. This news was something that she could have easily communicated to Evan by phone or email. Yet here she was, driving to a quaint little restaurant to meet him for lunch.

When the sign for Hector's came into view, Brenda started looking for a parking space. She was lucky and found one just past the restaurant and on the side of the road she was traveling on. Parking quickly, she noted that it was two minutes after 1:00PM and wondered if Evan might already be there. Grabbing her shoulder bag, she stepped out of the SUV and with no cars coming, headed directly across Charleston Blvd and to the front door of Hector's.

Upon entering, Brenda glanced around looking for Evan. Not surprised to see him there, he was sitting in a back booth on the left side where his view was looking out toward the front of the restaurant. Thinking he had not seen her come in as his gaze was out the south wall window at the moment, she tousled her hair and smoothed her business suit, pulling down on the skirt to help mask the creases from sitting during the drive. She went to adjust her solid color pale blue blouse, but instead just pulled her jacket closed and secured a button when she realized her high beams were on. Again, she thought to herself, "What am I doing here?" She was committed to the charade however, so she put a small smile on her face and confidently walked toward the booth.

Evan had seen her come in. He also saw her drive past the restaurant as he watched out the window and recognized her driving the silver Lexus SUV. Seeing her behavior in the foyer made him feel good and he was flattered that she was taking the time to check her look. When she finally moved toward the table, he slid out of the booth and prepared to give her a hug. As Brenda approached, she extended her right arm and offered Evan her hand. Not sure what to make of the greeting, he obliged her and shook her hand while Brenda said, "Hi Evan. Good to see you again."

Evan responded with, "It is good to see you again, too. I've been thinking about you," and gave her a mischievous look. They dropped each other's hand in a timely manner, but held each other's gaze for several moments longer.

Before the silence between them lasted long enough to become awkward, Brenda said, "Yes, well, I can understand that you would be thinking about our business, and the report Herkel & Grayson submitted to your potential Buyer."

It seemed clear to Evan that she was hoping to move past the other night. Disappointed, but not one to dwell too long on missed relationship opportunities, he shifted to business mode and said, "I hope you're here with good news. But before we talk business, let's order lunch. I've been looking at the menu and they have some great sounding sandwiches."

"OK, let's order. I've been here before and already know what I want. Check out the Broiled Halibut Hoagie, number six on the menu."

Evan read through the description of the sandwich and then closed his menu. "That looks delicious. We'll make it easy and order two," he said. "Are you having anything to drink?"

Brenda thought for a second and was tempted to have a glass of wine to settle her nervousness, but she opted to pass on the alcohol and said, "I think I'm just going to have water and maybe a glass of iced tea."

The waitress was prompt and she set them up with silverware, napkins and water glasses. From seemingly out of nowhere, she produced a tall slender glass pitcher filled with ice and water and set that on the table. She then filled the glasses from yet another water pitcher. Wasting no time after filling the glasses, a small tablet somehow materialized in her hand and said, "Hi, my name's Linda. Welcome to Hector's. Are you guys ready to order?"

Brenda spoke up first and said, "Yes we are. We'll have two of the number six sandwiches. Plus I'd like a glass of iced tea."

Evan added, "And for me Linda, I'll have a glass of lemonade."

Linda asked if they needed anything else at the moment and getting an answer in the negative, she turned and headed directly for the kitchen.

With greetings and the ordering of lunch out of the way, all that was left was for Brenda to deliver her news. She had tried on the drive to Hector's to come up with creative stories to justify the meeting, but she knew that what she had to say would be brief. So she took a deep breath and started, "I know you're aware my law office has been working on a business acquisition report for Dungeness Technologies. We completed the report and submitted it to our Client three business days ago." She paused for effect and to give Evan a chance to interject. He did not, so she went on. "This morning, I received notice that the report had been reviewed and with no further questions or issues, our Client has agreed to the terms and conditions regarding the acquisition of Dungeness Technologies."

She stopped talking and took a slow sip of water. Evan watched her and smiled to himself thinking that the face to face meeting was really not necessary. He did not let on that he suspected, and simply said, "That's fantastic news! I seem to recall that the terms set a two week period to complete the financial obligations of the agreement."

"That's right," Brenda said. "In two weeks you'll be a very wealthy man Mr. Evan Mason."

Evan had been so busy with the business of the business, that he had not really considered what the sale of his company actually meant for his day to day life. As he looked across the table at Brenda, it started to hit him that the relatively small amount of money he has been getting from Dungeness Technologies as salary is going away soon. In its place he gets an amount of money that realizes the years of hard work that he has put in to building the business. Thinking about the structure of the deal, which includes a fifteen percent stake in Dungeness Technologies through stock issued in his name and a cash payment of nearly twelve million dollars, he was left wondering what's next. Creating the business and growing the value of his company gave him a feeling of pride, and he considered it bittersweet that he was giving it up. He said to Brenda, "Well Brenda, I'm actually a very wealthy man right now. It's just that the wealth is locked up in the business. I guess it will be good to free that money up, although I'm not sure what's next."

She nodded her head up and down slightly and said, "That is true, even if you didn't sell the company now, it clearly has significant value. As far as what's next, I'm sure you'll come up with something."

Evan could do nothing but agree with her statement, and said as much. The conversation turned awkward then with the business of the meeting concluded and the chemistry of sex seemingly strong in the air. It seems that neither could forget last week, but neither wanted to pursue the next step and really acknowledge the intense physical attraction that existed between them.

Fortunately, Linda arrived with the hot hoagie sandwiches which allowed Brenda and Evan to be distracted by the food and drinks. Very little conversation happened from that point forward. They enjoyed the fish sandwiches and commented on how nice the atmosphere of the restaurant was.

When Linda brought the check, Evan reached out and slid the check to himself and said with a smile, "I've got this. It's the least I can do after you traveled so far to bring me the good news."

"Yes, well, I appreciate you picking up the tab. One less expense I need to submit to accounting," Brenda said, trying to avoid talking about her traveling to Bremerton.

After Evan took care of the bill which included providing a large tip for Linda's efficient service, they made their way to the front of the restaurant. Once in the foyer, Evan put his arm around Brenda's shoulder and stopped her progress. He said, "Just want to thank you for all your help with the sale of the company." He pulled her in and gave her a hug that only lasted a few seconds. Stepping back, but still resting his hands on her shoulders, he looked into her eyes and said, "Thank you, and I mean that. I'm really glad that we had the chance to get to know each other a little. I guess you can just let me know if something doesn't go as planned."

Brenda looked back at him and acknowledged by saying, "Of course, I'll get in touch with you right away if the transaction doesn't go as planned, and it was a pleasure meeting you, too."

With that, Evan turned and headed for the restrooms. Brenda turned toward the front door and started moving in that direction. She was feeling flushed all over from the unexpected hug from Evan. She had felt the strength of his arms and the firm muscles of his chest when he embraced her, and that was now sending tingles through her body. Opening the door and stepping across the threshold on to the sidewalk, Brenda felt the cool breeze and could smell the sea in the air. The change in scenery and atmosphere snapped her back to reality and she hurried across the street to her SUV. With the vehicle started and ready to go, she sat at the wheel for a full two minutes reliving the lunch conversation, and was feeling like she was more indecision than she had ever been before.

Evan was out the front door of Hector's in less than two minutes. He glanced both ways then started to turn to the right in the direction of his Camaro, but he stopped turning and did a double take to his left. Across the street sat what he thought was Brenda's Lexus. At first he was concerned something had happened, or the SUV wouldn't start. Then he saw the left blinker come on and a few seconds later, the driver pulled out of the parking space. He watched the Lexus travel a little ways north and then perform a U-turn at the next stoplight. Evan was on the sidewalk right in front of the restaurant and could clearly see Brenda at the wheel as the SUV sped by. It appeared she had not seen him standing there on the sidewalk watching her drive by. Or maybe she did see him and simply ignored him? He couldn't quite tell where her head was at. Watching the vehicle drive away, he just shook his head sideways a few times and thought to himself, "not sure what's going on with her, but maybe better left alone."

Chapter 18

Monday evening found Evan, Michael and Katie together at Michael and Katie's place. After the near find at the bottom of the Tacoma Narrows Strait on Saturday, they were all anxious to complete the hunt and go for another dive as soon as possible. Diving at depths in excess of one hundred feet in water below fifty degrees with limited visibility was no joke, and everyone wanted to be sure there was a plan in place to minimize the chances of an accident. Assuming they can accurately drop down on the last flag they set, and with the search area limited this time, Evan estimated they would have nearly fifty minutes right at the designated spot.

The best image they had of the color anomaly was on a large thirty-two inch monitor almost centered on Michael's desk. After the most recent dive and the close interaction with the coral formations, Evan and Michael had a better sense of scale and both agreed that the spot of color represented an area approximately three by three inches in size. The shape however was not square, but rather ragged and irregular while still maintaining the general shape of an oval. On Michael's second monitor, while it was only a twenty-six inch screen, large images of Evan's pictures from Saturday ran in a slideshow loop with the pictures changing every fifteen seconds. All three were transfixed on the pictures and were leaning forward to help spot the image on the big screen, somewhere in the images of the past Saturday as they rotated through on the smaller screen. Katie broke the staring contest first and said with more than just a little exasperation, "Wow, my mind is numb, and it all looks the same to me now!"

Michael tried to keep her spirits up and with a positive edge to his voice said, "We're making good progress though. Look at the handful of images we've been able to eliminate as probable spots so we don't need to search there. It is a challenge for sure, because I agree, it's starting to look the same to me, too."

Evan suggested that they'd done enough for the night and Michael and Katie wasted no time in shutting down the operation. They had been working for almost two hours and had most of the pieces in place. Katie disappeared right away and Michael was pulling two bottles of Blue Moon beer from the mini refrigerator in the room. Evan considered that lacking any real specific "Position Two" details, they would each have to follow the mini search grids that they would establish around the target location. They wanted to avoid mistakenly retracing their search and would use small bright green flags to mark completed sections. They did not however, have a day and time nailed down for the dive.

The week's weather was forecast as mild through Wednesday, and would then turn to periods of rain for several days after that. The preferred day for the dive was Wednesday, but unfortunately, Katie would not be available to drive the boat that day. While relaxing in the big comfortable recliner intended for just that purpose, Evan had a thought that he liked, but wasn't sure he wanted to act on. His conversation with the woman named Deena that he had met yesterday at the car show came to mind. She had talked of boating on Puget Sound from a young age, and fancied herself a competent sailor, but also discussed with fond recollection a Sea Ray Sundancer her family had owned for years. Throwing caution to the wind, he said, "You know Michael, I might have an option for a boat pilot for us on Wednesday."

"Who are you thinking about?" Michael asked.

"Well, you don't know her. I guess I really don't either, but I met her yesterday at the car show, and I really got a good vibe from her."

"Yeah right, Evan. That's happens with all the hot women you meet," Michael said jokingly.

"While that may be true," Evan said with a smile, "Deena talked about doing a lot of boating and from what she described, she could handle Crab got Legs with no problem during our dive."

"Hmmm," Michael quipped. "Deena huh? I would have no issues with that, after all, it's your boat. Plus we can always swim to shore when we surface and there's no boat around."

Evan acted hurt by the lack of faith in his judgement and gave a great performance as a man just dejected. He said, "I think I can trust her with the boat. Although since we're talking about it, we may want to keep what we're actually doing there under wraps. We're hoping we'll find something of value, and if it is, for now, the less number of people that know the better."

"I would have to agree with that," Michael said. "What would be your cover story? And it's Monday night, kind of short notice don't you think?"

"Well you're right of course about the short notice. Plus I only have her work number, so I can't call her until tomorrow. But I do have her email. I think I'll send her an email tonight and then follow up tomorrow with a call." Evan explained as he worked it out while talking out loud.

"Maybe just tell her about the octopus we saw and that we're going back for another look," Michael suggested.

Evan liked that idea, and made a note to himself to include that in the email once he got home. Had he not left Deena's business card on top of his dresser, he could have done that right then.

Katie arrived back in the room just in time to catch the end of the conversation and asked, "What's that you say, you've found a replacement boat pilot for Wednesday?"

Michael spoke up and said, "That's right. Evan bumped into this woman yesterday and she mentioned that maybe she'd operated a Sea Ray years ago. So he wants to hand her the keys to his boat."

Katie turned from looking at Michael to looking at Evan kicked back in the recliner, and said with some concern in her voice, "Well, Evan, that seems kind of out of character for you, considering that the last dive was the first time I'd ever driven your new boat!" Katie was right to be concerned about the situation since it wouldn't be to just pilot the boat. Michael and Evan's safety is involved, and this woman would be their only topside support in the event of an emergency. The importance of maintaining the divers down flag in position on the surface could not be disregarded either. Katie stared sternly at Evan with her hands on her hips and the look in her eyes told him she was in serious mode.

Realizing she had concerns with the proposal, he attempted to reassure her of Deena's competencies as she had alluded to them during their conversation yesterday. He could tell Katie was getting more comfortable with the idea, but still apprehensive.

Katie said firmly, "Look Evan, I don't really care about your boat. My concern is Michael's and your safety, and how things would go in an emergency situation."

"Fair enough," Evan said. "This is all speculation right now anyway. Let me put the offer out there to her and see if there's any interest. If she wants to, and she can pilot the boat on Wednesday, then maybe tomorrow night we figure out how to meet up for, let's say, introductions. Wouldn't want her to think it's an inquisition," he added with a little smile on his face.

Katie's demeanor softened and she dropped her hands from her hips and walked over to Michael who was sitting on the edge of his desk. She put her arms around his chest and gave him a hug. Looking back at Evan, she said, "OK. If she agrees to drive, then I want to meet her first."

Evan nodded his head in the affirmative, took a drink of the cold Blue Moon beer that was within his reach and said, "I'd say we have a Plan A. I'll contact Deena tomorrow and hopefully she can help us out. Although, exactly what is it that I'm asking her? Is she going to think it's a date?"

Katie smiled broadly and said, "Yes, well, you'll have to figure that one out yourself lover boy."

Evan took another drink of his beer and contemplated the predicament he had just volunteered to put himself in. Thinking about Brenda's behavior at lunch today, and all the feelings and emotions that go with romantic relationships, he started to wonder how he was going to approach Deena with his request.

Chapter 19

The evening at Michael's and Katie's had lasted until just after 10:30PM and driving home, Evan decided he would forego sending Deena an email about Wednesday's offer of a boat trip. He realized that given he had just met her, as casual as he could phrase it, he still might come off sounding like a wacko and scare her away. So when morning came the next day, he simply took Deena's business card and got himself comfortable in his nautically themed office and prepared to make a call.

Evan had checked the weekday office hours for HG Enterprises and found that they open for business at 9:00AM. It being thirty minutes past their opening time, he expected Deena would be in the office. With his notes in front of him of what he wanted to say, he keyed in her numbers and pressed the Call button hoping she would answer, and also remember who he was. After the third ring, the line was picked up and a pleasant female voice came through Evan's phone speaker with, "Hello, HGE Enterprises, this is Deena Ardosio. How may I assist you today?"

"Hello Deena, this is Evan Mason. We met this past Sunday at the car show in Port Townsend," Evan replied and pausing just briefly, also added, "Does that sound familiar?"

Deena did recall, and her face lit up slightly remembering the entertaining Sunday afternoon with Evan. Although she had given him her business card, she was surprised by his call and took a few seconds to compose herself before saying, "Evan, yes, I remember you, the green Road Runner, right?"

"Good memory, yes, the Road Runner," he said, thinking he kind of liked what she remembered about him. He went on to say, "Anyway, I know you're probably busy getting your day going, but I'm planning a day out on my boat tomorrow and wondered if you might be available to go, and would be interested of course?"

Deena's slight smile disappeared and she thought to herself, "kind of rude isn't he, he's asking me to take a day off with less than a day's notice."

Evan heard only silence and volunteered, "To be honest, it's not just a day on the boat, it's also that I plan to spend about an hour underwater. You see my friend Michael and I have located a spot in the Tacoma Narrows Strait that is of, let's say just, interest. We're hoping to dive tomorrow to get a better look."

This piqued Deena's interest and she asked, "Dive you say?"

"That's right. It's really more of a dive trip and we're using a boat to get there. Our normally reliable boat pilot is not available tomorrow and the weather is supposed to turn on Thursday, so we're hoping to get the dive in before then. I know it's a wild chance calling you, but from our conversation, I gathered that you could handle a cruiser style boat and having spent some time talking with you, thought you might also enjoy a little adventure," Evan offered.

Deena was intrigued. A diver herself, she could appreciate the fun of searching the depths of the sea for treasure, buried or not. Now granted, Evan never said treasure, he had said a "spot of interest." Deena however had a vivid imagination, and it took her no time at all to conjure up an image of herself floating near the seafloor with an arm wrapped around a chest filled with jewels and gold. "Wow Evan! You've really made quite a second impression," she said with real admiration for his effort in her voice. "That's quite a day you've got planned for us."

"I called you for a couple of reasons, one of them being the prominent gold lettering that's on your business card struck a chord. I'm not saying its treasure that we've found, but the mystery of not knowing is part of the thrill for me," Evan said trying to entice Deena into taking a chance.

In her head, Deena was starting to picture the day and abruptly stopped when she realized she had no idea what kind of boat Evan was talking about. He had mentioned "cruiser style", so that was a pretty good clue. She decided to tip her hand and show her interest by asking, "What kind of boat are we talking about?"

Evan smiled on his end of the phone at the question realizing that she was starting to seriously consider his offer. He said, "It's a Chaparral Signature sunbridge cruiser, model 330."

Deena recognized the Chaparral name, and since generally the model number indicates the length of the boat, she surmised he was talking about a thirty-three foot boat. She said, "A thirty-three foot boat for a two person dive seems a little excessive. Are you planning on raising something from the seafloor?"

Still with a bit of smile, he replied, "As you have probably guessed, it is not a dive boat, but it is my boat, and it makes for a comfortable day on the water." Not forgetting her question, he added, "And I do have a small hoist that mounts to the swimstep if it should be needed."

Now thinking about her work schedule, she realized that she was leaning, incredulously, toward taking Evan up on his offer. Her Wednesdays were generally light, but her interaction of late with her boss brought impromptu assignments into the picture. However, tomorrow looked clear, but it was still early Tuesday. Making what she hoped wouldn't be a terrible decision, she answered Evan's response with, "Evan, you have grabbed my imagination! I will accept this boat trip you offer, and expect that I will enjoy piloting your boat. It is very short notice, so I will have to rearrange some things, but I will make myself available all day."

Evan's smile got bigger and he said enthusiastically, "You won't regret it. The sun is supposed to be out, and we're aiming for the dive to start right around Noon."

"Crazy I've agreed to this." Deena lamented.

"It will be great," Evan said. "Although, I think we should get together before hand, you know, to go over the logistics and the dive plan specifically. If you're available this evening, and if it fits with your schedule, that would work best for me."

"I am, and it does." Deena replied. "What are you thinking?"

"You mentioned that you live on Bainbridge, and if you wouldn't mind driving to my dive buddy's place south of Port Townsend, we can meet there. Around 7:00PM for a couple of hours, maybe less," Evan explained.

"OK, I can do that," Deena responded. "I'm going to give you my numbers and you can text me the address." She then proceeded to give Evan her personal phone number.

Evan jotted the number down on the page of notes he had in front on him and said, "Alright then, I'll send you the address. It's the home of my friends Michael and Katie Anders and they'll be expecting you. I really appreciate you standing in for Katie tomorrow as the dive boat pilot." Evan wanted to be sure to circle back to the main reason he called her to reinforce his intentions for tomorrow. Thinking about seeing her again, he did look forward to the adventure, and told her that, "I look forward to seeing you again. Until tonight then, goodbye Deena."

"Goodbye Evan. I'll see you tonight. And I'm assuming the text you're going to send me will be from your personal phone?" she asked.

"It will be," he replied with a grin on his face, and then they both hung up.

Deena got right to work to reschedule two afternoon meetings planned for Wednesday.

Although she had been working with Davis, he is actually her second level boss and his approval is not needed for taking vacation days. So she submitted to her immediate boss, Ben Lauren, a request for tomorrow as a vacation day. She was a bit late with the request in accordance with HGE policy, but Ben seemed to be a good boss and attempted to manage to the intent of policy, not necessarily to the letter of it. She anticipated no issues with getting the day off, and began to step up her pace of work in order to get more done before skipping out of the office on short notice.

Having hung up the desk phone, Evan leaned back in his executive style leather desk chair and pulled his cell phone from his pocket. He added Deena's personal and work numbers to his Contacts list and started a new text message to Deena's cell number. Thanking her again for helping with the dive and providing Michael's address, he capitulated on the wording of his text while holding his finger over the Send button for a few seconds, and then committing to his plan, he pushed the button to initiate the delivery of the text. He then called Michael and gave him the good news and told him to expect Deena around 7:00PM. Evan also said he would try to be there early, to avoid the awkward stranger encounter at the front door if he isn't there.

Chapter 20

Deena arrived at Michael's and Katie's place right on time at 7:00PM. Evan did not get there early and showed up a few minutes after Deena, but the awkward introductions had already happened. In part due to Deena's charm, the three had quickly gotten past initial introductions and had moved on to talking about the only common thread between them, Evan Mason. So when Evan entered the house shortly after Deena, he was surprised to find the three of them getting along in what sounded like a gathering of old friends. As he moved closer to the family room, he started picking up words in the conversation mixed in with the laughter. They were clearly discussing him, and in particular, one occasion when he'd mistakenly gotten in a Toyota Sienna minivan that looked like Michael's and Katie's while waiting in a ferry staging lot, and scared a soccer Mom out of her wits. Thinking it was time to change the conversation, Evan strode into the room and wanting to defend himself, he said, "While that story is true, and she was very frightened when I opened the passenger door and hopped in, the wait line was still settling in when I left Michael's van, and it was not in the same place when I returned."

"Come on Evan," Michael said with a wink. "You must have really had your head elsewhere to get in another person's vehicle."

"OK, I was probably thinking about work, but when I saw and heard a screaming woman in the driver's seat instead of Michael, I came around quick. I figured out fast that I was in the wrong van," Evan said making sure everyone knew he was quick to react to his mistake.

It turns out Michael was two lanes over in the ferry staging lot and witnessed the whole thing while laughing like crazy. He said, "It was one of funniest things I've ever seen. Evan practically flew out of that van door while looking confused as hell."

Evan explained, "Yes, well, before the ferry boarded, I went back to the van, approaching from the front of course, and apologized to the woman." He went on to add, "Once I explained the situation and pointed out Michael waving from an almost identical van just nearby, she relaxed and was able to laugh a little at my mistake."

Deena stopped laughing, but still grinning, looked at Evan and all she could say was, "That is hilarious!"

Glad that Michael, Katie and Deena were hitting it off, at his expense or not, he suggested, "Looks like introductions are all over and you guys are as thick as thieves already, so maybe we move on to the business at hand. Namely, let's map out our dive plan for tomorrow."

Moving to Michael and Katie's office at the back of the house, they assembled around a large rectangular table made from old timbers. The top of the table was a collection of thick planks of different woods and colors that were glued together and then planed to a smooth even finish on both sides. The edges were left rough and the whole thing coated with a clear durable semi-gloss urethane finish. The four legs were simply old solid six by six inch posts coated with the same finish as the top. It looked very rustic and sturdy, but the finished top gave it a modern look. On the table top, Katie had already arranged printed images from the pictures Evan and Michael had taken on the last dive, plus a large chart of the Tacoma Narrows Strait. Their objective tonight was to try and locate the odd color patch in the pictures. Fortunately, both Evan and Michael had taken a series of pictures moving left to right from their respective position. Now, the two sets of images were lined up on the table in the order that they had been taken.

Deena looked at the pictures on the table and a confused look crossed her face and she said, "These are all very nice pictures, but if I'm going to be any help here tonight, I'll need a bit more to go on."

Evan replied quickly, "Oh yes, right. I'm so excited to get going with this that I nearly forgot you're not up to full speed on what we're doing."

"I'm a quick learner, and I didn't mention it before, but I am a certified PADI diver," Deena offered to the group.

"Well, well," Evan said while nodding his head in an appreciative way. He added, "You're just full of surprises aren't you. And that's a good one! It's always fun to be in the company of other divers. Maybe that's why we connected at the car show."

Deena smiled at Evan, and gave him a wink and a look that said, "Maybe."

Michael had stopped at the dual zone wine fridge near the kitchen and selected two bottles from local vineyards. Both wines were from just east of Seattle in Woodinville, a chardonnay from the Columbia winery, and a cabernet from the Ste. Michelle winery. Katie followed Michael in with a cheese and cracker platter, plus four wine glasses in a carrying rack. Michael made quick work of the corks and soon they all had a glass in their hand and were toasting a successful dive.

Looking at the photos and then over at Deena engaged in an animated discussion with Katie, Evan decided to share some details of what they were doing, but would avoid speculating on what it might be. He called Deena over to the table and proceeded to describe in vague details the reason for all the pictures. Deena reacted in an unexpected manner by simply saying, "I thought so."

Evan asked, "What's that you just said?"

"I said, I thought so," Deena repeated a bit louder. She elaborated with, "I don't really know of course, just wildly speculating about finding treasure."

"Fair enough," Evan replied. "You know I would also like to find some treasure, but realistically, the chances are slim to none. But I will be diving anyway," he said with a broad grin on his face.

The hard, tedious work of scrutinizing photos now commenced. Evan had described to Deena what to look for, and also showed her the magnified blurry image of the target location so she could get a sense of what color to look for. While Evan, Deena and Katie sat at the table, Michael was at his desk reviewing digital images of the photos. He would occasionally call out, but then would follow up soon after with "never mind." He was clearly getting anxious to find the needle in the haystack. Over an hour after first starting the effort, now it was Evan's turn to call out and he followed it up with, "I think I've found it!"

That got Michael out of his chair and over to the table. Katie and Deena had both moved around to get a better view of what Evan was seeing as well, and Deena moved in tight so that Evan could feel her body press against his left side. His mind momentarily abandoned the treasure hunt and fixated briefly on Deena's fragrant scent and the warmth coming off her body. Michael's loud, "I don't see it!", broke the spell and Evan gathered his thoughts and pointed to one of the pictures from Michael's camera. "I've convinced myself this is what we're looking for," Evan said while circling a small blue section on the photo."

Michael leaned in close and moved his head from side to side to change the way the light hit the photo. After what seemed like a long time, but really only about ten seconds, Michael declared, "I do believe that is what we're looking for."

Evan pulled back some and Deena squeezed in closer to get a look. She stared intently at the picture Evan had pointed out and after a few moments, let out an, "Aha, I see it now! It's incredible that you guys have been able to narrow the search down to just a relatively small area now. I would have to agree the blue color does look out of place, and I hope it really is something worthwhile finding, but I do love an adventure, so worth it or not, I'm looking forward to tomorrow."

Katie took off to the kitchen with the dirty glasses and the empty cheese platter with only a few crumbs left behind. Michael had retreated to his desk and was busy with finalizing the time of day schedule. They were at the mercy of the tides, and had to pick a time that would permit a near vertical descent at slack tide right at the GPS coordinates that are stored in the chart plotter memory of Crab got Legs. For Wednesday, he was finding that the tide change that occurs just before Noon looks like the time to dive. The weather conditions are still predicted as slight overcast, no rain, with a slight breeze to the north, so the weather conditions look good. Evan made his way to Michael and looked at his computer screen. He said, "I agree, the slack tide around Noon looks to be the best time."

"Alright then, not much else to do now but get our gear bags ready to go. I'll fill the tanks tomorrow and bring them with me when I come over. What time do you think we need to head out?"

Evan looked over at Deena, still gazing at the photos, and couldn't help but notice her toned body as she leaned over and stretched out across the table to see the images. Smiling to himself, he was glad he had asked her to join them on the dive trip. Not really wanting to interrupt her, but doing so anyway, he said, "Hey Deena, we're planning on being at the dive site probably ten minutes before Noon tomorrow. I figure it will be easiest for Michael and I to pick you up from a marina or public launch somewhere near your place. What do you think would be a good pickup spot?"

Deena pulled herself from the table and cocked her head to the right slightly as she turned to look at Evan. Tapping her finger against her chin, she said, "Well, let me see, the closest place might be too small as there's only a tiny floating dock and the depth there could be too shallow. I do see fishing boats on trailers all the time there, but none appear much longer than eighteen feet. The best place would probably be the Bainbridge Island City Dock, right near where the ferries come in from Seattle."

"I know where that's at. It will be easy to get to as we come around the east side of the island," Evan commented. "That's about an hour from the Narrows at cruise speed, so let's plan for picking you up no later than 10:45AM."

Deena nodded her head yes to acknowledge the pick-up time and said, "I'm excited now that I've seen everything you're doing." She paused briefly and then added, "By the way, what is you think you've found?"

Michael and Evan looked at each other, and then back at Deena. The silence started to get awkward and Evan said, "We don't know. We're hoping for some kind of artifact, but it could all be a wild goose chase. I really appreciate you helping us out, regardless of what we find."

"Like I said, I'm looking forward to see what tomorrow brings," Deena noted and then headed toward the kitchen to see if she could help Katie.

Evan and Michael went right into detailed planning mode now that they had all the information they needed to map out the day. Most important was the plan of action once they were back at depth in the strait and floating next to the orange flag they had planted to identify "Position Two." They established two rough search grids that slightly overlapped based on the collective images that they had available, and tried to use unique looking coral and rock formations to establish the grid boundaries.

Katie and Deena were just coming back into the room as Evan and Michael were finishing up with the dive plan, which would include a decompression stop at twenty-five feet for six minutes. Deena was first to talk, and with a sly smile said, "Well, Katie has filled me in on my assignment. Sounds like I might be in for a boring hour of idling and drifting back and forth in the boat." Behind Deena, Katie was smiling broadly and giving Evan a double thumbs up to indicate her approval of Deena as the dive boat pilot.

Evan caught Katie's approval and grinned, then looked surprised and replied, "What, Katie said she had a great time topside looking after the dive boat!"

"Yes Evan, that's what I said, but it was a bit of an exaggeration. After the thrill wore off about fifteen minutes in, I was starting to get a bit stir crazy," Katie admitted.

"I get it. The fun and excitement is below the surface of the water," Evan said acknowledging the mundane nature of what he was asking Deena to do. "But the boat is nice, and it will be fully stocked with refreshments and food, so it should be an enjoyable day. You just have to pay attention and stay on station at the dive location."

"I'm just teasing you. I'm sure it will be fine and I'll enjoy the day," Deena replied. "My question now is, what about this boat I'm supposed to pilot singlehandedly?"

Evan gave Deena a small smile and proceeded to tell her about his Chaparral 330 Signature that he'd named "Crab got Legs".

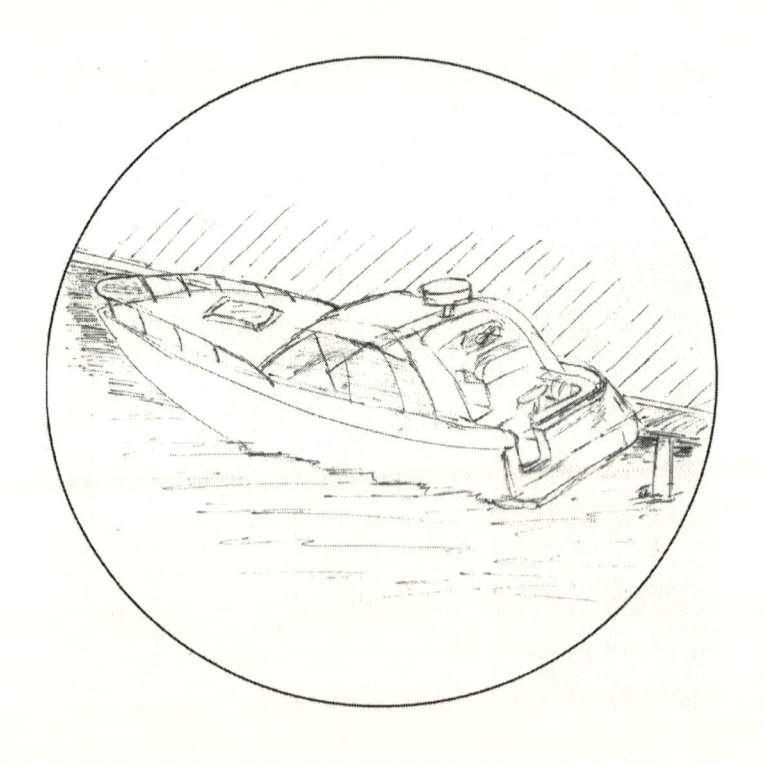

Crab got Legs at Bainbridge Island City Dock

Chapter 21

Michael was anxious to get going with the dive and was up early on Wednesday and he started by helping Katie get her things together for the business trip she was taking to central Washington. After Katie left around 8:00AM, he headed to the attached three car garage to fill four SCUBA tanks and assemble his dive gear for the trip to Evan's place in about an hour. Having decided to dive with the drysuits again, his wetsuit was left behind. With the air fill nearly complete, Michael finished packing and moved his now bulky gear bag to the cargo area of his Toyota Highlander SUV. He made sure to position the bag in the center so he could lay two tanks on each side before securing everything with straps. The last thing he wanted was for something to happen that could damage the tanks. At three thousand psi, a SCUBA tank becomes an out of control projectile if the valve is broken off. Hearing a change in the tone of the air compressor, Michael moved back to the third garage bay turned man cave and finished the fill process for the four tanks.

Looking at his vintage clock trimmed with blue neon and the Ford logo in the center, he realized it was time to get himself ready and he wasted no time moving the four tanks to the Highlander and strapping them in place. Double checking that all the valves were clear, he closed the liftgate and made his way to the upper level of the house where the master bedroom was located. Tossing his sweat pants and T-shirt in the hamper, Michael entered the luxurious bathroom and then thoroughly enjoyed the drenching rain coming from the showerhead that he and Katie had spent hours and hours searching for.

Michael had preplanned for today and already had his dry bag packed. It had his long underwear that he would wear under his drysuit and also two large towels for after getting out of the water. He also had the basics like a hairbrush and a mini package of Kleenex since one's sinuses are often empty after a dive excursion. Grabbing the dry bag and a bottle of water from the kitchen, he selected his medium weight Eddie Bauer brand jacket from the coat rack in the mud room, and proceeded to his SUV that was parked in the middle bay of the garage.

Tossing the dry bag and jacket in the rear seat, he got in the comfortable leather driver's seat that was already positioned to his preference and opened the garage door. Starting the vehicle that had thus far shown itself to be very reliable, he paused briefly for the engine to warm up, and then backed straight out. A slight turn of the wheel to the left and he was positioned to drive right out his driveway. Shifting to Drive, he did just that and noted the time as 8:57AM, which was three minutes ahead of his plan. A good start to the day he thought to himself.

About fifteen miles away to the west, Evan had his own preparations going on. He had taken care of outfitting the boat first thing with the supplies he had picked up last night. His dive gear and dry bag were all packed and all he had left was to get himself ready for the day. Not taking much time, he showered and dressed in jeans and a comfortable long sleeve pullover V-neck shirt.

Now almost 9:30AM, Michael should be arriving soon and then just a ride to the boathouse and by 9:45AM they would be on the water. Just as Evan was finishing his thoughts, he heard Michael pull up at the front of the house. Knowing that Michael was bringing his own gear plus the tanks, Evan headed out front to help by way of his garage. He pulled his large dock cart with him as he made his way to Michael who had the SUV's liftgate open and two tanks already out of the back.

"Good morning Michael. Did Katie get herself out of town OK?" Evan asked.

"She did," Michael replied. "I haven't heard anything since she left, so I'm assuming all is going fine."

"That's good," Evan commented. "Let's load this cart up with the tanks and then we'll use the other cart for the gear bags. Are you ready for this?"

Michael had a serious expression on his face when he looked at Evan and said, "Damn right I am. Today, we're going to have some success and find that strange blue spot in the reef."

Evan grinned at Michael and nodded his head in the affirmative. He then hefted a SCUBA tank up and laid it flat in the dock cart. He followed that with the other three tanks while Michael finished getting his gear out of the SUV and locking it up. Together they made their way around the garage to the backyard, Evan pushing the heavy dock cart and Michael trudging along with his gear bag. Once in the backyard, Michael happily loaded his bag in the other dock cart already loaded with Evan's gear that was sitting near the steps up to the rear deck.

"Go ahead and take the gear cart down and I'll be down with the tanks after I lock up the house," Evan told Michael as he took the few steps up to the deck.

"Sounds good," Michael said. "I'll see you down at the boathouse."

Evan quickly went through the house and made sure all was secure. On a whim, he grabbed his backpack style case with the DJI Phantom drone in it that he kept ready to fly, and headed out the back door of the garage. Setting the drone case on top of the tanks, he pushed the cart to the now waiting tram that Michael had returned to the top. The tram had plenty of room for Evan and the dock cart, and with a pass through design, the cart would just push straight out of the tram at the bottom. As he neared the boathouse, he could hear Michael prepping the boat to leave, so he must have already stowed the gear. As the tram eased to a stop at the dock, Michael appeared in the boathouse doorway and said, "Not much else to do now but secure the tanks in the transom rack. I checked the galley and looks like we're not going to go hungry or thirsty."

Evan smiled and said, "Yes, I pretty well stocked it up. You know I like to keep things full with food and drink when heading out on a trip."

"And head out we shall!" Michael exclaimed.

He then hefted a tank out of the cart and disappeared into the boathouse. Evan lifted the second tank and when he turned around, Michael was there and he handed it to him. They repeated the process two more times and all four of the tanks were aboard. While Michael secured the tanks in the rack, Evan went through his pre-departure routine and was soon ready to disconnect shorepower and get underway. Michael had already opened the bay doors behind the Chaparral, so the interior of the boathouse was brightly lit by the sun as it rose in the eastern sky. The angle of the sun at the moment was causing a glare on the dash, so Evan slipped his sunglasses on even before casting off. Now with both engines idling smoothly, Evan gave Michael the go ahead to release the lines from the dock and climb aboard.

Having already verified that both outdrives were centered, Evan shifted into Reverse and Crab got Legs responded immediately. While moving at barely over two knots is generally considered slow, in a boat near fixed structures like docks and buildings, barely moving seems fast since boats have no brakes. Evan skillfully maneuvered straight back and cleared the bay doors without incident. Once in water open, Captain Evan relaxed and shifted into Forward gear while also spinning the wheel to the right. Pushing both throttles forward half way, the Chaparral settled at the stern and with the props furiously thrashing the water below the swimstep, the thrust lifted the bow and accelerated the boat out of the hole. Quickly reaching a cruise speed of twenty-seven knots, both Evan and Michael settled in for the trip to Bainbridge Island to pick up Deena.

It was late September in the Northwest, but even today's bright sun and unseasonably warm weather did not bring out the boaters. So Evan and Michael had the Puget Sound nearly to themselves as they headed south. Their only company was a few fishing boats and the Washington State ferries making their crossings, and with the calm conditions, they made great time to Bainbridge. Evan consulted his chart plotter for the exact location of the city park marina after making a turn to starboard at Wing Point to head into Eagle Harbor. Adjusting slightly to the north, he steered a course to the west on a bearing of two hundred and eighty degrees.

As Crab got Legs idled toward the dock at the city park marina, Evan called Deena's cell phone hoping she was would pick up and let him know that she was close by. After the third ring, the call was answered and Evan recognized Deena's distinctive voice come through the speaker he was holding to his right ear.

Evan responded to the "Hello" with, "Hi Deena. We're floating just off the dock at the marina. Let me know if you can see the thirty-three foot blue and white Chaparral cruiser. Not too many boats moving about, so I think I'm pretty visible."

As Evan watched the park, he heard Deena say, "Yes! I see you!", and at the same time, caught sight of a person waving their arm in the air. Putting the sight and sound together and identifying Deena's location, he shifted to Forward and idled to a spot on the dock to pick her up. Deena was just stepping clear of a crowd of people when Evan brought the starboard side of his boat alongside the dock. And it was a smooth docking too, with no panic and without the need to make any sudden moves to avoid a collision.

Evan watched Deena make her way to his boat and couldn't help but appreciate the saunter to her walk as her auburn hair swung slightly in time with each step she took. She was looking very nautical and dressed for the occasion with a navy blue wind resistant hooded jacket over a long sleeve light blue V-neck pullover top. She wore a pair of light gray jeans that fit great, but were maybe a little bit too tight for boating, but Evan was OK with that. Her shoes were the sensible non-slip deck shoes often favored by sailors and Deena's pair were well worn by the looks of them. Evan called out to her, "Hello Deena!"

"Ahoy there Evan and Michael! Permission to come aboard?" Deena called out in reply.

"Absolutely, come on aboard. Looks like you're traveling light today," Evan said to Deena noting that she was only carrying a Victorinox brand backpack.

"Not too light. I have what a woman needs for a few hours on the water," she replied with a mischievous smile on her face.

Evan could tell Deena was no stranger to boats as she gracefully stepped from the dock to the swimstep never missing a beat. She moved to the port side of his boat and stepped through the transom door like she'd done it a thousand times. Clearly the woman had sea legs, as well as beautiful regular legs, he thought to himself. Michael secured the transom door and with Crab got Legs floating about a foot off the dock, Evan engaged the outdrives and the boat slipped forward through the calm water and away from the city park marina.

Turning to the east once clear of the no wake zone, Evan eased the throttles down and brought the boat to a steady fourteen-hundred RPMs which gave a speed right at eight knots. Before getting on plane and going to cruise speed, Evan wanted to show Deena the boat and he had Michael take over at the helm. Evan said, "Grab your backpack Deena and you can stow it below in the salon. Plus I'll give you a quick tour of Crab got Legs."

"Catchy name, Crab got Legs," she said. "You'll have to tell me the story behind that some time."

Evan smiled and said, "Not too much of a story. I'm just a fan of crab legs for eating, and my boat here has a few extra ponies under the engine hatch, so she has legs to run, if you might know that expression. So Crab got Legs is just a fun play on words."

Deena smiled back and said, "I like it."

Making their way below, Evan took Deena's backpack and stowed it in a cabinet in the amidships berth under the bridge. He showed her where he had put it so she would know when she went looking for it. Deena marveled at the elegant galley and the fine appointments of brass and chrome with plenty of exotic wood finishes. Evan made sure to show Deena the operation of the head which was located aft of the galley on the starboard side. Forward of the galley was the large V-berth stateroom, that was great for tall sleepers as it afforded an extra-long queen sized bed with room on both sides for small cabinets.

Deena was taken by the luxury of his boat and Evan could hear it in her voice when she said, "This is so nice. I can't believe how beautiful some of the boats are these days. This one definitely is more of a yacht than a boat."

"I would have to agree. In fact I prefer to call her a yacht, and she probably runs better for it," Evan said in a matter of fact way. "We're going to have a great day. The galley is stocked and the weather looks to be good all day. And by the way, can I get you anything to drink right now?"

"I would like a water," Deena requested.

Evan opened the refrigerator and lifted three cold bottles of water from the side door. He handed one to Deena, intended to give one to Michael, and would keep the third one for himself. Sweeping his left arm out, he said, "Ladies first," indicating it was time to head back outside to the bridge so they could get underway to their destination just below the Tacoma Narrows Bridge.

Chapter 22

On the bridge on the boat, Michael guided the Chaparral east toward Puget Sound, still maintaining their speed at eight knots. They were nearing the end of Eagle Harbor and an expansive view to the south was opening up as they rounded Bill Point. Deena and Evan were just coming up from the salon and upon her arrival on the bridge, Deena stopped short and stood staring through the windscreen at the incredible view. Evan noted her reaction to what he routinely enjoyed and the majority of people never get to see, an unobstructed view across the water in every direction. He asked Deena, "See something you like?"

Deena nodded her head and said, "I do. It's been awhile since I've been out on the water like this. In a small boat that is, with water and incredible scenery all around. I take the Bainbridge-Seattle ferry every day for work, but sitting in my car during the crossing does not compare to this." She broke her stare at the horizon and turned to look at Evan, who was still standing on the steps to the salon. She continued, and with real sincerity in her voice, said, "Thank you so much for the offer to join you today."

Evan responded by saying, "I should be thanking you. You're definitely helping us out a lot by handling the dive boat." Then with a big grin on his face, he said, "Any chance I can join you guys on the bridge?"

Deena laughed slightly and said, "Oh, I'm sorry, I did kind of trap you there on the stairs."

"No worries Deena. It's a boat after all, and the tight quarters are just part of the charm," Evan said.

Deena moved clear of the salon steps and sat down on the large passenger helm seat. Before Evan could step to the bridge, Michael said, "Hold up there Evan, let me get out from behind the wheel and you can take over."

"Sounds good," Evan replied. He continued with, "I'm thinking I'd like to keep going with Deena's tour of the boat and in particular, the helm. So slide on over Deena and take your place in the Captain's seat."

A big smile appeared on Deena's face and she slid herself over behind the wheel as Michael moved aft to the lounge area behind the bridge. Evan sat down next to Deena and first asked a series of questions to gauge her familiarity with power boats. With the exception of understanding the intricacies of adjusting the trim tabs for optimum performance and the use of the bow thrusters, she was well versed in the controls. She did admit that she had never operated a twin engine boat, so that would be new for her. Evan thought it was important that she get the feel and maneuverability of a boat with two engines and suggested that she should start her training with that. So Evan told Deena to take the wheel in her left hand and put her right on both throttles. He instructed her to ease both throttles back at the same time and shift to Neutral and then shift both drives to Reverse to bring the boat to a stop. Deena followed Evan's guidance and soon the propellers at the stern of Crab got Legs stopped spinning. Briefly after that, the reverse thrust from the props brought the boat to a stop.

The boat drifted in the calm water and Evan explained to Deena, "OK, now we're going to rotate in place by using the engines to spin us. Start by centering the wheel and then shift the port drive to Forward and then quickly after that, shift the starboard drive to Reverse."

Deena followed the instructions, and soon Crab got Legs was rotating in place in a clockwise direction. "That's impressive," Deena remarked. "I can see how that kind of control would be very useful in tight quarters."

"Oh absolutely. Now trying using the bow thrusters," Evan suggested. "You'll find that the starboard thruster will slow our rotational speed while the port one will increase it."

Deena reached out with her left hand and pressed the starboard bow thruster button. She held it down for a few seconds and then the boat started to noticeably spin a little slower. "Very nice," she commented.

"OK, enough fun at slow speed," Evan declared. "I think you'll have no problem handling the boat while we're diving. It really is like Katie explained, an hour of drifting and idling."

"I'm sure I could do with more practice, but if you say I'm ready, I'll go with that," Deena replied.

"Alright," Evan began, "go ahead and put both drives in Neutral once we're at a bearing of around one-hundred and eighty degrees. Once lined up, then shift both drives to Forward and bring the RPMs up to fourteen hundred. I'm going to have you bring the boat up on plane."

Deena turned to look at Evan and asked, "Are you sure you want me to do that?"

"This Chaparral is a pretty well behaved boat and unless you're whipping the steering wheel around, it will be just fine," Evan reassured her. "The trim tabs are still set from when we were cruising before picking you up, so just mash the throttles forward, jump up on plane, and then pull the throttles back and set the RPMs at thirty-two hundred. Just remember to keep the throttles together when you advance them to avoid a course change due to prop thrust."

"I'm anxious to try it, but a bit nervous," Deena admitted.

"I'm right here, and like I said, the boat handles very well," Evan stated.

"OK then," Deena exclaimed, "let's go to Tacoma!" And with that, she mashed the throttles forward and the RPMs of both engines rose quickly as displayed by the gauges at the helm. The boat was already accelerating smoothly out of the hole and it lifted up at the bow as it climbed the large wave in front of it. Deena was smiling ear to ear and both Evan and Michael could tell she was really enjoying being at the wheel. Crab got Legs reached cruising speed in no time at all and as Evan had instructed, Deena pulled the throttles back and set the engine RPMs at thirty-two hundred.

She turned to look at Evan in the passenger helm seat and asked, "Now what?"

"Now we enjoy the water, weather and company as we cruise south to Tacoma, probably about an hour away," Evan offered. "Go ahead and stay at the wheel and I'll go below and bring back some light snacks. I do have plenty of beer, wine and spirits, but Michael and I will have to wait until after we finish the dive. Can I get you anything besides water right now?"

Deena replied, "No, I'm good for now. Thanks anyway."

With that, Evan stood up and quickly disappeared down the steps to the salon. He didn't need to do much except pull the already prepared veggie and fruit platter from the refrigerator and pull off the plastic wrap. He added a small bowl to the platter filled with ranch dressing and after cleaning up the galley, headed back to the bridge.

Evan brought the platter and three plates with him from the salon. The food looked good and tasted even better and the veggies and fruit disappeared over the course of the next twenty minutes. With the snack out of the way, Evan started thinking about the dive and the equipment that they would need to get ready. They had painstakingly planned this dive, and with their search grid at the bottom of the strait narrowing in on the target location, today Evan hoped to find out what that odd blue patch they had identified really is.

After cleaning up, Evan was ready to take over at the helm, but wanted to first make sure Deena was comfortable with the operational aspects of the boat. He asked her, "So how are you feeling with piloting the boat?"

Deena looked relaxed and not tense at all and consistent with her demeanor, she responded, "Pretty well actually. The yacht handles beautifully and all the controls seem easy to understand. With no need for the trim tabs at idle speed, I believe I'm ready to solo!"

Evan was glad to hear that she was now comfortable handling the boat. He didn't expect any problems or trouble topside while he and Michael were below the surface, but knowing that Deena was competent with his boat set his mind at ease, a little bit. Letting both Michael and Deena know their expected time of arrival, he declared they were about twenty minutes from their destination. He indicated to Deena that he would go ahead and take over the helm now and finish the last leg of the trip to their dive spot. They switched seating positions and Evan happily sat down in the Captain's chair to take over the controls.

The rest of the trip was uneventful and the Tacoma Narrows Bridge soon came into view to the south. Michael had already begun getting the dive gear out and both of the buoyancy compensators were ready to go with the tanks attached. The location they wanted to stop at was just coming into view on the screen of the chart plotter, so Evan pulled the throttles back and let Crab got Legs slowly drop off of plane. Maintaining eight knots the rest of way, they were quickly at the marked location and Evan brought the boat to a stop. As they had planned, their arrival was just before Noon and there was very little current. What current there was, was in the southerly direction and in about fifteen minutes, that would cease and begin to reverse to the north as the ebb tide begins.

Michael and Evan were moving fast to finish getting things ready to go which also included getting dressed in their drysuits. Before Evan went below to change, he informed Deena it was time to take the wheel. She gave him a playful salute and hopped behind the wheel. She looked down at the chart plotter and asked, "So I see we've drifted off the Mark. Should I bring us back to the position?"

Evan glanced at the screen and nodded his head slightly up and down while saying, "Yes, go ahead and bring us closer. Continue on past the Mark though so when you shift to Neutral, the boat will drift back to the position. As the tide changes, the boat's "forward" direction will change for you too."

"I'm excited," Deena confided as she shifted the boat into Forward gear. "It feels like a treasure hunt!"

"I don't know about treasure, but this will be my third dive here and I can tell you this, I'm bringing something up, even if it's just pretty looking rock!"

Evan replied sounding very much committed to his plan.

That got a giggle out of Deena and she added, "Maybe you should grab two rocks for all your trouble."

"Very funny Deena," Evan said with a big smile on his face.

Michael was finished in the salon and Evan headed down to put on his drysuit. They were about five minutes away from stepping into the icy water and just thinking about the cold made Evan shiver. Putting on the long underwear helped, and once the drysuit was on, he started to warm up quick.

In the cockpit, all the gear was laid out and Michael was waiting on his dive buddy Evan to help get his tank on. Having been dive buddies for years, they knew the drill and in very little time were ready to go. Deena was monitoring the chart plotter and had the boat just off the Mark. Like Katie, Deena had one of Evan's DiveCom units for surface and near surface communications with the divers. She had been impressed with the system and even more so when Evan admitted that it was his technology.

Now ready to dive, Evan and Michael stood on the swimstep waiting for Deena's signal that they were at the identified location. There was essentially no current as slack tide was happening and Evan anticipated a nice straight drop to the seafloor.

At just a few minutes before Noon, Deena shifted to Neutral, turned off the engines, raised her left arm and shouted, "OK boys, we're here! Time to get wet!"

Evan and Michael grinned and looked at each other through their dive masks and gave one another the OK sign. Looking aft toward the north and the direction they had just come from, and while positioned almost right under the bridge, Michael took a giant step over the water in the port direction, and Evan took a giant step over the water in the starboard direction. With air in their buoyancy compensators they surfaced quickly and floated in the calm cold water while acclimating to the rapid change in temperature. Seasoned divers, they knew what to expect and were soon ready to submerge. Evan confirmed his DiveCom unit was up and running and sent a note to Deena to verify she had her unit turned on and could communicate back. Shortly after sending his message to Deena, she responded with, "All good." He looked over at his boat, that had now drifted south by some thirty feet primarily due to the wind conditions, and saw Deena waving at him from the helm. Evan lifted his right arm up and out of the water and waved back. Confident he would have a ride to dry land when he surfaced, he gave Michael the thumbs down signal for "time to descend". They both released air from their buoyancy compensators at the same time and within seconds disappeared below the surface in two furious displays of bubbles.

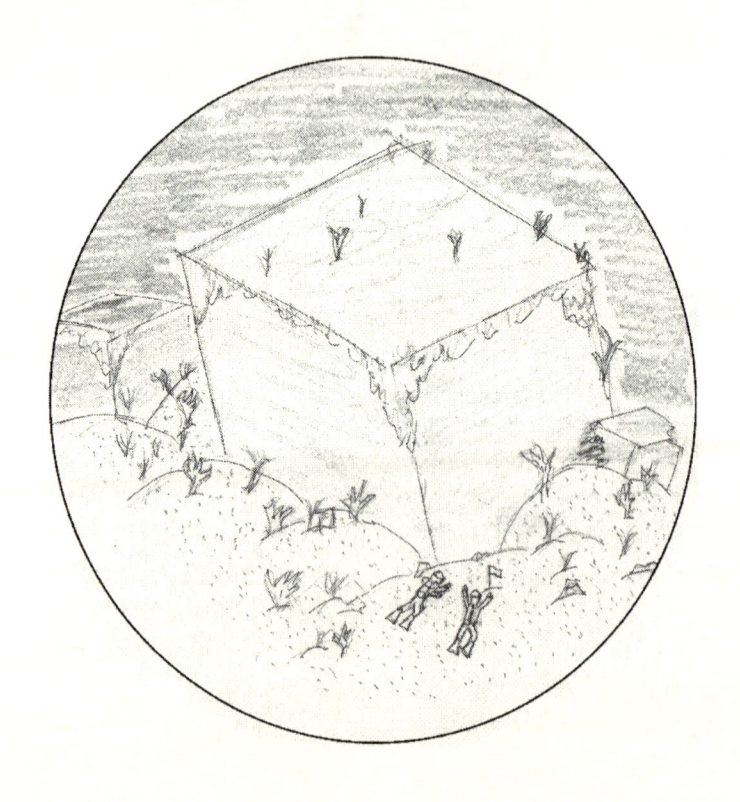

Evan and Michael at Position One

Chapter 23

Unnoticed on the western side of the strait by the occupants of the boat named Crab got Legs, a white Ford pickup truck pulling a small dilapidated dinghy on a single axle trailer drove south along the shoreline. Billy Desary had seen the blue and white Chaparral while lunching at his favorite "turnout with a view" location overlooking the water. Never one to miss an opportunity, Billy had started towing a "disposable" dinghy last week after he had observed a nice candidate boat to be hijacked being piloted singlehandedly by a woman. As the boat had gotten closer today, he recognized it from earlier and decided it looked like a recurrence of last week. There were three people onboard, two of them divers. Billy was no math whiz, but he could subtract two from three and know that only one person would be left onboard to pilot the boat. So deciding to take the risk, he called his boss at his legitimate place of work and told a lie about getting ill over lunch and needing to take the rest of the day off. Once that was done, a wicked grin came across Billy's face, and together with his haunting eyes, gave a glimpse of the psychopath hidden within.

The surge of bubbles from Evan and Michael's departure to the seafloor had dissipated quickly and no evidence was left that they had ever been there. Deena looked a little worried at first, knowing she had the controls and there was no one around to help her. She had been quite comfortable with Evan sitting next her, but now her confidence waned a bit as she looked at the myriad of buttons, switches, knobs, screens and dials located at the helm right in front of her. She remembered Evan's words, "drift and idle, drift and idle", and that helped calm her nerves.

Looking at the chart plotter, she saw she was about sixty feet south of the Mark. The boat had spun to drift bow first with the current, so Deena turned the wheel full to starboard and shifted the port engine to Forward. Showing the agility of a much smaller boat, the big cruiser turned sharply as the thrust from the spinning port side propellers helped nudge the boat around. Once on a bearing almost due north, she engaged the starboard engine and straightened out the wheel. Her speed settled at just under three knots as she watched the icon of Crab got Legs advance toward the Mark shown on the chart plotter screen. Now focused on the task at hand, Deena was able to move past her jitters and started to feel her confidence return.

Below the surface, with their exhalation bubbles trailing over their heads, Evan and Michael were slipping smoothly down into the darkness with just the sound of the bubbles to accompany them. They had covered fifty feet quickly, and both had turned on their dive lights and had them pointed them down hoping to get a glimpse of the seafloor at the earliest opportunity. From out the darkness below, differences in color began to materialize. Shortly after that, definition was possible and Evan thought he spotted a straight line feature indicating a possible manmade object. Confirming his thinking, at a depth of one-hundred and ten feet, a large block of concrete filled the view out of his dive mask window. As he scanned the area, he wanted to let out a "whoop, whoop!", but that was not possible with the regulator in his mouth. So he simply pumped his right arm in the water above his head congratulating himself for finding the orange flag that he had planted ten days ago to mark Position One.

Michael however, did not share Evan's enthusiasm for their arrival at the concrete block. He had his DiveCom unit out and was just finishing a message. Evan's DiveCom unit came to life and displayed a single word, "octopus".

Looking up, Evan saw Michael swimming smoothly in his direction using big powerful leg kicks. What he saw made him freeze in place and just stare. Looking past Michael, a very large Giant Pacific octopus, presumably the one they had encountered earlier, was spread across the seafloor and methodically advancing toward their location. Not one to normally panic, the situation was testing Evan's ability to keep it together. He had seen how fast the octopus could move and definitely wanted to avoid a repeat of their first meeting. Using hand signals, Evan communicated to Michael that they should retreat, quickly, around the far side of the concrete block. With no hesitation from Michael, he continued on his swim and was soon out of sight around the corner. Evan glanced at the octopus that appeared to be slowing its advance and then pushed off the seafloor and turned to follow Michael around the edge of the block.

Once out of sight of the octopus, the feeling of imminent danger subsided some, but still lingered as both men knew that they might simply be playing hide and seek with the giant of the deep. Plus getting their bearings was difficult since they were not able to see the orange flags that were somewhere out there in the dark marking Position Two. Evan looked at Michael and could tell he was on edge as his eyes were wide open and darting around, clearly on high alert. Given the situation, it was probably not a bad thing that Michael was being vigilante. It allowed Evan to focus on the task at hand right now, which was finding the orange flags. Communicating via the DiveCom units, Evan had Michael stay where he was and to alert him if he saw that the octopus had followed them. Evan planned to swim up to the top of the block for a better vantage point to try and locate the flags. Michael acknowledged with the diver's OK sign and Evan nodded back. Then he pushed off from the sediment laden seabed and left a small cloud of slit swirling in his wake as he ascended the vertical reef wall that was the concrete block.

Once on top of the block, Evan scanned the area all around. He had his dive light muted and at first saw nothing. Adjusting the light to full strength, he scanned the area again and was relieved to see that his initial observation was correct. That is, he still saw nothing. Now having his bearings with respect to the block and the flags marking Position One, he added a little air to his buoyancy compensator and lifted slightly to achieve neutral buoyancy. Aiming himself in the direction he thought most likely correct, he kicked with small strokes of his dive fins and moved closer to the edge of the block.

As Evan approached the edge, his view below expanded to include more of the seafloor near the block. Intently scanning the reef formations beyond the block, Evan was taken by surprise when his dive mask window filled with the color red and before he knew what was happening, he was struggling to breathe as a large octopus arm had surrounded his chest and air tank. The octopus continued to exert pressure and while Evan could breathe out, the intense squeeze of the octopus's arm did not allow his lungs to expand and he could not breathe in. His mind was racing, but his body was frozen and he considered the irony that he may die of suffocation with a SCUBA tank full of precious air strapped to his back.

Starting to feel lightheaded, the effects of no oxygen to Evan's brain were becoming pronounced. His chest was burning and he mustered what strength he had left to try and draw air through the regulator in his mouth. With no way to expand his lungs against the crushing squeeze of the octopus, only a small puff of air came across Evan's lips and he felt himself losing hope. His vision was narrowing and a deeper blackness seemed to be moving in on him. He shivered involuntarily and was aware enough to feel the octopus tighten its grip just a little bit more. It was shortly after that that Evan's eyes drooped shut and he lost consciousness. Had Michael been aware of what was happening and been able to see it, the macabre scene of a Giant Pacific octopus holding his friend in a death grip suspended above its body would have been something he never would have forgotten.

Once Evan fell into unconsciousness, he went limp and slumped inside the strong embrace of the arm wrapped around him. Shortly after that, the octopus unwound its arm from Evan's body and released him to float free in the water. His neutrally buoyant body showed no signs of movement, and after a period of time when the octopus appeared to be simply observing, it slowly lowered itself below the top edge of the block and disappeared.

On the other side of the concrete block, Michael watched both of the vertical edges of the block in front of him for any kind of movement. Several minutes had passed since Evan had left, and now feeling less out of control, Michael used his DiveCom unit to send an "are you OK?" message to Evan. Five seconds passed, and then ten, and after fifteen seconds with no response, Michael felt a chill run through his body. Trying to be optimistic, Michael considered that Evan was just out of range or that the block of concrete was obstructing the DiveCom signal.

Realizing that there was probably a simple explanation for the lack of response, the thought calmed him and he decided to venture after Evan in search of a better signal between the DiveCom units. Rising up from the bottom, Michael kicked slowly with small strokes of his legs and was soon over the top edge of the block. In the distance, he saw the faint glow of Evan's dive light coming up from below the edge of the far side of block. Shining his own dive light around, a mask of horror spread across his face when his light beam illuminated Evan's motionless body, floating face about forty feet away.

Chapter 24

Roughly twenty minutes had passed since Deena had taken over as Captain on the Crab got Legs. The drift and idle procedure now seemed quite easy and she felt she had mastered the maneuver, even as the current began to flow at a noticeably faster speed. Enjoying the fine weather and scenery, Deena felt lucky to be outside enjoying a day of boating instead of stuck in an office building wishing she was outside. During the cruise from Bainbridge Island, and even during the time so far on station at the Mark under the bridge, there had been very little boat traffic, so Deena easily spotted the small boat as it headed in her direction.

She could not really make out any details given the distance away, but the small boat appeared to be floundering. As the boat drew nearer riding the ebb tide flowing to the north, she saw a single occupant waving their arms frantically and pointing at a small outboard motor mounted on the transom. Everything screamed that this was a boat in distress and Deena had every intention of helping. Checking the time, she estimated it would still be at least half an hour before Evan and Michael surfaced, but she didn't want to leave her position where she was keeping the dive flag visible. When she looked up, the small boat was noticeably closer and she considered it lucky that the boat was drifting in her direction.

With the small boat about two-hundred yards away and clearly in trouble, Deena made the decision to abandon the dive spot and help the wayward boater instead. The current continued to sweep the boat north and Deena idled to the east on an intercept course. Soon she was within one-hundred feet of her target and spun the big Chaparral to port and shifting to Neutral, started to drift in line with the much smaller boat, except about fifty feet ahead of it. The boat's occupant waved at her and then quickly huddled down to prepare a line that could be secured to the aft port side cleat of Crab got Legs. Deena continued to watch behind her as the small boat closed the distance to her boat.

The current was running at almost two knots, so there was sufficient movement between the boats that it was making it difficult for the small boat's Captain to get the line around the cleat. Deena had no steerage with the drives out of gear, and in bare feet stepped quickly aft into the cockpit and motioned for the person in the small boat to throw her the line. With her arms outstretched, Deena caught the line on the first attempt and within just a few seconds, had leaned down and secured the line to the cleat. When she stood up and turned around, she was surprised by how fast the rescued boater had come aboard. Already the person was standing on the swimstep just at the threshold of the transom door. Deena's first reaction was to offer them her help, but when she saw a glint of sunlight reflect off the shiny blade of a large knife in the now unwelcome guest's left hand, she stopped talking in mid-sentence.

Looking up from the large blade, Deena took note of the unkempt clothes and slumped posture, but was confused when she saw ex-U.S. President Bill Clinton staring back are her with dark beady eyes. Deena's confusion swiftly cleared when she recognized the situation for what it was, a crime of some sort with her as the victim. The intruder started to wave the knife around wanting Deena to back up and she was in no position to resist. Slowly, while watching the intruder, she side stepped closer to the center of the cockpit. As the masked intruder attempted to enter the boat's cockpit, Deena's Taekwondo training that she did for exercise and self-defense flipped a switch in her head. Taking no time to reconsider, she crouched down slightly and then leapt up with a clockwise twisting move that torqued her body around and she delivered a powerful Hook Kick to the side of the intruder's neck. Along with the sound of the impact, there was also a loud sickening crunch as her right heel indiscriminately crushed a few vertebrae in the intruder's upper spine.

Deena then landed lightly on her feet and was able to watch the intruder stumble back and fall into the small boat trailing behind the Chaparral. Now Deena had the advantage and grabbing the boat hook, stepped to the port side and prepared to rain down blows with the four foot long aluminum club. The intruder recovered quickly however and was scrambling to get up from the floor of the small boat.

As Deena pulled back for the first swing, the intruder lunged forward with the knife and cleanly cut the line attached to the Chaparral's cleat. The boats began to separate almost at once, but were still close enough that Deena's swing connected solidly with the right shoulder of the intruder and she felt some satisfaction when they cried out in pain. Now with the boats too far apart for another swing, Deena noticed the awkward cant of the stranger's head, and she knew she had done some damage with her kick. She watched as the intruder fumbled with the outboard motor and then after two pulls of the starter cord, the beat up looking outboard sputtered to life. No warmup today for the little motor though, as the intruder immediately shifted into Forward gear and spun the throttle up on the tiller. The little boat veered hard to the west and Deena stared at it speeding away wondering what the hell just happened.

Shaking her head back and forth trying to make sense of it, she was still too stunned to comprehend the real danger she had been in. Her reaction had been uncharacteristic and it sort of frightened her that she had been able to lash out like she did. Shaking her head again to get back to reality, she remembered why she was on a boat under the Tacoma Narrows Bridge in the first place. Stepping back up to the helm, she took her position in the Captain's chair and looked first at the chart plotter to see how far she had moved off the Mark. She panicked when see didn't see the position identifier, but then realizing the scale of the screen was zoomed in tight, she zoomed out two scale sizes and finally saw the Mark.

At first she didn't believe it, but getting closer to the screen, she confirmed the scale was 1 inch = ¼ mile. With the Mark almost three scale lengths from the center of the screen, it was easy math to know she was nearly three quarters of a mile away. Shifting both drives into Forward gear, Deena pushed the throttles forward and within seconds the boat was up on plane and barreling in on the physical position represented by the Mark on the chart plotter screen.

Nearly a mile away and more than one hundred feet below the surface, Michael wanted to scream Evan's name when he saw his friend floating motionless, but couldn't with the regulator in his mouth. Instead he pumped his legs furiously and accelerated toward Evan's seemingly lifeless body. Covering the distance quickly, Michael checked Evan's face and the bluish color of his skin told him Evan had been without oxygen for a while. Pressing his hand on Evan's neck, he felt a very faint, slow pulsation. Knowing there was just seconds left before Evan succumbed to the lack of air and suffocated, he checked Evan's tank for pressure and saw it better than half full. So air was not the problem. Thinking quickly and trying not to panic, Michael decided an emergency blast of air to Evan's system was his only chance.

Since Evan was unable to draw a breathe of air on his own, the regulator in his mouth did not function as intended. Recognizing this, Michael reached over to Evan's regulator, and very carefully and slowly, just slightly tapped the purge valve. A blast of air escaped the mouthpiece and Michael saw Evan's cheeks puff up. He gave some time for the air to spread throughout Evan's body and then tapped the purge button again. He did this six times and was about to activate the purge button for the seventh time when Evan's regulator actuated normally. He stared at Evan's face through the dive mask glass and thought he saw a flicker of movement. The regulator actuated again and now he was sure of it. A few seconds later, Michael saw Evan's eyes twitch and then his eyelids slowly opened.

The relief on Michael's face was clearly evident when Evan looked up at his dive buddy, but he was not yet out of danger from the near suffocation. Having been underwater for only about half of the planned time, Michael figured no decompression stop needed, so he shifted Evan in such a way that he could control Evan's buoyancy compensator. Once in position, Michael added some air to the bladders and Evan slowly started to rise. Michael then added air to his own buoyancy compensator and together, they began the ascent to surface.

Chapter 25

A torrent of bubbles preceded Evan and Michael's return to the surface and when they arrived, they practically exploded into the sunshine. During the ascent, Michael could tell from Evan's lack of movement that time was of the essence, so he had taken a risk with both of their lives and further inflated the buoyancy compensators to provide a very fast rise rate. Now having survived the trip up without incident and floating on the surface, Michael moved immediately to get the regulator out of Evan's mouth and his dive mask off his face to make breathing as easy as possible. Sitting high in the water with the fully inflated compensator, Evan was able to rest unaided by Michael and he focused on getting air into his lungs. His breathing was shallow, and his rib cage hurt from the battle that he had fought with the octopus, but he was breathing again. It did occur to him that the battle was clearly no contest for the octopus, and he found a bit of humor in that.

As the fog in his head began to clear, his ears were picking up noises that began to sound like words, that turned into his name and he recognized Michael's voice.

"Evan! Evan! Can you hear me?" Michael was screaming at nearly point blank range.

Evan opened his eyes and in a low voice, but clearly and firmly said, "I hear you buddy. No need to yell."

Evan saw by just looking at Michael that he was badly shaken by the turn of events. That made Evan that much more thankful that Michael had responded to the emergency the way that he had. Evan understood all too well that if it had not been for his friend, he would surely be dead right now. Since he did not die, now all he wanted to do was get on his boat. He couldn't quite see all around him, but he was surprised that Crab got Legs did not appear to be close by.

In the distance, in the general vicinity of the Mark on the chart plotter, Deena witnessed a disturbance on the surface of the water and then something was left floating when the water settled. She suspected it was Evan and Michael, and since they were returning early, she hoped it meant that they'd have good news about a successful treasure hunt. Running at twenty-eight knots, she realized after seeing the men surface that the boat would cover the remaining distance quickly, and she pulled the throttles back to drop the boat off of plane. Pausing at sixteen hundred RPM to allow the following wake to first hit the transom, she then brought the engines to idle speed and watched the wake she'd created dissipate. It didn't take long since the current running in the opposite direction helped squash the neatly ordered waves created by the boat's passing.

At roughly fifty yards away, Deena prepared to maneuver the boat to let the men drift into the swimstep. With them floating toward the bow right now, she needed to get turned around, so using the move she'd performed all day, she briefly put the starboard outdrive in Neutral, then shifted it into Reverse. The boat's momentum carried the boat on its course until the starboard propellers grabbed the water hard enough to create an opposing thrust to the port side props. Deena wanted the boat turned quick and she used the port bow thruster to shove the bow around. In a diameter of less than forty feet, just barely larger than the length of the boat itself, she had made a one-hundred and eighty degree turn and now Evan and Michael were just twenty yards away from the swimstep.

When Deena finished the turn, her momentum left her on a stern first southerly course, but the north flowing current soon slowed the boat's GPS speed to zero. With Evan and Michael coming at her at over two knots, it looked like they would crash into her and she considered a touch of forward thrust to avoid the collision. Before she could put her hands back on the throttles to act, she felt the water take control of Crab got Legs and reverse her direction. Soon the force of the water against the transom was sufficient to push the boat up near the speed of the swimmers and the hard impact was avoided. Deena shut the engines off, but stayed at the helm and watched first Evan, and then Michael, grab ahold of the boat and then climb up on to the swimstep. Unexpectedly, they embraced in a clearly emotional hug and her spirits soared with the leap of faith that treasure had been found. "Surely a congratulatory hug associated with a great discovery!" she thought to herself. As the excited conversation filtered through the clanging and banging of the SCUBA equipment being stripped off, she picked up words like "suffocate", "octopus", and "death", and she realized that she could not be more wrong.

Shocked from the elation of a possible treasure find to now hearing talk of death, Deena simply blurted out loudly, "What the heck happened down there?"

Both Evan and Michael turned to look at Deena and she could tell that Evan was hurt in some way. With the way he was grimacing and holding his chest, he had the appearance of someone that had just walked away from a bad car accident.

Michael spoke up and said, "We had some trouble. Ran into the Giant Pacific octopus that appears to live around here, and it decided to take an interest in Evan."

"Michael's right about that. We had the octopus's attention right away and it just seemed to track us. Thought we were OK once we were out of sight, but that was not the case," Evan said while shaking his head slowly back and forth.

"OK, that sounds terrifying," Deena said impatiently, and then asked, "So why are you hurt?"

Evan looked at Deena and locked eyes with her and said, "I was literally in the death grip of the octopus, but it let me go. And thanks to Michael, I survived to see another day."

Deena's eyes opened wider and her jaw dropped slightly. Her face was projecting a look of disbelieve, so Evan elaborated and said, "I thought I would try looking around from a higher vantage point. So I was on top of a large concrete block just scanning the area, and before I knew what was happening, the beast reached up from below and wrapped an arm around me. Then put the squeeze on and after a brief struggle, I passed out and woke up some time later with Michael shining a dive light in my face."

"That's incredible!" Deena exclaimed.

"It's even more incredible than that," Michael added. "When I found Evan, he was floating face up and had a bluish tinge to his skin. I knew there was no time to get to the surface, and since he was unconscious, buddy breathing was not an option. So I tapped the purge valve of his mouthpiece a number of times to send fresh air into his system and after doing that six times I think, he came around enough to draw shallow breathes from the SCUBA tank by himself. Then we did a fast ascent to the surface. It was odd though, that you and the boat were nowhere to seen. What was up with that?"

Evan added, "Yes, what was up with that? You kind of left us hanging there for a while."

Deena looked at both men and acknowledged that she should not have left. Then she briefly recounted the events that occurred while they were below the surface and hoped that it sufficiently justified her decision to leave the dive site.

Evan was quiet for a few seconds after she finished talking and then said, "Wow Deena, I'm so sorry that this trip has not gone as planned so far. I am really glad though that you're not hurt. You took quite a chance tangling with a knife wielding low-life criminal. Although, I wish I could have seen you land that kick."

Deena's mouth broke into a slight smile and she said, "I couldn't believe I did that. I've never used my Taekwondo skills for anything except exercise, but in the heat of the moment, it just came to me as a very good option."

"I'm certainly glad it worked out," Michael commented. "Although, I am wondering what it was they were after with such a bold move in the middle of the day?"

"I don't know Michael," Evan said, "but let's get out of these drysuits, store the gear, and get ourselves underway."

"Agreed," Michael concurred.

"What can I do to help?" Deena asked.

"For starters," Evan replied, "since you were the eye witness, let's call the Coast Guard and let them know what happened to you while we were diving. The phone number is right there by the VHF, and this boat's registration is WN8569CT since I suspect they'll want that." Looking sympathetically at Deena, he added, "You can also stay at the wheel and we can start heading back to Bainbridge. Just slow for now until Michael and I get everything stowed away and then we can speed up."

Deena provided a "Sounds good," and then swiveled around in the Captain's chair, started the starboard engine first and then the port engine right after. The twin Mercruisers quickly settled to idle RPMs and Deena shifted both outdrives to Forward gear. Crab got Legs responded to the spinning propellers by immediately stabilizing itself and that stopped the boat from wallowing aimlessly in the current. Already pointed to the north, Deena held the wheel in position and the three of them left the dive site with a strong sense of failure for today's effort. Taking out her phone, she called the Coast Guard. Her call was answered by a younger sounding woman, and after a few minutes of reliving the harrowing encounter she had had with the masked boarder, she hung up realizing just how dangerous the situation had really been.

Three minutes later, the men had everything stowed and secured and were ready to get under way at cruise speed. Deena relinquished the helm to Evan and then sat close to him on the passenger helm seat. Michael made himself comfortable on the large lounge in the cockpit and tried to relax. It wasn't easy considering everything stressful that had happened in the last half hour, but he was going to try. Evan brought the boat up on plane and with very little conversation along the way and running at fast cruising speed, they were soon just outside of Eagle Harbor.

While making their way to the Bainbridge Island City Park dock, Deena asked, "So what now? Is this how it ends?"

Evan had been contemplative on the cruise north and said very little, but with Deena's question, he launched into a plan of sorts. "Well Deena, so far today has been tough going, but if I can convince yourself and Michael, I'd like to try again at the next slack tide, right around 6:00PM this evening. At this time of year, we'll have good light until 9:00PM at least."

Deena shifted quickly in her seat and spun to look at Evan with an incredulous expression on her face.

Evan smiled and said, "I can see that the idea takes you by surprise. However, with bad weather coming as early as tomorrow, and us with two full SCUBA tanks right now, I'm thinking we make another attempt today."

"Aren't you hurt right now? How can you possibly dive?" Deena asked.

"I'm feeling better and my breathing is much easier. There's some lingering pain in my chest, but again, much better now. So if you can hang out and try again tonight, I would certainly appreciate your help," Evan expressed in a very sincere tone.

Deena shook her head side to side in small swings clearly indicating she thought Evan was crazy, but counter to the movement of her head, she said,

"If you can convince Michael to dive again, I'll go with you guys."

Evan smiled broadly at Deena and simply said, "Thank you."

Chapter 26

Evan did convince Michael to dive again. It was not without some creative reasoning to be sure, and even Deena offered her two cents to justify the second dive. After finally accepting that the case for another dive today was just too strong, Michael had agreed. Having the extra full tanks aboard made it convenient, so instead of racing around to fill depleted tanks, the hours between dives was spent relaxing on Bainbridge Island. Deena had gone home and returned with some cards and a couple of board games to pass the time, but in the end it all went unused as the three treasure hunters talked at length about possibilities and dreams of discovery.

Around 3:00PM, they strolled through the city park to a clustering of quaint eateries. Deena made the choice for them and they entered one of the many Teriyaki themed restaurants in the Northwest. The late lunch was excellent and satisfying, and not too heavy for the dive coming up. After a nice casual walk back to the boat that helped stretch their legs, it was time to shift gears into treasure hunting mode.

There was essentially nothing to do with Crab got Legs except let the bilge blowers run for a bit and then start up the engines and leave the dock. Since they were approaching the allowed dock time for transient moorage, it was time to depart anyway. Evan sat at the helm with Deena by his side, and with

Michael tending to the lines, they smoothly slipped away from the dock.

Evenings in the Northwest will often bring calmer water, and today was such a day. The winds of the early afternoon had dissipated and the seas had smoothed to glassy conditions with just the occasional large undulating swell to disturb the surface. The boat slipped through the calm seas pushing a bow wave that transformed the peaceful water and created a steady spray that shot into the air and fanned out around the boat as it moved along. The fine mist that reached the helm brought the smell of the sea with it, and Evan was thoroughly enjoying the moment, even with the lingering pain in his chest from earlier. With Deena leaning close, he could also smell the fragrance of her hair and could feel the stray strands that would whip his neck lightly if the breeze blew around her just right. Thinking about her ordeal with the thief, hijacker, rapist or worse, he couldn't help but be impressed. Granted, he only has Deena's story for why she was not on station when they surfaced, and the boat shows no evidence of any major scuffle or trouble, but he believed her nonetheless. The small section of rope he had taken off the aft port cleat appeared to be the only physical evidence that something might have happened. After all he thought to himself, "Who would make up such a story?"

Once they had actually gotten underway, it looked like they might be arriving ahead of the planned time, so Evan had slowed the cruise speed by four knots. It was a lazy, beautiful cruise with the sun providing plenty of warmth on the way south to the dive site. Now closing in on just a few miles from their destination, the atmosphere onboard the boat was changing. Evan found it hard to describe, but it felt like nervousness, or just like being on edge waiting for something to happen. There was good reason for the feelings considering that of the three dives at this site so far, two included physical encounters with a Giant Pacific octopus.

With the Tacoma Narrows Bridge looming in front of Evan as he looked through the boat's windscreen, his nervousness turned to a chill running through his body when the memory of the last dive came rushing back to him. Shaking it off, he realized that the weight on his left side was Deena leaning close and it occurred to him that over the day, they had just become more comfortable with each other and the closeness seemed very natural. That thought thankfully diverted his focus from the upcoming dive and he was able to dispel the anxiousness he was feeling.

Evan's slight shiver got Deena's attention and she sat up a bit straighter. "Feeling a little cold?" she asked.

"Not really," Evan replied. "I just flashed back to earlier today and how that dive went. Things will go great this time though. Second times a charm, isn't that what they say?"

"No Evan, that is not what they say," Deena said with a bit of a comical scowl on her face, which actually looked quite good on her. "They say that the third time is the charm."

"Well OK, maybe that doesn't apply for today. But I'm feeling good about our chances for success anyway," Evan offered, trying to sound convincing. In his head, he knew that technically, earlier today was really the third time, and he kept that to himself considering that in this case, number three was definitely not a charm.

As usual, Michael had efficiently handled the prep work and things were ready to go in the cockpit. The drysuits were dry after lying out for a few hours in the sun, so the shocking effect of the cold water would have to wait until they actually got in. The tide was still in ebb tide mode, but just barely. According to the tide tables for the Tacoma Narrows Bridge tidal zone, slack tide was ten minutes away, and with Crab got Legs just arriving at the Mark, Evan turned to Deena and said, "We have arrived. Are you ready to take over as Captain again?"

Deena nodded her head in the affirmative and replied confidently, "Yes, I'm ready. It really is a nice boat to pilot. I promise to stay the course this time and not venture off, but today left me feeling kind of vulnerable. Might you have any suggestions on how to fend off boarders?"

"Well," Evan said as he pondered her question, and also got a bit angry that she even had to ask such a question while boating in Puget Sound. "The boat hook as a club is a good idea in close, but if want to stop someone farther away, then I suggest the flare gun. And don't forget about the Coast Guard and other boaters. If it looks like trouble is headed your way, use the VHF radio to put out a call."

"It's crazy that I just asked you that, right?" Deena asked to confirm what she was thinking.

"I agree," Evan replied. "It is definitely unnerving that we might have someone thinking they're a modern day pirate here in Puget Sound."

Deena appreciated Evan's advice, and she was sincere in asking the question. However, what she neglected to disclose to Evan, was that in addition to the cards and board games from home, she also brought aboard her 9mm Glock 43 handgun. The gun was small, but powerful, and carefully positioned in her purse to be hidden, yet readily available. She thought of earlier in the day and felt better knowing that if the same scenario played out, she would be bringing a gun to a knife fight.

Deena pulled her legs up on the seat and Evan stood up to move past her so he could get ready to dive. Once Evan was clear, Deena slipped into the vacant Captain's chair. Evan headed straight for the salon just as Michael was coming up, already dressed in his drysuit, so he stepped aside to allow Michael access to the bridge. Then he went below and quickly dressed for the frigid waters of Puget Sound.

With Evan and Michael ready for the dive, the atmosphere on the boat could best be described as exciting, but tense. The evening sun was just starting to cast shadows of the tall cliffs along the west side of the strait onto the smooth water near the western shoreline, and in combination with the stillness of the slack tide, the effect created an eerie scene. Evan shattered the stillness with his giant step entry into the water and then Michael's splash a few seconds later sounded almost like an echo. Both men were floating essentially motionless in the water as they gave Deena a wave and simultaneously released air from their buoyancy compensators. The escaping air from the compensators created a froth of bubbles, and it covered their heads as they slipped below the surface for the second time today.

Deena watched them disappear and a shiver ran down her spine. She thought that it was not a good sign, and opted to chalk it up to the evening coolness and a coincidence on the timing. She started both engines and then scanned the helm station, first making note of the fuel level and then the oil pressure and voltage to assure herself that all systems were go. It was early yet, but she turned on the navigation lights anyway. Spotting the horn button, and not having heard it before, she went ahead and pushed the button briefly. The horn mounted in the bow let loose a one-hundred and fifteen decibel blast and even though Deena had pushed the button, it startled her just the same. With the men now underwater and an expected time to surface of fifty minutes, she settled in for what she hoped would be an uneventful hour of piloting Crab got Legs.

Below the surface, light from the sun penetrated no farther than fifty feet, so the dive lights were already on as Evan and Michael descended toward the bottom. They were also being more cautious this time and dropped at half the descent rate that they had used for the first dive. They had discussed at length the octopus and its behavior, and both felt that with the repeated sightings and attacks, there was really no other explanation then its den was close, very close. Keeping that in mind was paramount considering what happened this morning. So they were keeping their heads on a swivel and taking it slow.

The slack tide afforded a nearly straight drop from the surface position identified by the Mark on the chart plotter and hopefully they would be close to their flags. In his head, Evan thought about the location of Position One on the bottom and hoped to gain valuable knowledge about its bearing and distance from the Mark displayed by the chart plotter. Assuming they find the flag for Position One, that information could be helpful for a better starting dive position if they dive the site again.

The blackness outside the reach of the dive light beams hid anything and everything. So Evan and Michael kept the lights moving trying to illuminate the largest volume of space within their field of view. Soon the bottom seemed to rise up to meet them and they landed in an open portion of the seafloor where the view of the seascape looked almost identical in all directions. The good news was that none of the views included a Giant Pacific octopus.

"So far, so good," Evan thought to himself. Now on the bottom, that helped with reducing their vulnerability and the frantic scanning of the dive lights ceased. Instead, both Evan and Michael slowed their scanning speed and peered into the tunnels of light they were creating.

After a few minutes of just trying to get a bearing on a direction to go, Evan spotted what appeared to be the color orange in the distance. There were other bright colors in the reef when the light hit them to be sure, but the neon orange flags had a unique look, and Evan felt he had located one of the flags they had set earlier. Position One or Position Two he did not know, but he took a reading on his compass that showed the orange color patch was located due east. With Michael following close behind and keeping a watchful eye on the surroundings, Evan pointed his light at the orange color in the distance and they cautiously advanced toward what he hoped was a flag.

Gliding smoothly above the seafloor, Evan kept his light steady and pointed straight ahead while Michael moved his light around in a wild fashion hoping to get the earliest possible warning of impending trouble that might come from any direction. Unfortunately, he was moving his light so fast he failed to notice the large octopus camouflaged almost directly below them amongst rumble from the old bridge. Scanning in wide, random arcs, Michael's light lit upon the tip of an octopus arm that swayed with the slight current that was just beginning to become noticeable. Due to Michael's heightened state, he had missed seeing the undulating arm of the octopus and an important element of their surroundings went unnoticed. The octopus altered its color slightly and began to move away from the entrance to its den. Evan and Michael continued on their journey, oblivious to the danger now just beneath them.

Chapter 27

From a distance, the orange color Evan had spotted was barely noticeable. As they advanced toward the color splotch, clarity through the dark water improved and the better vision provided that they had indeed found one of their prior locations. As they closed in on the position, Evan was able to discern that the color patch of orange was the flag they had planted with the large number "2" on it, confirming that they had located Position Two. Michael couldn't see Evan's face, but if he could have, he would have seen a man with a very wide smile.

Once Evan stopped pumping his legs, his dive fins stopped providing thrust and he slowed to a stop. Seeing Evan slow down, Michael did the same thing and they were soon hanging motionless in the water with the orange flag between them, drifting slightly to the south with the start of the flood tide. Using his DiveCom unit, Evan let Michael know that it was time to start a detailed search for their main target in their respective areas. Both men wasted no time pulling out three of the smaller bright green flags they would use to mark the completed sections in the search grid they were about to establish. Evan went one way from the orange flag and Michael went in the exact opposite direction, both swimming out about fifteen feet. Then each man planted a green flag so that the imaginary line through the two green flags and the one orange flag established the boundary between their respective search areas.

At thirty feet away from each other, they could still see each other OK and Michael saw Evan give him a wave. He waved back and then each man turned to their right ninety degrees and swam out approximately fifteen feet and planted another flag. They did the same thing again, but this time turned left and swam approximately thirty feet before planting the third flag. Now they had the outer boundary of a thirty foot by thirty foot search grid, and each man promptly adjusted their buoyancy to drop slightly lower and went to work painstakingly studying small sections of the reef.

Topside, Deena was starting to get a little bored with the back and forth handling of the dive boat. She was also feeling a bit warm as the bright sun, the relative stillness of the boat, and the lack of wind made the current weather conditions feel more like summer. She had a cold bottle of water just out of the refrigerator and while sitting at the helm, she rubbed it on both sides of her neck and then held it firmly on the back of her neck as she arched her head backwards. The coolness felt good, plus several drops of water dripped from the outside surface of the bottle and trickled down her back, offering some relief from the heat before being absorbed by her shirt.

Deena thought about creating her own wind, and considered pushing the throttles forward and taking a quick spin around in a large circle just to feel the breeze. Knowing that would not be a great idea, or even a good idea, she opted instead to extend the range from the Mark a little bit before making turns, and ran under power in both directions. Setting the throttles at slightly higher engine RPMs, a small breeze appeared and Deena stood up to catch the day's elusive wind against her upper body as it cleared the boat's windscreen. After a few cooling cycles around the Mark, she stopped fixating on the heat and returned her attention to her surroundings and the piloting of the boat.

Shifting her attention to the surroundings brought back the memory of earlier today, and Deena thought about her handbag that she had carefully placed near the helm station once Evan and Michael had started their dive. She reached into the large center cubby with her left hand and massaged the soft leather bag finding the hard outline of the Glock quickly. Feeling the gun right where it should be, she sat back reassured that between her resourcefulness, the VHF radio's access to the Coast Guard, her trusty 9mm Glock, and Evan's fast boat, she would be OK. She had never intended to deceive Evan about bringing the gun aboard, but when it came time to actually get back on board after her trip home, she legitimately forgot she was carrying it. After that, she just decided to keep it a secret as she was still unsure about how trusting she should be with Evan and

Michael. Then she got hot again, but now it was because she didn't feel safe in her own backyard, and she was angered by the prospect of that.

Deena physically shook herself to rid the thought from her head and the feeling from her body, and that action had the intended result. She moved on, or tried to anyway. The beauty of Puget Sound was all around and she found some comfort in the boat rocking lazily on the water. Deena considered however, that she was waiting alone on a strange boat with her gun, for two men she barely knew, diving for who knows what under the Tacoma Narrows Bridge. With the sun marching toward the western horizon and dusk coming soon, she furrowed her brow and thought to herself, "What have I gotten myself into?"

While Deena was considering, and maybe second guessing some of her recent decisions, Evan and Michael were nearly complete with a detailed look at roughly one third of the grid. Michael had at one point sent Evan a DiveCom message that moved a shot of adrenaline through his system, but while preparing to mark his grid exit point, Michael followed up with a "negative on the find" comment. It felt to Evan like the adrenaline left his system as fast as it had arrived, and the result was a noticeable drop in his energy level.

Realizing that they were likely trespassing on the home turf of a Giant Pacific octopus, both men would periodically stop searching the reef, and search their surroundings instead. They had talked about it before the dive, and both felt it a prudent thing to do given the prior encounters with the octopus. Coordinating their efforts, they timed the periodic scanning of the surroundings such that they alternated the role, which left the other available to continue to search the reef.

Evan and Michael continued in a consistent fashion like that until Evan stopped the process, and sent Michael a DiveCom message, "check air – mine at 30". Shortly after that, Evan's DiveCom unit came to life and displayed, "mine 20", letting him know that Michael's air volume was down to twenty percent left. "Not very much time to go", Evan thought to himself. Getting back to the task at hand, and with about two thirds of the grid yet to search, they both scrutinized the reef with renewed vigor trying to make the best use of the time they had left.

Another five minutes passed and Evan knew it was time to start wrapping things. As he reached out to place a green flag indicating that he had searched another two foot by two foot section of the reef, his eye caught an unusual color in the sea of greens, browns, blues, grays, reds and oranges. It was definitely in the blue color band, but not what Evan had been seeing so far on the dive. As he shifted his position, the color disappeared from his view, but he could still see the spot in the reef he had been looking at. Puzzled, he moved back to where he was before and the color appeared again. Studying the reef, Evan thought he was seeing a sort of navy blue color and reached carefully toward it with his right hand to explore what he was seeing. His hand found a small opening, but his hand was too large to fit in. He was however able to fit three of his fingers into the small gap in the reef structure. His gloved hand could feel the roughness of the edges and he stopped trying to force things. Instead, he pulled back and sent a DiveCom message to Michael, "I have found it".

Evan could see that Michael got the message since almost right after the message was sent, Michael's light shown in his direction and he could tell it was getting closer. Evan checked his air gauge and noted the air volume at fifteen percent. He knew Michael was probably starting to breathe hard as the reduced pressure in the tank meant shallower breathes for the diver. When Michael did arrive, he was already holding his air gauge in his hand and indicating it was time to surface. Evan acknowledged, but also pointed to the opening in the reef and enthusiastically shook his head in an up and down motion. Using his DiveCom unit, Evan sent a message to Michael, "start the ascent, right behind you."

Reaching up to add air to the buoyancy compensator's bladders, Michael started to rise with just a small burst of air. He looked down at Evan and gave him a wave as he floated up toward the surface. Evan did not inflate his compensator right away however. Instead, he turned his attention back to the opening in the reef. Crouching close to the opening, he directed the beam of his dive light into the opening. Looking carefully, he could see the blue color clearly and got excited when the color resolved into a recognizable manmade object. Evan was not sure what it was, but it was definitely not native to the seabed. He didn't want to rip his drysuit, or the gloves for the suit, so he quickly located a rock that would help enlarge the opening enough for his hand to fit through. He positioned the wedge shaped rock in the opening and proceeded to push with a fair about of force as his knees provided the anchor. He was very surprised when the rock moved more than just a little bit and the opening split apart. Evan saw right away before a cloud of silt flared up and obscured the area, that the rock had enlarged the hole considerably.

The current had been steadily increasing to the south so Evan didn't have to wait long for the area to clear as the moving water quickly swept the silt away. What he saw was confusing. The reef had separated and now there was clearly an opening that went deeper. Evan used his dive light to illuminate the space and was rewarded with the sight of the object they had been looking for. It was a piece of blue cloth, probably discarded or lost years ago, that had made its way to the bottom and become lodged among the outcroppings, fissures and depressions of the reef. Over the years, the piece of cloth simply became part of the reef. Evan shook his head back and forth and smiled at the discovery. "All the effort for a piece of cloth", he thought to himself, "what else should I have expected from a treasure hunt, right?"

With the little bit of extra pull required to get a full breathe, Evan could tell he was running short of air and time, and by now, Michael and Deena were probably wondering, "what's taking him so long to surface?" Since they had come so far, Evan wanted to take the prize with him and he reached about six inches in below the edge of the reef with his right hand to retrieve the cloth. As he expected, the cloth was somewhat stuck and he pulled harder to free it. He was surprised when the cloth appeared to come free from the reef, but was still difficult to lift out. Thinking it was still stuck, he reached deeper and felt around behind the cloth. He could feel the coarseness of the reef through the cloth, even with the material of his gloves between the cloth and his skin. What surprised him was that the reef felt almost crumbly beneath the cloth. Realizing it was time to go, he spread his hand wide and simply grabbed as much of the cloth that he could and pulled. The cloth came free, and so did some of the reef, or so he thought because of the weight in his hand. When Evan actually saw what he had, his eyes lit up. It was a blue cloth alright, but this cloth was wrapped around something else.

A quick examination revealed that the heavy cloth material, was in fact a portion of a larger garment which was indicated by two intact buttons near a finished edge. The other edges were ragged, and had clearly been subjected to considerable force in order to be torn free from the piece that Evan now held in his hand. Of particular interest though, was that the roughly fifty inch square swatch of fabric in Evan's hand contained a pocket, and the pocket was full. Evan had no idea what was in the pocket, but it was heavy and felt like rocks. He wanted to take the time to open the pocket, but in the dark by himself one hundred feet below the surface, it was not immediately obvious how to do that. Right about then, Evan got a sense he was being watched and he suddenly felt very nervous. He waved his dive light around in all directions and saw nothing in his immediate area. Still, he wanted to get going and tucked the heavy item carefully inside the straps of the buoyancy compensator. Then he took several of the green flags and firmly planted them right in front of the opening that he had pulled the cloth from. Satisfied that the spot was well marked, he added some air to the compensator and began to rise from the sea bottom.

As Evan made his way up, he kept his dive light moving in all directions. When he cleared the rubble of the old bridge and rose slightly above the large concrete blocks, his light landed on a sight that chilled his blood and he felt real fear. No more than thirty feet away on the top of a large block, a Giant Pacific octopus, more red than brown at the moment, seemed to be watching Evan ascend. Without taking his wide open eyes off of the octopus, Evan tried not to panic, and added more air to his compensator to hasten his escape to the surface.

Chapter 28

When Michael surfaced nearly an hour after he and Evan had gone in the water, Deena had him picked up in less than a minute of his arrival from the bottom of the strait. As she went about helping to get him aboard, she kept looking to the water for the eruption of bubbles that would signal the location of Evan's return. Deena was not an expert diver, but she was experienced enough to know that dive buddies surface together, so something must be wrong. She found it odd though that the lack of urgency from Michael was sending a different message. Anxious to know the outcome of the dive, as soon as Michael had his dive mask off and had pulled back the hood of the drysuit, she asked with some concern in her voice, "Where's Evan? Shouldn't he be with you?"

Michael nodded in the affirmative and explained, "Normally yes, that is the diver's code. However he thought he found the area in the reef that we've been looking for and wanted to set some flags to mark the spot. He'll be right behind me."

"What does "right behind" mean?" Deena asked with even more concern in her voice.

"Evan's an expert diver and won't put himself at risk. I only surfaced because I was getting dangerously low on air and had to come up." Michael offered.

"I don't know. I don't like it. We don't even have a spare tank to try and go down and check on him." Deena fretted.

"I'm sure he's on his way up. Send him a DiveCom message just to say hello. He'll be happy to hear from you," Michael said trying to make light of the situation. The truth was, he was also starting to get concerned. He expected Evan to literally be right behind him. Maybe thirty seconds to plant the flags, and having different ascent rates could factor in, but it was now going on two minutes since he had surfaced, and a worried look crossed his face.

The perceptive and observant woman that she was, Deena did not miss the worried look and called Michael out on it. "You're worried too aren't you?" she said, giving Michael a stern look.

"OK, a bit," he reluctantly agreed.

Deena grabbed the DiveCom unit and traced out the letter "A", for Arrival, on the touch screen. The letters "ETA" with a "?" were displayed and she prepared to hit Send. Michael had been looking over her shoulder and noted that Evan's icon was not displayed in the status banner, which indicated he was not yet in range for connectivity with the DiveCom units on the surface. He furrowed his brow, but didn't say anything to Deena. She was clearly already worried. She sent the message and then held the unit for some time in her hands before asking, "Should I send the message again?"

"That won't be necessary," Michael provided. "The system keeps broadcasting until Evan's DiveCom unit accepts the message or we turn it off from here."

One hundred and twenty feet below the surface, Evan was hugging the seafloor. He was trying to hide from the very large octopus that had just made an attempt to stop his ascent to the surface. When the octopus left the top of the concrete block, it did so in a hurry and Evan had no doubt about where it was going. Anticipating the move, when the octopus shot up toward him on an intercept course, Evan extinguished his light and at the same time, purged all the air from his buoyancy compensator. The result was an immediate stop to his movement toward the surface, and between his own body weight, the SCUBA tank, the weighted dive belt, and the heavy item he had retrieved from the seabed, he dropped quickly back down to the bottom.

The descent was faster than Evan expected and he twisted his left ankle slightly on impact with the irregular seafloor. He knew that his exhalation bubbles would certainly give him away if the octopus chose to track the bubbles in the dark, so he was just hoping that it was the light that kept getting the octopus's attention. He was trying to remain motionless and planned to wait for a brief time before attempting to surface again. As he focused on being still, he felt the beginning of the end of the air in his tank. Breathing was starting to take more of an effort, so time was short. Knowing he would need a brief decompression stop at thirty feet, Evan decided he had waited long enough. As he was preparing to depart, in the back of his mind, he saw an image of the large octopus that seemed to be hunting him. It set his senses on edge and he decided that he wanted to make a quick exit. There was a bad feeling creeping in on him, but he wrote it off to the darkness and the tricks that his mind was playing. Evan really wanted to flick his light on for an instant just to confirm that he wasn't going to launch himself straight up into the giant, but opted instead for the cover of darkness to make his escape.

As ready as he was going to be, and with the intent to accelerate quickly to arrive at his decompression stop as soon as possible, Evan added more than just a little air to the buoyancy compensator. At the same time that the air started to lift him up, Evan pushed off hard from the seafloor with his legs and immediately began a series of powerful kicks. Once Evan was on his way up, he was tempted to turn on his dive light and scan the area to allay his fears that the octopus had moved on. He decided it best to remain in the dark rather than risk alerting the octopus to his location, if it was still around, so he continued to ascend in total darkness. Had Evan chosen to turn his light on and scan the seafloor upon leaving, he would have been shocked to have seen that the Giant Pacific octopus had been very close, and that it was actually in the process of reaching toward him with two of its massive arms when he lifted off from the seafloor.

Michael and Deena were past being worried. In fact, Michael was thinking hard about making an emergency call to the Coast Guard when Deena screamed out, "Evan's icon just showed up on my DiveCom unit!"

Michael stepped quickly over to her and looked at the screen for himself. Sure enough, there was Evan's smiling face displayed against the white background of the circular icon. Both of them just stared at the screen, trying to will the device to display a response from him. Five seconds passed, then ten, then twenty, and right after that, the screen displayed the words, "decompression stop" and Evan's small icon illuminated. The relief was clearly evident on both of their faces and although essentially strangers, Michael and Deena hugged each other in a strong embrace celebrating the short message that they had just received.

Knowing that Evan was about ready to board the boat, Michael made quick work of cleaning up the cockpit and getting his equipment stowed and out of the way. Deena was spinning her head around in all directions waiting and watching for the first sign of bubbles to appear.

As Evan rested peacefully taking slow breaths while drifting with the current during the decompression stop, light was filtering down from the surface and he couldn't resist lifting the item he had recovered free of the buoyancy compensator to get a closer look. It was heavy, easily weighing two pounds and likely a little more. He was being careful and held it firmly in both hands while rotating it around in order to lessen the chances of it returning to the bottom of the sea. The two buttons held a story not yet unlocked, and Evan felt sure that the remnants of the intricate patterns on the buttons he could barely discern would provide a clue to the cloth's origins. His mind wandered and he considered what it was that he was holding and how it came to be stuck in a hole in the reef.

With the current running at almost three knots on the surface, at thirty feet deep the water was turbulent and full of eddy currents that circled around in all directions. Evan could feel the water swaying his body around randomly and he took notice of a stronger push from the swirling water that brought him back to reality from his daydream. When he moved his eyes off the recovered item, they picked up motion beneath him. Locating the moving object, he realized he was in an actual nightmare when he saw the giant octopus that he thought he had left behind, coming right at him from below.

Not really panicking, but certainly a bit frightened at the sight, Evan thought to himself, "decompression stop over, got to go" and he quickly tucked the item in his hands securely under the straps of the buoyancy compensator again. He then added more air to the compensator, and started kicking hard. As he glanced up, he could see he was nearing the surface and prepared for the transition. He just hoped his boat was right there as he wanted out of the water in a hurry. With the compensator bladders full of air and Evan kicking hard, he thought he might breach the surface he was moving so fast. That did not quite happen, but he did get nearly out of the water to his waist. Settling back in the water and then floating on the surface, he kept his legs moving while ducking his mask underwater to try and watch for the octopus.

When Deena spotted a torrent of water spouting into the air about fifty yards to the southwest, without sitting down in the Captain's chair, she shifted both drives to Forward. Crab got Legs responded to the thrust of the props and Deena rotated the wheel to the right to change the boat's course to head directly at the disturbance. As Deena brought the boat in closer, she could see it was indeed Evan, but he was engaged in some odd behavior instead of watching them move toward him. Suddenly, Deena let out a scream, "Oh My God! The octopus is on the surface!"

Michael immediately dropped what he was doing and rushed forward to see what Deena was talking about. As he looked through the windscreen, he saw the dark reddish color of three of the octopus's arms waving around within twenty feet of Evan. The beast was huge and Evan looked to be not much bigger around than one of the arms. Michael just watched in horror as for the second time today, Evan did battle with a Giant Pacific octopus. This time however, Crab got Legs was in a position to help, and help she did.

Deena expertly maneuvered the boat to the downstream side of Evan, then shifted to Neutral and allowed him to drift toward the starboard side of the boat. Now with the boat in the middle of the battle, the octopus started thrashing about in an even more agitated fashion. Going on the offensive, it tried to resist the boat's progress and reached up and grabbed the port bow rail, partially lifting itself from the water. Deena watched in terror as the octopus threw its arms across the boat with one landing solidly on the windscreen with a loud crash, and hitting with such force that she felt the wheel vibrate in her hands. The weight of the octopus was putting a heavy strain on the rail mounts and the boat was listing hard to port when the rail broke free of the deck mounts. The octopus did not release its grip on the rail and fell back into the water taking a large section of the boat's bow rail with it.

While the action on the bow was happening, Michael had extended the boat hook to Evan and was guiding him around to the stern of the boat. Once Evan had his hands on the swimstep, he quickly pulled his dive fins off and handed them to Michael. Then he took ahold of the boarding ladder and even laden with the SCUBA gear, climbed aboard as fast as he ever had. Michael looked past Evan and caught sight of the octopus coming around the aft port quarter and wasted no time giving Deena instructions, "Evan's aboard, let's get the hell out of here! Go Deena!"

Deena shifted to Forward as Michael reached over the transom and took ahold of Evan to keep him from falling backwards off the swimstep. He also watched the octopus flail its arms in the air as they motored west and away from the giant of the deep. Before submerging, the octopus rose up out of the water sufficiently to expose the top of its body, and Michael could swear that it was staring right at him with its dark slit eyes sending a "do not come back here again" warning message. Michael planned to heed that warning, but what Evan was about to share with him would make keeping that promise very difficult.

Chapter 29

At about the same time that Deena was watching a Giant Pacific octopus try and climb aboard the boat she was piloting, her second level boss, Davis, sat at his expansive desk in the HGE building fretting about his personal net worth. He already had more wealth than most people in the world, but it was not enough. He was not sure what drove his craving for more money, but he did know that he thoroughly enjoyed the power and privilege that money provides. He felt the old saying about "money making the world go around" still applied and he intended to confirm that. While most might consider greed a vice, Davis considered it a virtue and an enabler for his plans.

Part of Davis's concern right now was the transaction he was trying to work for the fictitious company he had established. The company was really nothing more than a holding company for some of Davis's personal assets. In this case, the company dealt in the buying, selling and storing of precious metals. An audit of the second set of books that Davis kept would reveal that the company dealt mainly in gold, and did very little selling.

The transaction had been going fine, but the HGE analyst that was helping him had neglected to include a key document with the final Purchase Agreement for a large amount of gold at extremely attractive pricing. Now the transaction is in jeopardy and the analyst involved is nowhere to be found. Davis had already read the riot act to one of his Managers earlier today for allowing the woman to take a vacation day on such short notice. Citing company policy, he had gone off the deep end with the reprimand, but he did not apologize, and had left the Manager standing amongst his coworkers nearly in tears from the verbal lashing. The behavior cemented Davis's reputation around the company as an asshole. Consistent with his character, Davis didn't give a shit.

Davis finally leaned back to take a break in his expensive leather office chair that was more art than function. He shifted around uncomfortably in the seat, feeling tightness in his muscles, and particularly the muscles in his shoulders and neck. With the office closed for the day and the floor pretty much empty of workers, Davis leaned forward and opened his top center drawer. Pulling the drawer out nearly all the way, he reached in and opened a small box and removed a small vial that was half full of high grade cocaine. He also removed a small mirror, a razor blade and a tightly rolled one hundred dollar bill.

Two fat lines later, Davis was ready to rock and his mind and metabolism were running a mile a minute. The initial rush of the coke lasted for only a brief time and feeling invincible and wanting some air, he decided to step out on to the small ledge outside his window for a breath of the fresh air he was craving. Standing twelve stories up on the ledge looking over Seattle, typical of a cocaine high, Davis felt his confidence swell and considered that he could do just about anything. Thinking about his options with the gold transaction, there was only one option in his mind, get the gold. The acquisition costs were incredibly attractive since the shipment was comprised of smaller lots of gold stolen from much bigger shipments. Not sure how it was done and didn't care, he just knew that the gold was not traceable and he wanted it.

Davis was aware the analyst named Deena that he had been working with was scheduled to work tomorrow, and he planned on talking with her first thing. It was unfortunate that she was not available today to complete the work, because tomorrow he will be very impatient with her and probably a bit angry. He thought about his handling of the policy infraction by Ben Lauren and smiled to himself because he actually enjoyed humiliating the man.

Tomorrow though, Davis needed Deena's support until the documentation required for the gold purchase was in order. Once that was complete, then he would be free to discuss her poor vacation day planning skills. Having a plan for tomorrow was step one, and Davis believed that he now had a path forward to achieve his near term gold purchase goal. Feeling much better with the cocaine coursing through his veins, Davis took a series of deep breaths and then climbed back through the window into his office.

Miles away in a nondescript house in the suburbs north of Seattle, Ben Lauren sat in his comfortable Lazy Boy recliner thinking about his day at work. It was horrendous. No doubt about it, Davis was an asshole. He hadn't cared for the man before the "incident" earlier in the day, and now, he hated him. Ben had felt completely torn down mentally after Davis had laid into him about letting Deena take a day of vacation on short notice. "Really," he thought to himself, "over a fricking vacation day!"

Given the situation and the possible wild man antics of Davis, Ben felt that he owed Deena some notice of what to expect at work tomorrow. He thought it a good idea, but still he had been debating all afternoon whether to involve himself any further in Davis's policy administration methods. In the end, he believed telling Deena was the right thing to do and he picked up his phone and dialed her home number. After the fourth ring, the line picked up and Ben was greeted by a voicemail system. He briefly explained the situation and suggested to Deena that Davis is likely going to want to speak with her, probably first thing when she gets in. Then he hung up and rested his head against the comfortable chair back trying to get the image and sound memories of Davis yelling at him out of his head.

Chapter 30

Once Evan, Michael and Deena were safely aboard the boat, and the boat was clear of the territory clearly claimed by the octopus, the three adventurers began to relax from the tangle with the giant beast. Deena shifted both outdrives to Neutral and she let the boat drift south with the current. With the excitement of getting Evan aboard, both Michael and Deena had neglected to notice the odd bulge in the left side of Evan's buoyancy compensator. After Evan had his mask and hood off, he lifted the blue item from its secure position.

Deena and Michael stood still with their eyes transfixed on the item in Evan's hands. Now free of its dark cold resting spot far below them, the waning sunlight revealed a piece of heavy weight dark blue fabric of an irregular shape and roughly six inches by nine inches in size. There were two buttons approximately three inches apart next to a long, single finished edge. The rest of the piece was ragged at the edges and there was a frayed hole where it looked like another button might have been. Everything about the appearance of the piece suggested the garment had been subjected to considerable destructive forces. Michael finally gathered his thoughts and nearly shouted, "Is that what I think it is?"

Evan beamed ear to ear and nodded his head up and down slightly while saying, "If you're thinking it's the blue color splotch we've been looking for, I'm going to say that you'd be right!"

"Holy shit!" Michael exclaimed.

"And that's not the best part," Evan said quickly, but then provided nothing further. Instead, he flipped the item around and displayed the stuffed pocket attached to the fabric swatch. Now Michael and Deena were mesmerized and were locked in on the discovery. Evan moved the pocket around in large sweeping motions and he saw them both follow it perfectly with their head and eyes.

"I think what we have here is a pocket, but there's only a small portion of what's left of the jacket or coat attached," Evan volunteered.

Deena spoke up and provided, "Must be a coat of some kind. I do see that there are two buttons attached to the fabric there. Although, could it be that the pocket might just be full of silt and mud?"

"Possibly, but I did look briefly when I was below and again now, and it is not like the pocket is wide open for easy scooping up of debris. In fact, it's still not obvious how to open it," Evan said sounding excited by the intrigue.

"What a great find Evan, but let's save that for that later," Michael suggested. "The sun is going down now and we have about an hour until twilight. Probably best that you get changed out of your dive gear and we'll get ourselves underway. We'll be able to drop Deena off on Bainbridge Island before dark."

"I agree Michael, good plan," Evan replied.

"I mostly agree," Deena interjected. "To the part about dropping me off, yes. To the part about opening the pocket later, no," she communicated most emphatically.

Evan raised his eyebrows, smiled at her and asked, "You want to open the pocket right now?"

"Yes, I want to open the pocket right now!" Deena replied right away.

"Then let's do it. But let me get changed first if that's OK?" Evan responded giving Deena a wry smile.

Evan instructed Deena to turn on both the navigation lights and the interior lights for the bridge and cockpit. Against the deep purple sky and darkening water, the bright LED lighting of Crab Legs made the boat visible for miles. Then leaving the discovered item in Michael's capable hands, Evan stepped through the bridge area and down to the salon. Michael set the wet piece of fabric carefully in a bucket and placed the bucket on the small table in the lounge area on the port side of the cockpit. Then he busied himself rinsing and stowing Evan's tank, compensator and regulator. Deena leaned over the back of the helm passenger seat and stared longingly at the object Evan had retrieved from the sea floor, wondering what treasures and mysteries it might hold, or maybe nothing of interest at all.

Turns out she didn't have to wait long. Evan was as anxious as Deena was to open the pocket and in less than two minutes after dropping down into the salon, he returned to the bridge dressed in the clothes he started the trip in. "OK," he said, "Let's find out what it is I've brought up." Turning to look at Deena and at the same time motioning toward the lounge area in the cockpit, he asked, "Care to join us Deena?"

Deena did not have to be asked twice and was quickly up and around the helm seat and stepping into the cockpit almost before Evan finished his question. While she was quick to change seats, Evan did have enough time to not miss the agility of her moves or the sensuous way she maneuvered past him on her way to the lounge. Evan was distracted from the task at hand by Deena and he hesitated briefly before following her to the lounge. When he looked over, he caught eyes with Michael who was shaking his head sideways slightly with a smile in his eyes and his mouth was forming the words, "you are hooked." Evan gave a small smile, shrugged his shoulders slightly, and continued on his way to the lounge, sitting down on the "J" shaped bench seat on Deena's right side. Michael sat on her left side, and all three of them were wide eyed sitting around the table as Evan lifted the discovery from the bucket and placed it on a large serving tray he had brought with him from the salon.

With Michael providing additional light from a handheld LED flashlight, Evan inspected the entire pocket paying particular attention to where the pocket and the ragged fabric appeared to be connected together. The entire piece was still wet and there were small reflections from the light bouncing off the water droplets as Michael tried to hold his light steady in spite of his excitement level. Pulling the piece close, Evan leaned in and pulled at a loose fiber near the pocket to fabric connection, and was surprised that the fiber did not pull off easily. Instead, he noted that tugging on the fiber caused the pocket to fabric connection to pucker slightly. As Evan tugged a few more times, he recognized the puckering pattern for what it was, the result of pulling on the end of a stitch.

The fiber Evan had been pulling on was essentially the same color as the fabric, but once he realized that the pocket had been deliberately sewn shut, he focused his inspection on trying to follow the fiber. As he studied the sewing work that had been done, he located two spots where it looked like a stitch had been completed and then used needle nose pliers to help expose the stitch. Using wire cutters, he then carefully clipped both of the stitches that he had found. Releasing the entire piece from his hands, the filled pocket slumped down on the serving tray. From the small hole created by Evan's clipping of the two stitches, four dull yellow colored rocks spilled out on to the aluminum tray, making a muted, but distinctly metal on metal sound.

Nobody said a word. Instead, they all just stared at the four rocks lying on the tray apart from the fabric. Deena was first to reach out and take one of the rocks into her hand. It was barely the size of a pea, but was considerably heavier than a pea. She transferred the small yellow rock from hand to hand several times and then declared, "This is no ordinary rock. It is tough to tell for sure, but it seems to weigh more than a same size piece of granite would." She then let the rock drop from her right hand from just above the tray and they all heard the metal on metal sound when it landed on the tray. Deena continued, "No doubt about it, this, and the three rocks just like it right there, are all unrefined gold in its raw condition. That's right guys, these are real gold nuggets!"

Evan's face lit up with a huge smile and while happy with her assessment, questioned Deena on her pronouncement, "Are you sure?"

"Absolutely," she said with conviction. "If you recall Evan, I'm an analyst at HG Enterprises in the Precious Metals Division, plus I have a Bachelor's in Geology. So I feel confident that we're looking at gold." To further prove her point, she reached out with her right hand and picked up the rock she had previously dropped on the tray. She then held the pea sized piece between her thumb and index finger and proceeded to place it between her left front molars. Then slowly, but firmly, she bit down.

"Yes, it's gold alright," Deena said after setting the piece of gold back on the tray. "Gold is quite malleable in its native form and my little test told me what I wanted to know. As I exerted pressure with my teeth, I could feel the material give way slightly, which indicates there is some softness to the metallic material."

"This is incredible!" Michael added.

"And that's only four nuggets that happened to spill out of the pocket. Now that I've got it started, I say we open the pocket the rest of the way," Evan suggested with a big grin.

They all agreed, and after Michael finished a series of pictures and video, Evan proceeded to open the pocket all the way. Michael was taking video of the now clearly historic moment, but was having a hard time keeping his phone from jiggling he was so excited. With a small opening already started, finding and clipping the random placement of the remaining stitches was straightforward. Evan then lifted the bottom of the pocket enough for the contents to start spilling into the tray. When he was done, they were staring at nearly one hundred gold nuggets, in sizes that ranged from small peas to large olives.

The pocket was now empty of gold nuggets, but something was still inside. Opening the pocket, Evan used the small LED flashlight to light up the interior and he peeked inside. Lifting his head up and looking first at Michael, and then at Deena, with the tone of his voice hinting at something very exciting, he said to them, "This looks very interesting."

Deena was quick to ask, "What, what looks very interesting?"

"I think we've found a ship's log book," Evan said, almost disbelieving his own words as he said them. Then he stood up abruptly and as he moved toward the salon, said, "I'll be right back."

Michael and Deena looked at each other a bit puzzled and both shrugged their shoulders slightly.

Michael took advantage of the break and stopped with the video and pictures, but soon Evan returned with a few quart size Zip-lock bags and a pair of nitrile gloves. He explained, "If that really is a ship's log, it's been in salt water a long time, and it should probably stay that way for now. Chances of the pages being intact are slim, but who knows, and I have a friend at the MOHAI that can help us with preservation and maritime history. That's the Museum Of History And Industry in Seattle by the way."

Then Evan put on the gloves to avoid touching the artifact with his bare hands, and carefully reached in to the pocket and pinched the edge of the small book between his right index finger and his thumb. The book was small, but heavy as it was water logged through and through, so Evan had to pinch hard in order to lift the book. Once lifted, the book slid right out of the pocket and Evan laid it on the tray. There in front of them, resting in a small pool of water from Puget Sound, sat a four inch by six inch leather bound book with the words "Bonita Joya" embossed on the cover.

Chapter 31

Thursday morning came early for Deena since her day off from work had turned into more than she had bargained for. She realized she was already running a bit late since she was waking to her alarm. Normally, she would wake before the alarm. Rolling over and reaching for her phone, she picked it up from the nightstand and quickly stopped the noise that had interrupted her slumber. Since her commute to work included catching the 8:10AM ferry to Seattle, she had no time to waste and threw back the covers and sat up. That move brought a throbbing to her head and she had to sit still for a bit before getting up. She then made her way to the bathroom and headed right to the medicine cabinet for some Tylenol. "Oh Deena, I think you may have had too much wine last night," she thought to herself.

Then the prior day came rushing back and the thrill of it all put a big smile on her face. Aside from fighting off an armed boarder, she had thoroughly enjoyed the day. Evan and Michael had dropped her at the city dock at a reasonable hour last night, but then she didn't leave right away. Instead, she stayed aboard with them for several hours as Crab got Legs rocked lightly in the calm water while tied to the dock. They had sat at the dining table in the salon, drinking wine from the collection that Evan had aboard, and considered the next steps for the

At Water's End 255

artifacts they had come to simply describe as "the treasure".

Feeling a bit foggy from the alcohol last night, Deena turned the cold water on at the sink, cupped her hands, and then splashed some of the water in her face. It felt refreshing and helped with the headache that had materialized this morning. She used a towel to dry her face and then immediately turned on the standalone glass enclosed shower and prepared to get in. Tossing her nightshirt and panties in the hamper, she stepped in before the water was fully up to temperature. The brisk water chilled her at first, but then she relaxed and enjoyed the feel and sound of the spray while the water warmed up.

By the time Deena had showered, dressed and nearly finished eating a small breakfast of dry toast, yogurt and a fruit cup, she was starting to feel like her normal self. The large cup of Kona brand coffee she had brewed probably helped some too she thought. Knowing the ferry would not wait for her, she hurriedly finished up with the breakfast and just left the dishes in the sink. Then she slipped her business casual jacket over the light gray blouse she had selected for the day, grabbed her leather tote and headed for the front door of her condo. As she was just preparing to step outside, the slowly flashing green message light of her landline phone system caught her attention, but given the time, she opted to hold off listening to the messages until later.

Once in her ten year old BMW M3 sport sedan and on the way to the ferry dock, Deena didn't worry about the time any more, but did proceed at a good speed along State Highway 305. Arriving at the dock after six minutes, she got in line with all the other commuter cars and the commercial trucks making their way across Puget Sound to Seattle by boat. After parking in the wait lot, she noted that she had ended up farther back in the line for the 8:10AM crossing than she usually did. She silently hoped there was going to be room for her on the ferry that was just coming into view around Bill Point to the east as it brought passengers, cars and trucks from Seattle.

After patiently waiting through the unloading process, Deena had her car running and was just starting to move forward. To her, it seemed like the loading process was taking forever, but in actuality, the WSDOT was quite efficient and always left the dock on time, and rarely left without a full load. As she crept forward, the ramp to the ferry came into view, but she was not yet past the single orange plank that served as a gate to separate the line of vehicles into the end of the 8:10AM group and the beginning of the 8:55AM group. She really, really wanted to get past that gate. If she did not, she would be late to work, and being late right after a vacation day taken on short notice just simply wouldn't be good.

To anyone that might have been looking at her when she passed the gate, they would have seen Deena physically change from very anxious looking to calm and serene. Now she was sure she would be on the 8:10AM ferry. Glancing in her rear view mirror, she saw a ferry dock worker step in front of the car that was two behind her. The gate came down and she realized that she was going to be the second to the last vehicle on the ferry. "That was way too close," she thought to herself, "better adjust my alarm to wake me up earlier."

The ferry ride to Seattle was uneventful and it gave Deena time to reflect on yesterday. It all seemed so surreal to her now that she was back in her regular routine. But it was real! They had tangled with a very large Giant Pacific octopus. The mangled bow rail and damaged windscreen that they had found when they inspected Crab got Legs at the Bainbridge Island city dock had confirmed that. Plus they did find unprocessed gold nuggets and a ship's log! And she thought, I really did spend the day with two attractive men that I just recently met, one of which is single and quite charming.

That got her thinking about Evan, and she realized she wanted to see more of him. They had crafted a plan last night to get together, so she already knew she would be seeing him Saturday morning at MOHAI to hear what his friend has to say about the find. She was anxious to learn more, and had hoped it would have happened earlier, but Evan's friend won't be back in town until then. She was abruptly pulled away from the daydream by the loud announcement for passengers to return to their vehicles. She had never left her car, so was ready to go and just needed the vehicles in front of her to start moving so she could get to work on time.

As Deena's ferry was disembarking the last of the passengers and vehicles at the Seattle ferry terminal in Elliot Bay, Ben Lauren was in his office at HG Enterprises waiting for Deena to arrive. He wanted to catch her right away before Davis did to be sure she was prepared for whatever Davis had planned. After a nervous ten minutes of ducking in and out of his office, he finally saw that Deena was coming down a walkway between two rows of desks toward her own desk. She had a smile on her face, greeting coworkers, and looking like she didn't have a care in the world.

Ben was understandably puzzled. He had thought his message made it clear that today was likely not going to be a good day for her. Although he did admire her attitude, he had figured that she would have at least been less noticeable upon her arrival in the office. As Ben stepped toward Deena's desk, he caught sight of Davis coming out of his office. Davis turned his head in Ben's direction and then promptly turned his whole body when he saw Deena. With a serious look on his face, Davis started striding briskly in Deena's direction. Ben hurried his pace a bit, but not enough to look obvious, and was able cut Davis off before he reached Deena's desk and he asked, "Good morning Davis, what can I do for you?"

Davis practically glared at Ben and in addition to dismissing him with a wave, he said, "Nothing. I need to speak with Deena." Then he moved past Ben and headed toward Deena. Ben turned and followed him.

Just arriving at her desk, Deena put her tote down and was just taking off her jacket when she noticed Ben and Davis nearby. As she went to sit down, she saw that both men were now moving, and both were coming in her direction. She felt a twinge of panic, kind of like what one feels when a police car's flashing lights turn on while it is driving behind you. As she looked at Davis coming toward her, the twinge got worse as his contorted face seemed to scream frustration. When he glanced up and noticed Deena looking at him, his expression changed in the blink of an eye to that of a man with not a care in the world. Deena knew it to be a lie, but chose to go along with the façade and shook off the slight panic attack, then took the offensive. "Good morning Davis. And Good Morning to you too Ben," she said with a cheery voice and a smile on her face. "How can I help you gentlemen?"

Davis was first to speak and got right to the point, "Welcome back Deena," he said with an odd edge to his voice. "It's about the project you've been working on for me. We seem to have hit a snag and I could use your help to get things sorted out."

"Anything I can do to help?" Ben asked enthusiastically.

"No, nothing for you to do Ben," Davis provided. Looking directly at Deena, he continued, "I see you just got in, but there is some urgency, so if you can join me in my office, we should be able to take care of the issue right away."

"Oh absolutely," Deena said almost immediately. Then things got uncomfortable as Davis did not return to his office as Deena was expecting. Instead, he stayed right at her desk clearly intending for her to go with him back to his office. She looked at Davis and asked the obvious question, "You mean right now?"

"Yes Deena, right now," Davis repeated with that slight edge to his voice again.

"Maybe I should join you guys," Ben volunteered.

Davis was quick to provide a response and with no explanation included, simply said, "No, that won't be necessary." Then Davis turned on his heels and walked away from Deena's desk.

Deena stood up and grabbed the notepad she had on her desk, and a pen, then gave Ben a slight shrug of her shoulders and followed Davis to his office. Once Deena was inside, Ben heard the door close. He thought Deena a pretty cool character given the description of Davis's behavior that he had provided her. Unfortunately for Deena, the description Ben provided was still waiting to be heard in a voicemail tied to her landline phone.

When Davis closed the door behind Deena after she came in, the uncomfortable feeling she had just moments ago came flooding back. She was beginning to believe it was maybe just Davis as a person that was giving her the heebie-jeebies. Pushing that to the back of her mind, she sat down in one of the four chairs at the round table in his office, the one closest to the door, and Davis joined her at the table.

Without any preamble, and without any real specifics, Davis began explaining why the lack of completed paperwork was putting his gold deal in jeopardy. As he went on, the real issue was finally brought to light and Deena relaxed some when she realized it was only a single document that he required. She recalled seeing it, and inserted herself in Davis's one-sided conversation with, "I know the document you're talking about."

Davis stopped talking, and for a few seconds just looked at Deena wondering if she was telling the truth, or was just anxious to leave his company. She continued, "I recall seeing it, and will get it completed and added to the purchase contract right away."

Davis wanted this deal done, so opted to trust that she would have the paperwork completed as soon as possible. Switching to a friendly version of himself, Davis said, "Well that will be fine then. Glad we'll be able to get this taken care of today." He paused briefly and then continued with, "It surprised me to find you on vacation yesterday. I do hope it was a good day off of work. Did you do anything special?"

That last question caught her by surprise. It was rare that she ever heard Davis ask anything about someone else. Hearing the question left her feeling like a deer in headlights, and she froze for a split second. Lacking a good impromptu story, she volunteered bits of the truth. Deena was trying to be vague, but the story seemed to intrigue Davis and he asked seemingly poignant follow up questions. After a few minutes discussing her day off, Davis took on a contemplative look and seemed to fix his gaze to look right through her. Deena started to feel even more awkward and broke the silence with, "If that will be all, I'd like to get going on the paperwork."

The sound of Deena's voice snapped Davis back to the present and he said, "Yes, yes, by all means, take care of finishing the purchase contract right away so our Customer's operations are not impacted."

Davis then stood up and walked behind his desk and prepared to sit down. Deena stood up at nearly the same time and walked across the room toward the closed door. With barely a hesitation to stop and open the door, she breezed across the threshold like she had a tailwind at her back. Once outside of the office and away from the door, she slowed down and took several deep breaths as she tried to walk casually back to her desk.

Chapter 32

Throughout the day, Davis kept drifting back to his conversation with Deena about her day off. He couldn't have cared less about her, or what she did for fun, but her story had elements that meshed with an old story he had heard that could be a legend, a myth, a fairy tale, or maybe even the truth. Davis knew that much of the planet's gold supply was still undiscovered. However a large percentage of the gold supply has already been discovered, gathered together, and then a considerable amount of that gold lost to the bottom of seas. Davis found that as gold collector, he is indiscriminate about where the object of his desire comes from, so all sources are open to him. Sunken and buried treasure are included, and Davis had spent hours and hours doing research on candidate shipwrecks that, if physically located, had a high probability that they carried gold.

In the case of Deena's story, the location that she said her friends recovered the "artifact", she had called it, brought to mind a story Davis had heard almost all his life. The story tells of a shipwreck in waters that would seem to describe a north-south passage in Puget Sound that today, Davis believed to be in the area of the Tacoma Narrows Strait. According to the feeble timeline he had for the story, the wreck would have happened hundreds of years ago. The ship supposedly carried gold that was literally picked up off the shores of Puget Sound. His research would indicate the scenario possible, and when Deena's description included "something old and nautical discovered in the Tacoma Narrows Strait," that had piqued his interest.

Thinking back to the discussion with Deena, Davis realized that since he had no real interest in her day off, he wasn't really listening to her, at first. He had only asked about her day to try and seem personable so that she would get the paperwork done faster. As she used certain words however, Davis had become interested, and started to listen intently and even asked a few questions. He was now suspecting that maybe there was more to her story than she was letting on, and he considered that a follow up conversation, as casual as he could play it, would be in order.

Later in the morning, well after her meeting with Davis, Deena had gotten a feeling that she was being watched. She knew exactly who she suspected was watching her too, but never actually saw anyone watching. Maybe it was just paranoia from mentioning the diving that Evan and Michael had done in the Tacoma Narrows Strait yesterday. Thinking about it, she felt fortunate that she hadn't just blurted out the whole story given how nervous she was and how awkward the conversation with Davis had been. Unfortunately, she did mention that an artifact of some kind had been found. Deena thought to herself, "Why did I talk so much? Why was he asking about my day? Was he hitting on me? That was just weird."

With the required documents for the Purchase Agreement that Davis needed almost complete, Deena leaned backwards in her chair to stretch her back and neck muscles. Looking at her watch, she realized that she had been working nearly nonstop for just over three hours. The watch was indicating the lunch hour, which shifted her thoughts to lunch, but she was not really hungry at the moment. Deena did decide that she wanted to get out of the office though.

After setting her Instant Messenger status to "Lunch" and then locking her screen, she stood up and headed to the restroom for a long overdue break. Once back at her desk, she slipped on her jacket, picked up her tote and headed for the elevators. As she rounded the corner to the elevator bay, one of the two elevator doors was starting to close and she called out, "Hold the elevator please!", but the door continued to close and was fully shut by the time she was in front of it. Slightly exasperated by missing the Just in Time ride down, she stabbed at the "Down" button on the elevator keypad to make sure it lit up.

After just under thirty seconds of waiting, the other elevator arrived and Deena was able to make a two stop trip to the parking garage. Her BMW was off to the left of the elevators and she walked there directly as soon as the doors opened. Unlocking the car from a short distance away, she didn't lose a step as she opened the driver's door, got in the seat, and closed the door in one fluid motion. Being in her own space did help to calm her down some. It had been a crazy day so far and sitting in her car allowed the HG Enterprises work to float away. Reclining her seat slightly, she rested her head against the seat back and closed her eyes.

With her eyes shut, her mind started filling up with images from yesterday. Thinking about the excitement and danger of the adventure put a smile on her face, but that soon changed to a frown realizing that she had let their secret out. Telling herself that the discussion with Davis had meant nothing, she focused on her breathing to steady her nerves and to get herself under control.

When Deena was reclining her car seat, Davis was just slipping back into the parking garage elevator bay after making his way there through the numerous shadows in the garage. Having kept tabs on Deena starting around 11:00AM, he was hoping that she would leave the office and in particular, go to her car. When he saw her at her desk looking like she might leave, he took a chance and immediately rode an elevator to the garage. Davis wasn't sure why he wanted to know more about Deena, or what vehicle she drove, but for some reason he did. He had witnessed her exit the elevator and head off to the left, and then followed her covertly. She had gone directly to a vehicle, presumably hers, and he made a note of the older looking light blue BMW M3 sedan that she had opened and gotten in. The license plate was the standard Washington State design, number DHC-4235, and Davis wrote the number down on one of his business cards.

Later in the day, just before 3:00PM, Deena was able to complete the necessary paperwork for Davis and she immediately went to his office to let him know. Peeking in the door, she did not see anyone in the room. Turning away from the doorway to leave and look elsewhere, she found herself staring right at Davis. Somehow he had snuck up on her and that startled her a bit. Before she could say anything, Davis said, "Do you have something for me?"

Deena stammered out "Yes."

"Let's finish this in my office," he said, and ushered her into the room and right to the same chair that she sat in earlier in the day. Before he sat down, Davis closed his office door and that uncomfortable feeling hit Deena again. She was seriously starting to not like the man she was working for. Once Davis sat down, Deena wanted to start right into explaining the completion of the documents. However before she was really able to say anything, Davis opened the conversation with, "Thank you for handling this transaction. I know it kind of got dropped on you, but sometimes time is of the essence."

"I appreciate that," Deena replied, and began to sort through the pile of papers she had come into the room with.

Davis reached over the tabletop and laid his left hand on her right forearm, and said, "We have enough time for that. I'd like to hear more about your day off. That was quite an adventure you described this morning."

As soon as Deena felt the touch of Davis's hand, her skin began to crawl. Her gut instinct was telling her something wasn't right, but she could not put her finger on it. She did withdraw her arm with an obvious intent to let Davis know that his touch was unacceptable, and having considered that the subject might come up, she said, "Yes, well, I think my imagination must have gotten the better of me. I really embellished what actually happened to make it sound like a great adventure. I'm sorry for talking it up so much."

Davis sat back and stared at Deena with a perplexed look on his face. Then he leaned forward and his behavior suggested that he was trying to think of what to say next. When he spoke, he seemed like a different man. His eyes actually appeared darker and the haunting look that would frequently occupy his face returned. He was back to being all business and simply said, "Alright, let's see the completed work. The company can't afford to miss out on handling this transaction and it needs to be done by the close of business our time today."

That surprised Deena since she had not been told that there was a specific due date involved. Taking it in stride, she said, "No problem, just initial and sign where I've indicated and I'll take care of it."

Then she sat back and waited for Davis to complete his initials and signature. When she could tell he was about done, Deena started to gather her things and prepared to stand up. Davis finished up, laid the pen down on the table and said, "Hold on one second before you leave."

Deena didn't like the sound of that, but remained seated. Davis began to speak sternly at her and reiterated the company's policy regarding paid time off. His face was starting to get flush and his voice became elevated when he described the importance of the work he had trusted Deena with. He also lamented about how disappointed he was in her lack of consideration by taking Wednesday off without telling him. Then he stood up and walked to the closed office door and opened it roughly. Looking at Deena, he said, "Now head on back to your desk and finish what should have been done yesterday."

Deena stood up quickly, gathered everything up and lifted it from the table. Then with her head hanging low from Davis's reprimand, she walked past him and out of his office toward her desk.

Davis moved to his own desk and sat down heavily in his luxurious desk chair and started fuming. He could tell that the bitch was lying to him about her story and he was more convinced than ever that something had been found in the deep waters of the Tacoma Narrows. Not wanting to let it go, he started thinking about what he might do next to persuade Deena to disclose the truth about what her friends brought up from the seafloor.

Right around 4:30PM, Deena couldn't wait to be done with work, so she started watching the clock advance slowly toward 5:00PM. As it got closer to leaving time, she straightened up her desk and wasted a few more minutes with a nearly unnecessary bathroom trip. After all that had happened today, she did feel the situation warranted a final check that everything was OK with the work she had done. The last thing she wanted tomorrow was a repeat of today. Then hesitantly, she started walking toward Davis's office. She did take a meandering route though and was able to get a look through Davis's office doorway from farther away. He was not sitting at his desk and she breathed a sigh of relief.

Having taken care of what she considered the last loose end from the nightmare work assignment, Deena's mood brightened and she wasted no time getting back to her desk and closing things up for the day. Heading to the elevators, she passed a few coworkers that were still at their desks and made departing comments like, "don't stay around here too long" and "it's time to power down, the office is closed." Her coworkers barely looked up, but they did acknowledge with responses like "sure thing" and "thanks for the reminder."

Once in the parking garage, Deena's step quickened. She knew that if you reached the ferry terminal much after 5:25PM, she'd be in the same situation as this morning and at risk of missing her preferred crossing time. She had no plans and no schedule to keep, but did want to get back to Bainbridge Island at the earliest.

After she had unlocked and opened the driver's door, she reached in and put her tote on the floor just in front of the passenger seat, then removed her jacket and placed it neatly on the passenger seat. Sitting down in the driver's seat, she used the steering wheel for support and lifted her legs and rotated them into the car. Pulling the seatbelt across her chest and lap, she snapped the connectors together with a solid clicking sound confirming that she was buckled in. Getting ready to start the car, she glanced first in her side mirrors and then the rearview mirror to make sure it was clear to back up. Her eyes went wide and she froze with her hands gripping hard on to the steering wheel when she caught sight of a shadowy form reflected it the rearview mirror. When she heard Davis say, "Hello Deena," she let out a blood curdling scream.

Chapter 33

When Deena had started to scream, Davis had reacted instantly. It was all a blur as it happened so fast, but he recalled reaching around from behind her with his right arm and covering her mouth and nose with a cloth soaked in chloroform. The cloth muffled Deena's scream, but she was moving about in the seat and the chloroform takes time to work. He remembered yanking hard on the seatbelt and that pinned her back, but she was still trying to scream. When she released her grip on the steering wheel and started to go for the car horn, that's when he had dropped the cloth, pulled back his right arm, and then delivered a tight fist hard to Deena's right temple. Her head snapped to the left and then all was silent. At the same time, the tension on the seatbelt that he was holding tight had eased and he felt her body go limp in the seat. Wanting to make sure she stayed out for a while, he had held the cloth on her face for another four minutes while she breathed in the knock out vapors.

Now Davis sat staring at Deena while she rested comfortably in a recliner across from him. With the exception of the gag in her mouth, the bruise spreading on the right side of her head and her bound hands and feet, she looked like she was just in a deep sleep. Since Deena had not moved at all in the hour and a half since he had abducted her, he wondered if maybe he had hit her too hard or used too much of the chloroform. He also wondered if she would be more comfortable without her clothes on, but then decided that that would be more for his benefit than hers. The thought still appealed to him though as he pictured Deena naked, and so he filed the idea away for a different time.

His plan had been simple and all that he had wanted to do was demonstrate his power to Deena by showing he could gain access to her car. Davis figured it would make her more talkative. He had used one of his criminal contacts to help him and he easily gained access. The demonstration part worked, but Deena did not react as he had hoped and that caused him to resort to physically knocking her out. What her mood would be like once she came to was not really a mystery, so Davis kept the chloroform close by as he expected he would need it again.

Having to come up with a new game plan, Davis had been busy during the time since he had knocked Deena out. Now that he had initiated the plan, he was fully committed and that meant covering loose ends. He felt he had done that starting with leaving the HGE building since he had driven Deena's car out of the parking garage and then parked nearby in a Pay by Hour lot. He had left Deena out cold lying on the backseat floor of her car covered by her jacket as best he could. The dark tinted windows made it almost impossible for a casual observer to see her and with that complete, he had made his way back to the HGE building on foot. The HGE building does have security personnel on site, but there is no "check in" required to access the building, so Davis had walked right in the front door and headed directly to the elevators. A few minutes later he was back in his office.

Once there, Davis had quickly closed things up for the day, locked his office door on the way out and then walked briskly through the company office space on the twelfth floor. He was looking for people still working so he could be observed. It was after closing time, but there had been a few people still working. When Davis saw them, he had made suggestions like, "don't stay here working too long" and "time to close up for day." He had then proceeded directly to his Porsche Cayenne SUV in the parking garage and was soon parked a few spaces away from Deena's car in the Park by Hour lot. Then he transferred to Deena's car, and leaving his Porsche in the lot, had driven her vehicle and her unconscious body the six miles to Harbor Island. The mostly industrial island known as Harbor Island is located just off of the West Seattle Bridge in the southeast corner of Elliot Bay, and Davis felt sure he could use one of his storage facility offices as a temporary safe house while he sorted things out. With Deena's car safely tucked away in the warehouse, he just needed Deena to start talking, really talking, about her day off from work yesterday.

While Davis had been pondering the situation and thinking about next steps, he had missed that Deena had come around, so he was quite surprised when he glanced at her and she was staring at him with a smoldering fury that burned right through him. "This is not going to be easy," he thought to himself.

Thursday evening found Evan at home in his office staring at the artifacts from the last Tacoma Narrows dive. He was really anxious to meet with Audrey Richards, someone he had known for years and now worked at MOHAI on the shores of south Lake Union just north of downtown Seattle. Audrey was also a research nut for anything old and water logged. That is to say, she was obsessed with documenting shipwrecks and the equipment, supplies and cargo associated with the earliest days of sailing.

Evan was particularly interested in the ship's log, which had the name of the supposed ship embossed on the cover. Looking at the book in the bright light of his desk lamp, he was surprised that the leather of the cover and the gilding of the page edges appeared to be in very good shape. The lack of oxygen in the waters of south Puget Sound was actually beneficial for the preservation of most things, and the book appeared to be another case of that. How the writing, if there was any, had fared over the years was what he really wanted to know.

At almost 8:00PM, he heard his phone beep letting him know he had a text message. Thinking it was a good time for a break anyway, he pushed his chair back from his desk and then stretched his back and rolled his shoulders several time to chase away the stiffness. He noticed his large water cup was almost empty and stood up, grabbed the cup and headed to the kitchen. After filling up the cup with filtered water from the front of the refrigerator, he took a long drink of the refreshing clear liquid.

Pulling his phone from his pocket, he saw that the text was from Deena and a little smile came to his lips. Getting the text reminded him that he had enjoyed the day with her yesterday, and that he was looking forward to seeing her on Saturday. Opening the text, Evan read through it quickly and then paused since he didn't quite know what to think of it. He read it again, and again was surprised that Deena was proposing they get together in about an hour. There was not much of a reason provided except, "want to see you". He wanted to see her too, and along with yesterday's adventure that she probably wanted to talk about, he could understand her reason for wanting the late get together.

Evan decided to meet Deena, and sent an affirmative and asked where. Her reply was prompt and simply said, "city park by the ferry terminal, Jasper's Bar & Grill at 9:00PM." Evan knew of Jasper's but had never been there and replied with. "OK, see you soon." Shortly after that, Deena responded with "OK."

With about a forty minute drive ahead of him, Evan returned to his office to close things up and also to secure the artifacts that they had found on the dive in his wall safe. After freshening up, Evan headed for the garage with the keys to his Camaro in his pocket. As he backed the car out of the garage and the light rain started hitting the windshield, he had an odd premonition that something wasn't right. Pushing it to the back of his mind, he shifted the modern day muscle car he was driving into gear. Then with a light touch to the gas pedal to keep the rear wheels from spinning, he began his trip to Bainbridge Island for an evening rendezvous with Deena.

Just under forty-five minutes after leaving his house, Evan pulled into Jasper's and found a spot in the parking lot in front of the building. He looked around and realized that he didn't know what kind of car Deena drove on a daily basis and he suspected that in the rain and at night, it was not the Challenger. Assuming that she was probably already there given that she lived nearby, he pulled his jacket hood over his head, stepped out of the Camaro and walked briskly in the now steady rain to Jasper's brightly lit entrance. Once inside, Evan shook himself to shed the rainwater that had clung to his jacket and then removed his hood to look around.

The bar and grill was only brightly lit from the outside. Inside, the space was dimly lit, but not in a bad way. The effect was a restaurant bar that provided a nautical theme with an eerie feeling of being underwater. Evan suspected that as the patrons got drunk, the sense of being underwater and the light effects that emulated wave action had left more than just few of them puking their guts out. He stood in the entrance looking around, but mainly he was waiting for his eyes to adjust to the dark environment. When he felt his vision had adjusted enough and that he would be able to spot Deena, he ventured into the bar side of the establishment on a mission to find her.

In the bar section of Jasper's Bar & Grill, against the far wall, Davis sat on a barstool at a tall table cradling a glass of water, carefully surveying the people around him. Deena had provided, reluctantly, a description of the man named Evan Mason, and Davis intended to locate him and address the man like they were old friends. The personal information about Evan that Deena had volunteered should make it easy for Davis to gain his trust. After that, Davis wasn't sure where things would go, but the SIG Sauer 9mm handgun in his coat pocket made him feel confidence that he would get what he wanted.

When a tall man with wavy brown hair looking about the right age and build walked into the bar, Davis casually turned his attention toward the new customer. The bar was not full, but there were enough people that it could be considered crowded, and although Evan was expecting that he might hear his name, he was surprised when he heard "Hey Evan, Evan Mason!", in a clearly masculine sounding voice.

Evan spun around to the left looking for the source of the voice, but no one appeared familiar. Then he felt a heavy hand on his right shoulder and heard, "Hello Mr. Mason." Snapping his head around he found himself face to face with a man he didn't believe he'd ever met before, yet this unknown person knew his name. The coincidence of an apparent stranger being at Jasper's the same time he was supposed to meet Deena just didn't sit right, but he had no reason to think the two were related, yet, so he acted accordingly and said, "Yes, I'm Evan. And who might you be? I'm sorry, but I don't recognize you."

Davis was prepared for that question and responded with, "That would be right, we don't know each other. I'm a friend of Deena's and she's running a bit late. I spend most night's here and she called and asked me to let you know."

Shaking his head slightly up and down indicating he understood, Evan questioned the stranger on Deena's request, "Weird she didn't just call me and let me know she would be late."

Davis saw where Evan's thinking was going and quickly suggested that Deena must not have wanted to risk his safety while he was driving. It seemed that Evan was satisfied with that explanation and asked, "Did she say how late she would be?"

Looking concerned, Davis took this as the opportunity to try and get Evan alone, and in a very sober tone said, "Let's talk outside. It's less noisy and more private."

That sounded ominous to Evan and alarm bells started going off in his head, but he gave a slight nod and then Davis led the way through the crowd to the front door. Trailing slightly behind Davis, Evan wanted to try and get in touch with Deena and quickly sent her a text message asking, "got message u r running late, eta?"

Slipping his phone back in his pocket, Evan followed Davis out the front door and to the right toward the edge of the building. Standing under the cover of the oversized building eaves, the rain continued to splatter loudly on the pavement around them, but Evan still heard the stranger's phone issue a two pulse techno beat sound that Evan instantly recognized as the same one Deena uses for text messages. The lighting was poor away from the entrance to Jasper's, but with only four feet of space between them, Evan was able to see the stranger well enough to watch him pull a phone from his left coat pocket, and from his right coat pocket, a gun that he immediately aimed directly at Evan's chest.

"Very clever Evan," Davis said of Evan's sneaky attempt to contact Deena. "Unfortunately, Deena won't be getting your text message. She is safe I can assure you, but the tale she told of yesterday's dive at the Tacoma Narrows, well, I simply have to know more. Actually, let me rephrase that. I simply have to have what you found."

"I don't know what you're talking about," Evan said without hesitation, but hearing that the stranger seemed well versed regarding yesterday's find, left him reeling.

"Come, come now Evan," the stranger said. "I'm holding Deena's phone in my hand, and she is not here. As I've told you, I'm aware of your adventure yesterday and I know you recovered a small amount of gold. How I know that is none of your concern."

The statements just made by the stranger gave Evan pause to reconsider Deena's role in the current situation. He thought to himself, "Is it possible that Deena told this deranged looking individual in front of me about the gold and is part of all this?". He didn't want to believe it, but he had no information to the contrary to dispel the uncomfortable feeling. Evan recognized that either way, the stranger holding the gun on him at the moment knew way more than he should. So Evan's premonition seemed realized, and it was confirmed that something was definitely not right.

Evan decided to play the hapless victim and made it seem that he simply wanted to be done with the meeting and would do whatever the stranger wanted. The ploy worked and soon Evan noticed the stranger let the barrel of the gun drop slightly and he considered his chances of disarming the man. Realizing that as fast as he would be at closing the gap between them, the bullet would close the gap much faster, and while the stranger was less tense now, he was still highly alert. Accepting that he would not likely be able to physically take the man because of the gun, Evan listened attentively to the instructions he was being given.

Chapter 34

The meeting with the stranger outside of Jasper's left Evan fuming. Now back in his car and headed home, he tried to recall the words the madman had used to describe Deena's condition. He had said she "was safe", but given the man with the gun didn't appear too stable, Evan had his doubts. Evan also didn't know exactly what Deena had disclosed to the stranger, or if she had done it voluntarily, but the stranger had been right with enough details to convince Evan that the situation was for real.

The road conditions were not great, but there was little traffic, and with the rain coming down he kept the windshield wipers going at a medium speed to push the water aside. Once across Agate Pass and off of Bainbridge Island, Evan drove north toward Sequim at a good bit above the speed limit. The drone of the wipers was monotonous and Evan's attention began to drift to thoughts of the meeting at Jasper's. Questions kept coming up in his head about the stranger, and Deena, and what kind of relationship they might have. Was he somebody that had heard her talking about yesterday somewhere in public, did she know him, maybe Deena is not who she would appear to be? After all Evan thought, he had just met her five days ago, supposedly at random, and really knew very little about her. Although if she was the innocent victim in all this, Evan intended to avenge whatever wrongs that may have been done to her.

Shifting gears mentally, he started thinking about what he had been directed to do. It made some sense, but was wrong in one important way; there was nothing left to recover from the seafloor. The stranger, which Evan now thought of as the enemy, kept repeating "gold, more gold," like he was under the impression that more gold existed at the bottom of Puget Sound. In fact, he was so sure there was more gold that the direction provided was to dive the site again and retrieve it. The only explanation that Evan could come up with was that Deena had not disclosed everything, so the story she had told was incomplete. The ship's log book never came up at Jasper's, and that lent some credence to the idea.

Coming to grips with the situation, Evan opted to believe that Deena was not involved and that she was the victim of circumstance. Going forward and assuming he correctly guessed Deena's role, he had every intention of saving her from whatever plans the madman had for her, plus he was not going to give away the artifacts that they had worked so hard to find. With those two objectives in mind, Evan's brain started sorting through ideas that might work to achieve them both.

The stranger had said, "No Police." That's fine for now Evan thought, but the ideas forming in his head would require help, and with his phone already connected to the Camaro's media system, he said, "Call Michael Anders."

After three rings, Evan heard Michael's voice casually come across the line with "Hi Evan. What's going on tonight?"

Evan wasted no time with banter and just launched right into the situation, and his plan to deal with it. Michael listened closely once he realized Evan was deadly serious, and even wrote down a few notes while sitting comfortably at his office desk. When Evan stopped to take a long breath, Michael had the chance to interject, "Are you sure there is no other way?"

Taking time to consider the question, Evan replied, "Variations maybe, but ultimately the objectives and the outcome need to be the same."

"I understand, and you can count on me," Michael said with conviction.

"I knew I could. And we'll need Katie's support, too. As I see it, we don't know who that man was tonight, and we also don't know where Deena is and can't contact her, so we have almost no cards right now," Evan pointed out.

"Based on what you've told me, I would have to agree," Michael added.

Enthusiastically, Evan suggested, "Well then, let's get things started. I'm about twenty minutes away right now and we have a lot of work to do before I have to call that number the stranger gave me. He's expecting that at 8:00AM tomorrow I'll call to confirm that the Deena for gold exchange will take place. I wonder what would happen if I didn't call?"

"Are you prepared to take that risk with Deena's life?" Michael was quick to point out.

With a heavy heart knowing that his invitation for a boat ride has turned into a real nightmare for Deena, Evan answered, "No, no I am not."

Chapter 35

Precisely at 8:00AM Friday morning, Evan dialed the number he'd been given and waited four full rings before the line was picked up. There was no "Hello" or "Hi", or even "Who is it?", just silence. He waited about five seconds and then questioned, "Anyone there?"

The nasally voice he had heard last night came through his home phone's speaker and asked, "Do you have an answer for me?"

"I do, and it is yes." Evan stated emphatically.

"And you can meet at 11:00AM to dive the site?" the voice wanted to know.

"I would prefer later to avoid the strong current at that time, but yes, I can meet then," Evan reluctantly agreed.

The disembodied voice volunteered, "It should not surprise you Mr. Mason that I already know the location. I will see you shortly, right under the Tacoma Narrows Bridge." Then the line went dead and Evan stared at his phone, wondering how his fifth dive at the Tacoma Narrows in less than two weeks would turn out.

Arriving in Gig Harbor at just after 9:00AM, Evan, Michael and Katie rolled into town driving the Anders family van carrying two complete SCUBA diving setups and a large object covered with a grey heavily padded moving blanket. Michael knew right where he was going and after getting off State Highway 16, turned north toward the water. Navigating a series of turns as the road wound down the side of a steep hill, they turned left off of the hill road on to a road the followed the shoreline around Gig Harbor. One and a half miles later, materializing out of the drizzling rain, they saw the sign on the right side of the road for Charley's Boat & Watercraft Rentals. Evan had called first thing in the morning and arranged for the full day rental, so the two boats should be ready to go. He just needed to finalize the rental agreement and then they would be able to transfer their gear to the boats.

Michael pulled in to the dirt parking lot and stopped near the front door of the shop so Evan could jump out. Then he continued around the side of the building to the small marina behind and parked as near as possible to the top of the ramp that led to the rental boats. As he opened the van's rear doors, Evan exited the back of the building with an older gentleman that was well groomed, but wore clothes that were from another era. The look worked for him though and Michael was sure he recognized in the man years of hard learned lessons from time on the sea.

When Evan and the older gentleman made it to the van, Evan introduced the man as "Charley, Owner and Proprietor of the shop." Evan then introduced Michael and Katie and moved quickly on to the rental transaction saying, "I appreciate the two boat, full day rental on such short notice Charley."

"Not a problem," Charley replied, "never too busy around here this time of year, especially on a weekday when it's raining. I see you've got some gear to load, so let's get the boats fired up and you'll soon be underway. The gas tanks are full, so be sure to bring them back that way or I'll have to charge you for a refill, and my prices for gas aren't cheap."

Evan turned to Michael and said, "I rented two Grady-White twenty-one foot center consoles. Charley assured me the motors are tuned and the boats will do better than forty knots wide open. Let's hope that's fast enough."

"You and me both!" Michael exclaimed. Michael was a bit concerned since he and Evan had made a number of assumptions late last night as they devised the plan, one of them being the kind of boat the stranger would show up in. Another key one was that the stranger was going to show up in a boat. They had both dismissed the idea that "under the bridge" included the shoreline, so they proceeded to plan assuming the stranger would show up in a boat, and that the boat would have a top speed of forty knots or less.

The four of them walked down the ramp to the floating dock and once at the two Grady-Whites, Charley stepped aboard the closest one and first opened the fuel tank valve and then trimmed the gleaming black two hundred and twenty-five horsepower Mercury Blackmax outboard down into the water. A twist of the ignition key to the right and held briefly, and the nearly new outboard jumped to life and quickly settled to a smooth, quiet idle. Then Charley did the same thing to the second boat and just fifteen minutes after arriving at the shop, both boats were warmed up and each was loaded with a large gear bag and one set of SCUBA diving equipment.

As Evan surveyed the two boats resting quietly tied to the dock, they looked nearly identical. The registration numbers were different, but other than that, at a glance, the boats appeared the same. The last item in the van was only going to go on one boat, and that was the one Michael and Katie would be using.

Katie stepped aboard the Grady-White that Michael's gear was on and took a position in passenger helm chair out of the rain under the canopy. Evan, Michael and Charley walked back toward the van. Charley continued on his way back to the building and with both rear doors of the van opened wide, Evan and Michael threw back the moving blanket and pulled the item lying in the cargo area to the rear of the van. Each man grabbed their respective handholds located at either side of the three foot long by eighteen inch diameter oblong shaped item and lifted it from the van's cargo floor. The experimental Diver Propulsion Vehicle (DPV) they had brought from Evan's place only weighed fifty pounds, but it was awkward to carry due to its size and both men walked carefully along the dock to avoid an accident.

Once they made it to the boats, they loaded the DPV on Michael and Katie's boat and secured it for the ride to the Tacoma Narrows. Then Evan stepped on the other boat and quickly familiarized himself with the operation and instrumentation of the Grady-White. Looking over at Michael and Katie, he gave them a thumb's up and a smile. Both Michael and Katie returned the gesture in kind and acknowledged that they were ready to go. With that, Evan moved to the port side and released the forward line from the dock cleat and then moved aft and released the stern line. Stepping back to the center console helm, he shifted into Reverse and the boat immediately started moving backwards out of the slip.

Michael did the same with his boat and then they traveled together, side by side, moving through Gig Harbor at eight knots until reaching the lighthouse at the entrance to the harbor. At that point they separated when both boats got up on plane and Michael and Katie veered to the east, while Evan took a course with a more southerly route that followed the shoreline on his starboard side. When Evan rounded Point Evans, in the distance through the gray mist hanging over Puget Sound he could just make out the eastern support tower for the massive Tacoma Narrows suspension bridge.

For the most part the waters were deserted. Evan had only seen commercial traffic so far and even that traffic had been light. He was early for the meeting by almost an hour as intended in order to make the preparations needed for the plan they had devised. The bulk of the setup work was the responsibility of Michael and Katie. For Evans part, he would serve as a distraction to make sure Michael and Katie go unnoticed in case the stranger arrives early.

After fifty minutes of hanging out near the dive site, Evan saw some small movement to the south and fixed his binoculars on the motion. The cloud cover and the mist in the air together made for poor visibility, and even with the high power binoculars, Evan was uncertain what size and kind of boat was moving toward him. Watching with a steady gaze for several minutes, the object began to resolve itself in his field of view and at about three hundred yards away, Evan recognized the sleek lines of a Donzi 22 Classic.

Evan's confidence in their plan dissipated like a soap bubble popping as it touches the grass when he caught the sight of the Donzi brand boat, known as the Ferrari of the sea. Being a boat guy, Evan was aware that the 22 Classic in particular is considered a pocket rocket and that the deceptively fast "gentleman's speedboat" will hit speeds over seventy knots at Wide Open Throttle. So the forty knot maximum speed of his Grady-White would be no match for the Donzi in a boat chase, and that caused Evan an immense amount of angst. Pushing that feeling down, he had to proceed as planned, so he contacted Michael and Katie to give them an update, then continued to hold positon near the dive site directly under the Tacoma Narrows Bridge.

When the Donzi was one hundred yards away, Evan put his binoculars down, but continued to watch the boat motor slowly in his direction. Through the binoculars, he had seen all he needed to see. The stranger was piloting the boat from the starboard side helm and Deena was in the passenger seat. She sat at an awkward angle and Evan assumed her hands and feet were restrained since he could see a gag in her mouth. With the bimini top covering the boat's cockpit, Evan could just barely make out Deena's face, and she looked both exhausted, and terrified.

Evan was already in his wetsuit, and he had his gear set out in an organized fashion at the stern of the boat to make the meeting go quickly. He also had three fenders hung on the port side of the Grady-White in preparation for securing the boats together, which he really hated doing. However, he knew it was necessary given the increasing speed of the current as the water moved toward the southern shores of Puget Sound.

From twenty feet away, Evan heard his name being called and responded, "Let's get this over with." Then he prepared his port stern line to tie off on the forward cleat on the port side of the Donzi, which would put Deena almost within arm's reach.

The stranger spoke again, and very clearly said, "We're not rafting together."

"What?" Evan asked almost in disbelief. "I can't anchor here."

"Throw your forward line over and I'll tie it off on an aft cleat. I'll just tow your boat while you're taking care of business underwater," the stranger replied.

So Evan dropped his aft line and coiled his forward line in order to make the throw between boats. His aim and power was right on and the line landed on the engine compartment hatch of the Donzi. The stranger quickly grabbed the line and tied it off on the aft starboard cleat, leaving the boats roughly twenty feet apart. Evan allowed the Grady-White to drift with the current as he brought the boat to idle speed, and the line between the two boats snapped tight. Feeling nowhere near comfortable, but also realizing he had to trust the stranger holding Deena hostage to keep his boat from drifting away, he shifted to Neutral and then reached down and turned the ignition key to the Off position. The quiet outboard stopped right away and with the strong current, Evan's boat created a fair amount of drag on the Donzi causing it to list to starboard as it held the Grady-White against the pull of the water.

"So what now?" Evan asked the stranger.

"Suit up and go get the gold Mr. Mason. We'll be waiting for you. And once you hand over everything you've brought up, you and Deena are free to go," the stranger provided in an almost casual manner, but also made sure Evan saw the gun he had pointed in Deena's direction.

Evan looked at Deena and could see that she was pleading with him using her eyes. His heart dropped at the sight and he tried to reassure her with a slight nod. Then he turned away and prepared himself for another dive into the cold, dark water. He started with his weight belt, which happened to have an inconspicuous DiveCom unit attached, looking just like another weight. The he lifted his buoyancy compensator from the cockpit floor and setting it on the top of the transom, rotated himself into the vest and secured the chest straps. With the compensator in place, Evan pulled on his neoprene hood and placed his dive mask and snorkel in position on his head. Then he pulled on his thick dive gloves and sat down on the starboard gunwale to put on his dive fins. Once the fins were on, Evan called out, "I don't know how long it will take, or if I'm even going to find anything, but I do know my down time will not exceed fifty minutes."

"I have every confidence that you will succeed. After all, considering the current circumstances, you have many incentives to bring back what I'm asking for," the stranger said with an evil looking twisted smile.

Evan scowled at that remark and gave no response. Instead, he put his regulator in his mouth and then pulled his dive mask down over his face. While pressing the mask's glass firmly with his left hand, and holding a dive light in his right, he flipped over the gunwale backwards. With very little air in the compensator's air bladders, Evan quickly slipped below the surface and was soon completely out of sight of Deena and the stranger that was holding her for ransom.

Chapter 36

When Michael got the call from Evan that Deena and the stranger had shown up at the dive site, he was ready. He and Katie had arrived early at the Narrows Bridge and using a thick, one-hundred and fifty foot dock line, had rigged a makeshift harness around the north tower of the east bridge supports. The resultant harness provided a decent docking system that allowed their Grady-White to be tightly secured by both the forward and aft cleats. The arrangement also provided a steady platform to the launch the DPV in the strong current.

With the water flowing to the south, Michael had positioned the boat facing north on the east side of the support structure. This obstructed their view to the west, but more importantly, hid them from view by anyone near the dive site. With the swift current and turbulent conditions around the support, the boat did experience steady bouncing against the concrete bridge tower base, but the three fenders on the port side did a good job of protecting the boat. They had been secured in position for about thirty minutes and were starting to get antsy when Evan's call came in.

Moving directly to the DPV, Michael lifted it to the starboard corner of the transom and after double checking that the tether was secure, lowered it into the water. The six knot current quickly took ahold of the unit and snatched it out of Michael's hands. The ten foot long tether snapped tight and the DPV bobbed and weaved as the fast moving water flowed by it. Michael looked at the DPV and realized it was going to be a challenge getting into position, but he did not hesitate and proceeded to get the rest of his dive gear put on.

Fully suited up and ready to go, Michael planned to lower himself over the starboard side of the boat to get into the water. Then he would hold on to the tether and slowly slip back to the DPV. When he started to lower himself down, as soon as his dive fins touched the water his body felt the tug of the current, and it wanted to rip him off the gunwale. Pulling his legs back up, he realized he needed a different plan. Grabbing one of the dock lines, he wrapped it around his chest and tied a Kalmyk Loop knot to secure the line. Then he estimated ten feet of length and tied the free end of the dock line off on the aft starboard cleat. He expected that after getting in the water the line would tighten around his chest significantly once fully payed out, but with the non-jamming Kalmyk knot, he hoped to release the line easily.

Katie looked worried. She knew what Michael was trying to do was dangerous, and with the dock line wrapped around his chest, there were any number of things that could go wrong. Fully committed to Deena's rescue however, she helped Michael get into position and would make sure that the line did not get hung up on anything.

Michael was now back in the same position as before, lying on his stomach with his legs extended out over the water. As he lowered his dive fins into the water this time, when he felt the tug of the current, he pushed off hard with his arms and that lifted his upper body off the gunwale. As he slipped down into the water, Michael was swept immediately downstream to the south. The dock line went tight and he felt a sharp pain where it dug into his ribs. He also could feel the DPV moving around next to him and reached out to find the tether. Once he found the DPV's tether, he wrapped his left arm around it and then used his right hand to find the free end of the Kalmyk knot.

The water was flowing swiftly by Michael and was really buffeting him around as he tried to free himself from the dock line. With the heavy dive gloves on, finding the small piece of line was proving to be difficult. Finally, thinking he had the right piece, he pulled hard hoping that the knot would release. It did, and Michael immediately felt relief from the squeeze of the tight line around his chest, but also felt the current wanting to tear his left arm free of the tether line that he had it wrapped around. Katie had been watching Michael and immediately when she saw that he was free of the dock line, began to release the tether connecting the DPV to the boat.

As soon as the tether was free of the cleat, Michael and the DPV moved quickly south with the current and away from the boat. For Michael, he was moving fast with the current flow, but he was now still relative to the water and immediately got into position to operate the DPV. He looked around to get his bearings and saw two boats in the general direction of the dive site. He was more than half of a mile away, but he was confident the location of the two boats was his destination. He glanced at his compass for the three-hundred degree bearing he needed to take and then released some air from his buoyancy compensator. In a rush of bubbles, Michael and DPV disappeared below the surface.

Allowing himself to sink down in the water, Michael started putting air into his compensator at thirty feet deep. He cleared his ears as he went and at sixty feet, obtained neutral buoyancy. He flipped the main power switch on the DPV and feeling that he had drifted a bit farther south as he had descended, adjusted his bearing to head a bit more to the north. The DPV's steering and control was much like a Jetski, and with the modifications done by Evan to increase the motor's power, a new propeller blade was fitted that improved the top speed of the DPV. With both his hands firmly grasping the handlebar grips, Michael pulled in the throttle with his right two fingers and the DPV took off like a shot.

He held on tight as the unit picked up speed and he could feel the DPV's safety harness tow him along through the water. The muted blue lights illuminating the DPV's control panel showed that the batteries were fully charged, the trim system was in automatic mode, his depth was sixty-two feet, and his speed through the water was almost nine knots. If their estimate held, it would take Michael roughly four minutes to cover the half mile distance from the support tower to the dive site, and he settled in for the ride.

On the western side of the Tacoma Narrows Strait, Evan hung weightless in the water at a depth of sixty feet. The current at that depth was around three knots and he positioned himself with his back to the water flow, and then kicked steadily at an easy pace to stay in position. He thought he was close to the actual location where he had recovered the logbook and gold, but since he was not going there today, he dismissed the wild thoughts of the Giant Pacific octopus and concentrated on looking southeast into the dark water. He kept his dive light turned on in order to serve as a beacon for Michael when he got close to Evan's position, but pointed it down to avoid flashing any light to the surface.

After less than two minutes of biding his time, Evan picked up a faint humming sound. He was unable to locate the exact direction of the sound, but from out of the blackness, Michael materialized with the DPV pulling him quickly toward Evan's location. Flashing his light twice to signify to Michael that he had seen him, Evan made ready to put the next part of their plan in motion.

With the strong flowing current, which was increasing with each passing minute, maintaining position was getting more difficult, so Evan was thankful that the DPV had arrived. When Michael saw Evan, he had extended the DPV's three foot long retractable boom to his right side and a safety line was now trailing behind the boom by a few feet. When Michael slowed to match Evan's drift speed, Evan grabbed the line and clipped the line to his compensator's vest. He was flailing a bit at first, but soon got the hang of essentially gliding through the water and maintaining control with slight movements of his dive fins. The DPV maintained the desired course since Evan had specifically modified the DPV to serve as a tow vehicle. The modified design included an automated control system to compensate for the off center drag by directing the steering veins of the DPV to the left as needed. The DPV pilot, Michael in this case, maintained directional control as usual and the DPV moved forward with a sizeable amount of yaw control applied.

Evan used his DiveCom unit to remind Michael about the faster than expected boat that the stranger had arrived in, and expressed some concern that the plan would still work. They were counting on being able to elude the stranger while the Coast Guard made their way to the Narrows. Michael acknowledged with a nod and shrugged his shoulders letting Evan know he wasn't sure of the next move. Using his DiveCom unit, Evan sent Michael a message, "proceed as planned."

The DPV had a storage compartment and it had been preloaded with two items, a two-hundred and fifty foot length of three-eighths of an inch diameter polyester line, and an artificially distressed leather bag about the size of a half-gallon milk container. The leather bag had been distressed the night before and left to soak in a strong salt water solution overnight. At a glance, it looked old, and was now filled with pyrite, more commonly referred to as fool's gold.

The length of polyester line was intended to serve as an anchor line, but Evan first had to attach it to the stranger's boat. Once Evan had the length of line in his hands, Michael began to ascend to the surface. Moving toward the surface brought stronger current speeds and Evan could feel the pull in the tension of the safety line attached to his compensator. At ten feet below the surface, both Michael and Evan scanned the water above them looking for the hulls of the two boats. After traveling a fair distance north into the current, Michael spotted the boats off to his left and headed in that direction.

On paper, the idea seemed straightforward, but in the cold waters of Puget Sound, the plan to attach a line to a boat that was essentially moving at nearly seven knots seemed like a daunting task. Michael positioned the DPV to the port side of the stranger's boat and then ever so slowly, began to surface keeping Evan on the boat's centerline. When Evan's head cleared the surface, he immediately looked up to locate the bow eye on the prow of the Donzi 22 Classic. Michael did his part and matched the speed of the Donzi and when Evan felt he was close enough, he kicked hard with his legs and propelled himself up and out of the water sufficiently to reach the bow eye with his left hand. He tried to thread the free end of the line through the two inch diameter steel ring, but dropped back into the water with the free end still in his right hand. The maneuver caused Evan to bump his right leg against the boat's hull and he considered what a precarious position he was in. If the safety line broke, or the boom on the DPV failed, the flowing water would quickly sweep him along the keel of the boat and right into the spinning propeller. Trying not to think about that, he readied himself for another attempt.

Michael handled the DPV expertly after the miss and applied a bit of throttle to move them slightly ahead of the boat and into position again. Evan took advantage of having seen what he had to do once above the surface and prepared himself to act much quicker with the second attempt. With his dive fins nearly touching the hull, Evan began to pump both his legs together in a dolphin style kick and also guided his upper body in a steep ascent. He broke the surface just under the bow eye and quickly threaded the free end of the line through the steel ring with his right hand, and grabbed the end with his left hand before dropping back below the surface. Evan then tied a jamming Noose Knot to create a slip knot in the line and that completing securing the anchor line to the stranger's boat.

Maintaining the same speed and course in the water to stay right below the boat, Michael piloted the DPV to a lower depth and at forty feet, slowed their descent to hover at fifty feet. Here they would part company after transferring the fake treasure from the DPV's storage compartment to Evan, and the transfer was not going to be an easy task with the current flowing along. Determined to follow through with the plan, Evan looped the coil of line temporarily around the end of the DPV's boom and reached for one of the four five pound lead weights he had attached to his belt. Evan pulled a total of two weights from his belt and together, they nearly matched the weight of the bag. Michael had already opened the compartment's access panel, and while Evan reached toward the compartment with his right hand, he moved his left hand into a position to drop the two five pound weights in the compartment. As Evan lifted the bag from the compartment, he felt himself sink slightly as the DPV rose slightly. Wasting no time, he dropped the dive weights in the compartment and equilibrium was restored.

The next step was tricky and it would free Evan from the DPV, and then he would be at the mercy of the current running at almost four knots. To undo the safety line, Michael backed off the throttle and as the DPV moved south with the current, the tension on the safety line eased. Evan quickly undid the carbineer style attachment and immediately after, felt the wake from the DPV's drive blade as Michael pulled in on the throttle to get back under the stranger's boat.

Evan had the fake treasure tucked securely in his compensator vest and he got himself positioned facing into the current. He began to kick steadily with smooth strong strokes and could feel he was making some headway in the water. Moving north into the current flow for a few minutes, Evan estimated that he was close to being under the boats. The current at Evan's depth of sixty feet was strong and he was struggling with holding position. Turning on his dive light, he used it to scan the area around him and was pleased to see the line he had attached to the stranger's boat stretched tight in a large looping arc about thirty feet away. He smiled a bit knowing that Michael had done his part and connected the other end of the line to a large rock on the seafloor.

The line was to the west and Evan turned in that direction. He began kicking his legs and his dive fins pushed against the water to propel him toward the line that was suspended between the bow eye of the stranger's boat and the seafloor. Once he reached the line, Evan got in a position to kick into the current and was able to match its speed. Turning off the dive light and securing it to his compensator, he then switched on the headlamp style light he wore that freed up both of his hands. Evan then took a length of the line about four feet long and folded it back upon itself. Using the resultant two foot length as a free end, Evan used it to secure himself to the line using a Mooring hitch tied around the straps of his Buoyancy Compensator.

With the hitch knot tied tight and the free end positioned to make for an easy grab and pull to release the knot, Evan slowed his leg kicks and the line began to tighten up. When Evan stopped kicking, his full weight was hanging on the line and the extra drag caused the stranger's boat to slip to the south, but the slight movement went unnoticed by the occupants of the Donzi.

Evan was now essentially flying in the water as it moved past him at four knots and he reached around behind his back with his left arm and located the tank pressure gauge. The tank was showing that it was still half full and had plenty of air left for his planned fifteen minute rest. The rest period would allow Michael and Katie to get the other boat prepared for a fast departure. So Evan settled in for an eerie fifteen minutes. He left his headlamp style light on to watch for anything coming at him in the water flow, but also to help chase away the memories of the octopus that he was pretty sure was right below him. Evan was concerned about where his imagination might go with the memories of two days ago and he wanted to avoid thinking about it.

Chapter 37

After fifteen minutes of floating at sixty feet deep, Evan prepared himself to surface. He could feel the strength of the current and knew as soon as he released the knot keeping him anchored to the seafloor he would rapidly move to the south. Taking ahold of the line in front of him with both hands, he pulled it toward him and advanced up the length by almost two feet. Now with some slack ahead of the Mooring knot, he used his left hand to quickly pull the knot's release line. Knowing that the upper end of the line was connected to the stranger's boat, he pulled himself hand over hand up the line for a few minutes and was rewarded with filtered light making its way down to him.

Pulling himself along the length of line was getting harder. The current gained speed as Evan moved up and at twenty feet below the surface, he could barely hold on. He could see the outline of both boats as they bobbed and weaved in the flowing water and used powerful legs kicks to navigate toward the boat farthest south. Reaching up along the line, Evan made three more pulls and attempting a fourth pull, he realized he had very little strength left in his arms. Looking up he could see the surface was close and he was also forward of his boat. Moving any closer would be very dangerous since the line he was hanging on was getting closer and closer to the Donzi's spinning propeller. Deciding he was as near as he was going to get, Evan started kicking vigorously to try and reduce the relative speed of the water around him. Pumping his legs as hard and as fast as he could, Evan released his grip on the polyester line and he started slipping away from it.

The speed of the current exceeded Evan's ability to remain in position and he moved south at over three knots. Glancing to his left over his shoulder, he could barely see the Grady-White's hull coming at him. He knew the boarding ladder was down on the starboard side of the boat and Evan used his arms and legs to furiously make for the ladder that reached almost three feet below the surface. He surfaced about amidships on the starboard side and was able to touch the hull. The water swept him along the hull and he reached below the surface hoping to catch the ladder with his left arm as he moved past.

The impact with the ladder sent shooting pain into Evan's left arm and shoulder. Ignoring the pain from the wrenching of his left arm that had become stuck in a ladder rung, he brought his right arm around and took ahold of the ladder. Fighting through what felt like a broken forearm, he kicked with his legs and used his right arm to pull his body slightly forward. It was enough that he felt some relieve in his left arm and lifted the damaged limb out of the ladder. Maneuvering around to trail behind the ladder face down, he grabbed the left side vertical ladder support with his left hand and was immediately met with excruciating pain. With no choice but to hold on, he gripped as tight as he could and considered the next problem, how to get aboard the boat.

With his damaged arm, it was going to be difficult. First thing was to get the fake treasure securely aboard, so Evan looped his left arm over the top rung of the ladder and let it rest in the crook of his elbow. It hurt like crazy, but he released his right hand and quickly snatched the old looking leather bag from his compensator vest and heaved it up on to the small swim step next to the outboard motor. Then as fast he could, he released the three catches that were holding the buoyancy compensator to his back. He grabbed the ladder again with his right hand and eased his left arm out of the vest. Then back to looping his left arm around the rung, and when he released his right hand, the vest, tank and regulator were pulled off his body. Still holding on only by his left arm, Evan reached his right hand toward his dive fins and at the same time brought his knees toward his chest. He first took off his right fin and let it slip away with the current. Then he did the same with his left one. Now unencumbered without the dive gear, Evan put his feet on the lowest rung of the ladder and stood up.

Positioned as he was on the boarding ladder, he could just see over the transom and looking forward, could see two silhouettes under the low rise bimini top of the Donzi. He was also exhausted, and after lifting the leather bag into the cockpit, crawled into the cockpit himself, pulled off his mask, snorkel and neoprene hood and collapsed on the floor. Lying there on his back, Evan breathed deeply to calm his nerves and replenish the oxygen that he had depleted from his muscles during the ascent to the surface. After a few minutes, he looked at his dive watch and noted that it had been roughly forty minutes since he had entered the water under duress.

The next few minutes would decide his and Deena's fate. Evan was gambling that the ruse of the fake treasure, the anchor line attached to the Donzi, and his skill at boat handling would allow them enough time to make an escape. Evan also considered that it is hard to out run a bullet when it leaves the gun barrel at close to the speed of sound. Gathering his wits about him, and the leather bag, he stood up and shouted, "Ahoy!"

There was activity on the Donzi and the stranger appeared through the back of the bimini top. He shouted back, "Do you have the gold?"

Evan held up the leather bag, mostly with his right arm, still dripping the briny water of Puget Sound onto the deck of the Grady-White. He could see the expression of the stranger change from one of stern, hard features to one that sent a chill down Evan's spine. It was difficult to describe, but what came to Evan's mind was that of a manic, schizophrenic individual. He took away that it would likely not be possible to predict the actions of the stranger, and that reinforced the need for a fast getaway.

"Start your boat and bring it next to mine and we'll make the exchange, as we agreed," the stranger said with an edge of distrust in his voice.

Evan didn't need to be told twice and quickly had the Grady-White moving closer to the Donzi. When he has abeam on the port side of the Donzi and holding the throttle to match the boat's speed, Evan eased his boat to the east and inched closer to the stranger's boat. The stranger tended the towline and pulled it in as Evan moved closer. When the hulls came together with only the three fenders separating them, the stranger tied off the line on his forward cleat. Evan quickly moved aft and secured the sterns together by connecting a line between the two aft cleats.

When Evan looked over to the cockpit of the Donzi, he was met with the barrel of a handgun pointed right at him. "No need for that, you'll get what you want," Evan said with clear distaste in the tone of his voice.

"This just helps make sure of it," the stranger replied. Then added, "I understand you recovered some gold from a prior dive, I want that too."

Evan anticipated that the prior dive might come up and came prepared. He replied, "There was very little found, but I have that too."

Then he leaned over toward his gear bag to retrieve the gold and heard the stranger yell, "Stop right there! Not another move or Deena will get to watch you die right where you stand!"

Evan froze in place and shouted out, "I'm getting the gold! It's in my gear bag!"

"Do so very slowly. And just so you know, while you're out of my sight, my gun will be trained on Deena's head," the stranger growled with a menacing look that said he wasn't kidding.

Evan continued to the port side of his boat and opened his gear bag. He then reached in to retrieve a deep purple colored felt bag. The signature Crown Royal bag that normally holds a fifth of the fine whiskey, was now half filled with pyrite. Evan verified that the drawstring was pulled tight and that the top was still tightly shut. For extra difficulty opening the bag, he had wrapped the loose drawstrings around the opening and tied a simple square knot. Holding the bag in his left hand was painful as he made his way back to the starboard side of his boat, but his right hand was busy as it carried the ten pound leather bag he had just brought on board.

Evan didn't like that he was becoming slightly accustomed to having the weapon trained on him and he was growing impatient with the business of kidnapping and extortion. "How are we going to do this?" he barked at the stranger.

"Toss the gold over here and if all is in order, Deena is all yours," was the response he got.

That was not what Evan was going to do and replied, "I don't think so. This is going to go down at the same time. I want Deena on my boat before I turn all of this over," indicating the bags in his hands.

The stranger countered with, "Let's have the large bag first then, and I'll let Deena leave, but as soon as she is aboard your boat, I want the small bag."

Considering he was totally bluffing, Evan felt the negotiated arrangement would work. He agreed with, "OK. Get Deena ready to leave. Once she's ready to transfer over, I'll throw the bag."

Evan watched the stranger pull a tool of some sort from a cubby and lean over reaching toward Deena's feet. He came away with a large cut Ziptie and motioned for Deena to prepare to climb out of the cockpit and over to the other boat. Her hands were still bound, but the stranger had removed Deena's gag and as she rotated in her seat, Evan picked up the silent "thank you" that her eyes and moving lips conveyed. Then she turned toward the stranger and yelled, "I hate you, you son of a bitch!"

The stranger seemed unmoved by the outburst and simply said, "I would expect that to be the case, but I don't care. Our arrangement still stands."

"Fuck you!" Deena yelled and started to stand in order to get over to Evan's boat.

"No so fast bitch," the stranger said coldly as he pressed Deena's right shoulder down hard, forcing her back into the seat. "Let's have the gold Evan, right now," he said while pointing his gun at Deena.

Evan was reeling. The conversation he had just heard was brief, but said a lot. Deena did know the stranger! He even talked about some kind of arrangement that they had. The revelation shook his confidence in the plan. Was Deena just acting like the victim to gain his trust? To what end? There were many questions that came rushing to Evan's mind, but regaining the reality of the situation, his only question to himself was, "What's my next step?" Deciding to stay the course with the plan, he gave Deena the benefit of the doubt and assumed she would be working with him, not against him. So he heaved the ten pound leather bag in his right hand on to the stranger's boat. It landed heavy, conveying that with a loud thunk when the bag bounced off the engine hatch and into the rear seats of the Donzi.

Deena wasted no time and immediately after the bag stopped moving, was up and out of the seat. She rose high enough to shift her butt up on to the gunwale of the Donzi and move out from under the bimini top. This time the stranger did not try to stop her. Using her bound hands together, she reached across the gap between the boats and grabbed the Grady-White's hard top support tower that was made from polished chrome tubing. She held tight since the two boats were rafted together and were being jostled around by the strength of the water flowing by between them. Committing to the transfer, Deena swung her legs up out of the Donzi's cockpit and toward the bow of the boat. Once they cleared the Donzi's windscreen, she was able to extend them over the gunwale of the Grady-White and using just the strength of her arms, pulled herself aboard.

Evan was watching Deena get safely aboard and as soon as her feet touched the deck, he heard the stranger call out, "She's aboard. Let's have the rest of the gold!"

Wanting to be gone as soon as possible, Evan quickly transferred the Crown Royal bag to his right hand and tossed the bag into the cockpit of the Donzi. He watched the stranger carefully to see what his next move would be and as he expected, the stranger dropped his gaze into the cockpit's rear seat to study the bags of gold. Looking up, the stranger found Evan moving quickly to get Deena in a safe position in the bow of the Grady-White, plus he had already loosened the forward line from his boat leaving it connected to the Donzi.

The stranger spoke in a strange tone and said, "Leaving so soon Mr. Mason? We know what you've got in Deena there, but let's first see what I've got," and he made sure that Evan could see the gun pointed directly at his chest from less than eight feet away.

The stranger kept switching his view from Evan to the bags, and each time he was not looking at Evan, Evan moved slightly closer to the aft starboard cleat. When the stranger realized it was going to take more than one hand to open either bag, he brought his gun hand down briefly to use it to hold the large bag in place. Evan took that instant to calmly reach over with his right hand and let loose the line tied off on the aft cleat of his boat. The noise of the rushing water and the boat engines let the sound of the line dropping into the water go by unheard, but the stranger did not miss the sound of the Grady-White's outboard revving up or the motion of the hull as it began to accelerate away from him.

Taken by surprise, the stranger fired off two shots at the fleeing boat. One shot went wide, but the other one passed right by Evan on its way to hitting the windscreen and splintering it into a spider web of fractures. Evan was unfazed and kept the throttle on while adjusting course to head directly for the bridge's east support towers.

On board the Donzi, Davis grabbed the Crown Royal bag and let go of the large leather one. He frantically tore at the drawstring and after a few seconds, spread the top of the bag open and dumped out the contents on the passenger seat. The anger started deep inside him when he recognized the sharp corners and regular shapes of pyrite. He let out a loud scream and hammered the throttle of the Donzi to the stop. The stern of the boat dug in and the bow lifted quickly. Davis turned sharply to starboard and the boat started to gain speed. Suddenly the bow dove down toward the surface and the stern lifted up, spinning the boat partially around. Davis immediately pulled the throttle back not knowing what had happened and the strong current grabbed the boat, rotating the Donzi so it was hanging on the makeshift anchor line attached to the seafloor, with the bow pointed due north.

Davis was stunned, and his head was bleeding from a gash he received above his right eye when the boat came to an abrupt halt. The blow to the head left him dazed, but his greed and anger continued to feed his fury. Quickly assessing the situation, he realized that Evan had somehow secured a line to his boat and tied it off to something solid below the surface. Carrying the same knife he used to cut the Ziptie off of Deena's ankles, Davis leaned over the dash and opened the center section of the windscreen. Then carefully but quickly, he made his way to the bow and laid down with his right arm hanging over the edge of the boat. Grabbing hard with his right hand to the starboard side rub rail, Davis leaned his head and left shoulder over the port side rub rail. With his left arm fully extended and his hand clutching the knife, Davis had just enough reach to touch the line attached to the bow eye with the tip of the blade.

When the very sharp blade touched the line, it sliced right through it. Once the line was cut, the Donzi immediately started drifting to the south at almost eight knots. Davis partially stood up and scrambled back to the cockpit as the boat rotated one-hundred and eighty degrees to drift with the bow pointing south. Once back inside the cockpit, Davis slipped behind the wheel and got himself positioned in the helm chair. Then he shifted to Forward gear and kept on pushing the throttle all the way to the limit. The boat was up on plan in seconds and Davis steered to port to bring the boat around on a course to the northeast. Looking out over the bow, he saw the Grady-White was heading for the bridge's east tower supports and he pushed down harder on the throttle control that was already against the stop.

Chapter 38

After the near miss with the bullet, Evan's heart was beating fast and adrenaline was coursing through his body. His mind was clear however, and he picked up the roar of the Donzi's engine as the stranger took up the chase. Evan glanced over his left shoulder and roughly fifty yards away, saw the Donzi start to accelerate. Just as quickly, the boat came to an abrupt halt as the bow was pulled down to the water's surface. He smiled as the stranger's boat rocked wildly from the anchor line's effects, finally spinning to point north with the water flowing rapidly by the stationary boat.

Evan turned his attention forward and concentrated his effort on steering the boat in the poor visibility and swirling seas. About half way to the tower supports, he heard the Donzi's engine roar again and didn't need to look back to know what was happening. Instead, he leaned on the throttle trying to coax just a little more speed out the already screaming outdrive.

Moving at a speed of thirty eight knots, the bridge towers were soon looming overhead and Evan steered around the southeast corner of the giant concrete support structures. He also pulled the throttle back to half and as soon as he saw the other Grady-White, he cut the throttle to a quarter and tried to match the speed of the current. He expertly maneuvered his boat closer to the stationary Grady-

White and bumped the hull against the fenders hanging off the starboard side. Michael practically leapt over the gunwales and landed next to Deena in the open bow of Evan's boat. He helped her stand and then lifted her up and sat her on the gunwale of his boat. Deena then pulled herself aboard Michael's boat just like she did just a few minutes before and Katie guided her to a seat in the open bow. While the women got settled in the bow, Michael made his way back to his boat and was already at the helm prepared for their next move.

The support base holding up the westbound lanes of State Highway 16 two hundred feet overhead was a massive concrete block eighty feet long in the north-south direction and thirty-five feet wide. Michael and Katie had positioned their temporary dock just south of the midpoint of the eighty foot length to maximize their hiding position and Evan maintained a slight port direction bias to hold his boat in as close as possible to the support. With the sound of the roaring water flowing swiftly around the support, it was difficult to have any kind of conversation, so Evan practically yelled at Michael saying, "The anchor trick worked. Bought us some time, but he's coming fast!"

Michael acknowledged with a nod and wave of his arm. Then over the noise of the rushing water, the unmistakable sound of a gunshot could be heard and small pieces of concrete fell from the top of the concrete support into the water in front of the Grady-Whites.

On the western side of the supports, Davis was holding stationary midway along the length of the concrete support structures. He had watched Evan round the southern end of the tower support, but he did not reappear. Davis concluded that they thought they had eluded him and were hiding out. To let them know that was not the case, Davis had taken aim at the top of the north tower's concrete base and pulled the trigger a number of times. The bullets found their marks and exploded near the top of the concrete, just below the bottom of the three hundred foot tall steel structure. The impacts launched bits of concrete into the air and over the top. Davis waited briefly for a reaction, but nothing happened.

Davis had plenty of ammunition for his handgun and took aim as before and sent several more bullets flying into the concrete. On the eastern side of the support, everyone heard the gunshots and saw the debris falling from the support. The last two gunshots were the closest and the concrete shrapnel rained down on the two boats.

Evan looked over at Michael and gave him a look that said it was time go. Michael gave his friend a solemn look in return and nodded. Evan applied a bit of throttle and his boat moved north slowly. As he moved past the open bow of Michael's boat, he looked to port and down at Deena and Katie, huddled together trying to stay low. They both looked over at him and he could see the fear in their eyes. With a strong resolve to get everyone safely out of the situation they were in, Evan clenched his jaw, gritted his teeth and prepared to make a run for it. Last night, this part of the plan seemed like the simplest part of the operation, but now, with the stranger just on the other side of the support and letting the bullets fly, Evan wasn't so sure.

The Coast Guard had been contacted and Evan didn't expect to have to outrun the Donzi for long, but he considered the speed of the bullets and planned on driving fast and chaotic to not allow the stranger an easy shot at a stable target. As he moved his boat north and closer to the end of the north concrete support, he had to increase his turn to port to keep the boat going north since the water flowing around the support was forcing the bow to move to starboard. When he was within ten feet of the end of the support, Evan let the bow of the Grady-White move to the east with the flow of water. As the boat moved to a forty-five degree angle with the support, he slammed the throttle to the stop and the boat shot out of the hole, heading away from the bridge support on a northeast course.

Davis had been waiting for something to happen and when he heard the outboard motor of the Grady-White spin up, his lips formed an evil grin and he prepared to give chase. His handgun had a brand new clip of bullets and the speed of the Donzi would run the other boat down in no time, so he was confident he would have the chance to confront Evan about his deceit and trickery. Thinking about it now, just added to Davis's fury and his face contorted into an ugly mask of pure malice.

When Evan accelerated away from the bridge support, Davis was just approaching the north end of the tower base and the roaring water moving south was sweeping around the concrete support. The large standing wave created by the stationary bridge support started pushing the Donzi's bow to the west, in the opposite direction that Davis wanted to go. With Evan trying to make a run for it, Davis was ready to pick up the chase and turned the wheel quickly to starboard while pushing the throttle almost to the stop. The Donzi reacted poorly to the large amount of throttle input and while the stern initially dug in, the prop then started to slip badly as it tried to climb both the Donzi's bow wave and the standing wave.

The strong, steady current did not stop or slow down to let the Donzi recover. Instead, the standing wave lifted the port side of the boat and lowered the aft starboard quarter closer to the surface of the swirling turbulent water. Davis responded with more throttle and the boat managed to gain some forward progress, but the expression on Davis's face had changed from malice to panic as he realized he was in a very dangerous predicament. When the boat pitched forward as it crested the top of the standing wave, the prop struggled to gain purchase as it spun out of the water. Quickly surveying the situation, Davis saw he was now perpendicular to the current and the starboard gunwale was just a few feet from the concrete bridge support. Davis reacted by turning hard to port to move away from the support. The boat initially moved away, but as the Donzi's bow neared the east side of the bridge support, the bow started being pulled to the south by the current. Davis immediately turned the boat farther to port in order to try and correct his course.

From the shelter of Michael's Grady-White boat still secured to the makeshift docking system, Deena dared to peek over the cushions in the seating area and look forward to try and catch a glimpse of Evan as he sped away. Instead her attention was grabbed by the Donzi appearing at the corner of the bridge support. As she watched, the bow turned toward her and she yelled for Katie and Michael to "Get down!", afraid that they were sitting ducks for the handgun Davis was carrying. When she heard no gun shots, she raised her head just enough to locate the Donzi. What she saw caused her eyes to go wide and her mouth to gape open in disbelief.

When Davis turned the wheel to the left, the boat had reacted violently in the swirling current and the aft port quarter lowered quickly with the turn. The large standing wave created by the bridge support now towered over the rear of the boat and water was spilling on to the engine hatch. Davis continued to hold the wheel and throttle in position expecting the powerful motor to launch him away from the concrete. However the flow of the turbulent water was irregular, and when the Donzi's prop hit an air pocket, the effects of ventilation caused the boat to lose its forward thrust. In that instant of no thrust, the current took ahold of Davis's boat and slammed the starboard side into the concrete bridge support.

The boat initially rose up, and Davis's vantage point at the corner of the concrete afforded him a view of a boat tied to the east side of the support. When he recognized Deena in the bow, rage filled his mind and he momentarily forgot about his situation. He brought his right arm around and with the gun now back in his hand, took aim at Deena as best he could and prepared to squeeze the trigger repeatedly.

Before Davis was able to pull the trigger to send the first bullet in Deena's direction, the Donzi settled lower in the water after its initial collision with the bridge support and Davis could no longer see the boat tied alongside. With the low rise styling of the Donzi design providing little resistance to the steady flow of water pounding the port side of the boat, the cockpit began taking on water. The boat was quickly starting to roll to port in response to the water weight and when the top of the port gunwale dipped below the surface of the flowing water, the strong current forced the port side of the boat down hard. Davis dropped the gun and grabbed the wheel to hold on, but with the Donzi's prop free-wheeling out of the water and the engine screaming, the boat simply flipped over and slammed top down into the surface of the icy water.

The standing wave then took over control of the boat and held it briefly in position. In the upside down boat, Davis shook his head to clear it from the violent flip and took a deep breath. He quickly realized he himself was upside down and had only managed to get the breath of air from a pocket of the life giving gas that was trapped with him in the cockpit of his boat. His panic reached its peak and he decided to try and duck below the gunwale of the boat to try and escape. Before Davis could get into position to attempt the escape, the boat began to spin about its lengthwise axis. Once started, the wave action continued the spin while also submerging the boat below the surface. Inside the boat, when the rotation first started, the air pocket escaped the cockpit, but Davis did not. Instead, the full fury of the eight knot current slammed into the cockpit crushing Davis and breaking ribs, both arms and one of his legs at the femur. The pain was intense and when Davis let out a scream, the fast moving water flooded his mouth and quickly filled his lungs. In agonizing pain from the physical injuries and with his brain hungering for oxygen, Davis blacked out just before the strength of the current split the boat apart against the concrete support.

Aboard the Grady-White that was tied to the bridge support, Deena, Michael and Katie all watched the destruction of the Donzi and presumably the death of the person driving the boat. As they stared at the spectacle in front of them, the water took the boat below the surface. Seconds after that, they heard a loud crack and a portion of the forward section of the Donzi briefly appeared in front of them. The current quickly swept the debris toward them and they all heard the loud screeching sounds as it hit the hull of the Grady –White on its way south and to the bottom of Puget Sound.

Over one hundred yards away and still moving to the northeast at full speed, Evan dared to chance a look behind him. What he saw, or rather didn't see, was confusing to him. He was expecting to see the stranger's Donzi closing in on him and was even prepared for gunfire. What he actually saw was only one boat, and it was Michael's Grady-White still tied to the bridge support. The Donzi was nowhere to be seen.

Chapter 39

Upon seeing only one boat, Evan pulled back on the throttle and made a fast one-hundred and eighty degree turn to starboard. Coming around, he pulled his phone out and speed dialed Michael, let it ring four times and then hung up since he was now back within shouting distance of the other Grady-White. He took a wide turn under the bridge from the south and steered a course that allowed him to see the western side of the support structure. There was nothing there. As he closed on the east side of the support, he could see Michael, Katie and Deena, and they no longer had the look of fear about them. Evan pulled alongside the other boat and held his throttle to match the speed of the current, and coming to a stop next to the stationary boat, he shouted, "What happened?"

Michael was first to respond and cupping his hands around his mouth to form a simple megaphone, shouted back, "He crashed his boat into the bridge support! The water churned him up pretty good then broke the boat into pieces!"

"Holy shit!" Evan exclaimed. "Was there any possible chance he survived the crash?" he questioned.

"I don't think so!" Michael replied, and both Katie and Deena shook their heads "no" to corroborate Michael's response.

"Well it's time to get the hell out of here then!" Evan shouted back.

Michael nodded in the affirmative and began instructing Katie on the plan to disconnect from the tower support. Done wrong, they could end up like the Donzi and considering what he had just witnessed, Michael wanted no part of that. Deena looked over at Evan and without saying a word, he held out his left arm to help her over the gunwales and onto his boat. She moved swiftly and confidently between the two boats and was wrapped in Evan's arms in just a matter of seconds. He could feel her breathing deeply and shivering from the dampness in the misty air, so he held her tightly for a few moments and then whispered, "It's OK, everything will be OK now."

As Michael and Katie went about dismantling the lines securing their boat to the support, Evan continued to hold Deena as they settled into the helm chairs. He could tell that Deena was calming down as her breathing was becoming more regular and Evan was glad for that. He spoke to her and said, "The Coast Guard is on their way. We'll wait here for them and then give our statements. Michael and Katie aren't involved, it's just you and I, and the stranger that's no longer with us."

"That bastard!" Deena cried out.

Her outburst struck Evan, and he recalled her reaction to the stranger's comments when she transferred from his boat. He did recognize her fragile state, but needed to know what, if any, kind of "arrangement" she had had with the stranger, so he blurted out, "What was the arrangement that you had with the man that kidnapped you?"

Deena raised her head, looked Evan directly in the eyes and said, "He was my second level boss at HG Enterprises. I knew something was strange about that man from the day I started working there." Then Deena lowered her head again and assumed a dejected posture.

Her response provided new information for Evan, and he let his arms drop from around her body. He had settled on the explanation that the man was a stranger and had acted rashly, but now his mind moved to his thoughts from earlier and imagined that it all could have been planned. Deena picked up on Evan's reaction, as slight as it was, and asked, "What's wrong?"

"I guess I'm a bit confused. So how is it that the two of you ended up in a boat together waiting for me hand over gold that may or may not exist?"

"But it does exist! I saw you give it to Davis when you surfaced." Deena said excitedly. Then her face took on a somber look and she said, "Now it's back at the bottom of Puget Sound."

Evan wasn't sure where to go with the conversation and was glad when Michael interrupted their talk to let him know he was ready to release his boat. Evan gave Michael a wave to acknowledge the message and said to Deena, "Michael and Katie are heading back to Gig Harbor, but we're going to hang out in the area and wait for the Coast Guard. We don't have much time, so let's be sure we are on the same page with what happened. I thought you were kidnapped by some stranger that might have overheard you talk about the dive, but turns out you apparently told someone about it? I feel a bit betrayed."

Deena's reaction told him a lot about what might have happened, and he felt bad he had essentially accused her of collaborating with her boss to steal the treasure he'd brought up from the seafloor. He looked over at the other boat, and with Katie at the helm, Michael released the stern line first and the boat was moved away from the support tower by the water flowing past the port side. Evan reduced throttle and his boat slipped to the south and that provided room for the other boat to depart. Watching Michael lean out of the open bow to undo the last line, Evan noticed light gray pieces of concrete that were scattered across the top of the bridge support base and considered how lucky they had been. He thought to himself, "this could have gone really, really bad," and was very thankful to be leaving in one piece and with the people he cared about alive and well.

Once Michael released the forward line and hauled the free end aboard, Katie slipped the boat into Forward gear and brought the throttle up to about one third. The Grady-White stabilized in the swirling waters and headed north, directly into the waning current that was still running at over seven knots. Evan and Deena continued to drift south and separate from Michael and Katie to avoid involving them should the Coast Guard suddenly appear, and once they were a speck on the horizon, Evan increased the throttle to move toward the bridge towers.

While they drifted in the area waiting for the Coast Guard, the low lying, rain laden marine layer covering the Puget Sound waters began to clear and the sun started to peek through sporadically. The warmth of the short bursts of sun felt good and it took the chill from their bodies, but there was a chill in the air between Evan and Deena. Almost seven minutes after Evan had called in the incident, flashing blue lights appeared to the south of the bridge. During the time that they had waited, there was very little real conversation aboard the boat.

They both watched the Coast Guard response boat approach at a high rate of speed and breathed a sigh of relief that the ordeal was nearly over. The pilot of the Coast Guard craft expertly maneuvered to put his starboard side against the Grady-White's port side, and with a man standing both forward and aft, the two boats were secured together in no time. The Coast Guard pilot yelled out the cabin window, "Turn off your engine. We've got control now."

Evan did as instructed and replied with, "OK, we're shut down."

The man that secured the forward line moved closer to amidships and introduced himself to Evan and Deena, "Hello there, I'm Lieutenant Cayson. First things first, is anyone in need of medical assistance?"

Evan and Deena looked at each other, then back at the Lieutenant and said at almost the same time, "No, we're good."

"OK then. So are you Evan Mason, the person that made the call?", the Lieutenant asked, looking directly at Evan.

"Yes, that would be me. And this is Deena Ardosio," Evan responded.

"Pleasure to meet you both, and now that we have the pleasantries out of the way, I want to hear about what's going on out here. The recording of the call I listened to was vague and implied your lives were in danger. I'm looking around now and things look pretty peaceful," the Lieutenant said with a slight bit of irritation evident in his voice.

Deena spoke up before Evan could say anything and said with conviction, "This is my story to tell, and I need to tell it."

Evan did not object and Lieutenant Cayson made his way over the gunwales to join Deena and Evan in the cockpit of the Grady-White. After finding a spot to sit down, he pulled an Apple tablet from the lining of his jacket and made ready to take Deena's statement. Deena wasted no time and began telling the Lieutenant her story, starting with Evan's offer to take a boat ride on Wednesday, just two short days ago.

As the story unfolded, the true horror of what Deena had been through came to light for Evan. The man named Davis Garcia was not a good person, and he had used both physical and mental abuse in order to get Deena to crack and divulge what she knew about the gold that had been discovered. Evan felt a sense of pride when he realized through it all, she never did disclose the existence of the log book to Davis, or to Lieutenant Cayson just now. When she finally reached the end of what she had to say, tears were streaming down her cheeks. Evan for his part felt terrible for ever having doubted her, and told her that so he was sure she knew. The Lieutenant had been feverously taking notes as Deena was talking and did not say a word as he finished the last few entries. The he looked at Deena and said, "That's quite a story. You've been through a lot the last few days. Do you have any evidence of anything that you've described?"

Deena said nothing and just stared at him with her piercing brown eyes. Evan picked up the ball and volunteered, "The gold that went down at the bridge was not as it appeared. I handed over bags filled with pyrite, more commonly known as fool's gold."

In the blink of an eye, Deena turned toward Evan and faced him with a surprised look, and with an elevated voice said, "You what?"

"I handed over fake gold hoping to buy some time, but now I know why it didn't work. The person I handed it to must have identified it immediately," Evan explained. He also provided, "There's going to be physical evidence at the east bridge tower supports. He was firing a gun at the concrete and I know there's concrete fragments up there. There should also be some evidence of the sinking of his boat on the north side of the concrete base, and somewhere below us, the remains of his Donzi 22 Classic."

The Lieutenant entered more notes on the tablet and when he stopped writing on the touch screen, he said, "Well Evan and Deena, it's been a hell of a day if what you've described is accurate. No need for you to stay around here, but we'll stay and do some preliminary investigation to try and confirm what you've told us. I have your names and contact info for any follow up questions, so if there's nothing else, I'll let you guys get out of here." Without waiting to see if either of them had anything else to say, he stood up, then quickly and efficiently made his way to the Coast Guard boat. Once back aboard, he suggested that Evan do two things, get his engine started, and hold on to the real gold he recovered from the seafloor as the authorities will be wanting to know about that. Then he directed the man at the stern to release the aft line from the Grady-White. Nearly simultaneously, the Lieutenant released the forward line and Evan and Deena began immediately to slip to the south away from the other boat.

As they watched the Coast Guard boat, it moved north and closer to the east bridge towers. With the Grady-White's outboard now idling smoothly, Evan shifted to Forward and brought the throttle up while turning to a bearing of three hundred degrees NNW toward Gig Harbor. Deena sat next to Evan on the two person helm chair, but was quiet and withdrawn as they started back to Charley's Boat & Watercraft

Rentals. Evan could see she was distraught, and considering her last few days, that was understandable. He did not push for conversation and instead piloted the boat in silence.

Chapter 40

Standing next to the small marina at the back of Charley's rental shop, Michael and Katie had provided Charley a summary of what happened that included almost nothing of what actually happened. The damage to the Grady-White was mostly below the waterline, but the large gash along the forward starboard section of the boat provided the evidence of a collision. Upon further inspection, Charley also found that when he tilted the outboard up and out of the water, it was clear that the drive had taken a solid impact. After Charley was satisfied that he'd inspected and noted all damage, he stepped back on to the dock. While shaking his head slowly back and forth in a sideways direction, he said, "I would have thought the chart plotter would have kept you out of trouble. Some pretty good damage to the boat is visible, and I suspect there's more on the lower hull aft of that forward scrape. Nothing that can't be fixed with the insurance money though, but it's going to be a pain in the ass. I'm just glad you guys are OK, and that's the main thing."

"We appreciate that," Katie said, and added, "we're so sorry for messing up and hitting the rocks."

Charley continued his oracle and said, "The waters can be treacherous around here if you're not knowing the tides and shorelines. Many a ship and small craft have gone down just outside the entrance to Gig Harbor over there. That's even with the lighthouse throwing that beam of light out as a warning."

At the mention of ships going down, Michael and Katie shared a secret look, and Michael added to Charley's tale with, "Yes, we're aware that many ships have wrecked and sunk in the Sound. We feel fortunate that you charter the Grady-White brand of boat. A lesser boat may not have survived without taking on water."

Nodding his head in agreement, Charley said, "Well, I feel good about that too. You wrecked my dang boat though, and fixing it is going to take some effort!"

In the distance to the east, a boat was making its way into the harbor and slowing down slightly to reduce the impact of the its wake on the shoreline. Evan and Deena were now just minutes from Charley's and Deena finally decided to speak. Without looking at Evan, she said, "When I met you just five days ago, I could never have imagined everything that has happened since. I don't know about you, but for me, the last five days have been crazy."

"They've been crazy days for me, too," Evan agreed.

Almost as if she didn't hear him, Deena continued talking and said, "I enjoyed spending time with you at the car show and the dive trip was exciting, but after that, things turned really bad."

Evan didn't care too much for the sound of what Deena was saying, and her solemn tone had a sense of foreboding. Plus the chilly vibe she was giving off could not be missed and when she opened her mouth again, her words just confirmed what Evan was sensing. "Evan," she said, "my career may well be over since this will surely be a scandalous topic at HG Enterprises." After a long pause, she added, "I don't know what my future holds, but I've decided that it can't include you."

Expecting to hear something like, "maybe we should slow down", or "I hardly know you", Evan was taken back by the pronouncement that Deena was simply terminating the budding relationship. Looking at her now, with her hair in tangles, smeared makeup and a nasty bruise on the side of her face, he still found that she was a beautiful woman. The scowl on her face presented an odd contrast to that and Evan reflected on the juxtaposition for a moment.

Not really knowing what to say, he nodded his head in acceptance and said, "This experience has clearly left you worse off than when it started. I can only apologize for my part in the craziness and hope that the damage done can be repaired."

"Thank you," was the last thing that Deena said until they arrived at the marina and had tied up at the dock. Once tied up, Deena was quick to make ready to exit the boat, and having just the clothes on her back and the light jacket she had gotten from Michael, it didn't take long. Slipping the dark blue jacket with the Seattle Mariners logo embroidered on the back off her shoulders, she let it drop off her arms and caught it with her right hand. She folded it neatly and laid it over the back of the helm chair. "Would you please see that Michael gets this jacket back, I would appreciate it," Deena asked and instructed all in the same sentence.

"Of course," Evan replied.

For the first time since they had started out from the Tacoma Narrows, Deena allowed herself to look directly at Evan and into his eyes. What Evan saw in Deena's eyes was a woman lost in her emotions. In the first instant, he saw the Deena he recalled meeting at the car show in Port Townsend five days ago that was working hard to try and be carefree. An instant later, her look had hardened and she seemed to look right through him. Finally settling on a look of indifference, Deena put her right hand on top on Evan's left hand and said, "I'm sorry it has to be like this, I really am. I do have a favor to ask of you though." Without waiting for Evan to accept or reject the request, she continued with, "I'd like to use your phone to call a friend to pick me up."

Evan reached into the cubby at the helm and grabbed his phone. He quickly unlocked it and pulled up the phone app for her to use. After he handed it to her, she said, "thank you," and stood up and stepped over the gunwale and on to the dock. Without looking back, she started a call and walked slowly in the direction of Charley, Michael and Katie.

Evan watched Deena move away, and he wished things had gone differently. He really felt terrible that her life had gotten turned upside down and hoped that she was going to be OK. Maybe in some way he would be able to help her down the road, and he would sure like to know how she's doing after returning to work. Unfortunately, it seemed pretty clear to Evan that she was opting to move on without his help, and there was very little he could do about that right now.

From his vantage point of three slips away, Evan saw Deena talking in an animated fashion, but was unable to hear anything she said. When Deena's hands slowed down and her arms dropped to her sides, he saw Katie lean in and give her a hug. Michael did the same after Katie and then Deena appeared to shake Michael's hand. When Michael dropped his hand into the right front pocket of his jeans, Evan suspected Deena had returned his phone. As Evan watched the scene unfold, Deena reached up with her left hand and tossed her hair back while turning her head slightly to the left. Her gaze fell upon Evan, and when she realized he was watching her, she quickly dropped her hand and let her hair fall to block the view. He heard the words, "good-bye" used a few times and then Deena moved away, walked briskly up the dock ramp and was soon out of sight.

Still in his wetsuit and with no breeze to speak of, Evan was starting to overheat, so the first thing he needed to do was get back into his clothes. He peeled off the neoprene suit, dried quickly with a towel and was back in jeans and a T-shirt before Michael arrived at the side of his boat. He was sporting a sad looking face, which Evan took to mean that Deena had told them about her decision to move on. Thankfully, Michael did not bring it up and instead said, "Charley's not too happy with the damage to our boat, and not sure how he'll respond when he sees yours with the busted windscreen."

Evan didn't miss a beat and with a wry smile replied, "Guess I should have been more careful swinging the boat hook around."

Michael showed a small smile himself and nodded his head in agreement. Behind Michael, Evan could see Katie and Charley coming his way and he prepared to explain the damage to the boat. He noticed that Charley no longer looked to be the kindly old man he had met earlier today, but had a hard edge to his appearance. Before Evan had the chance to speak, Charley noticed the shattered windscreen and let the expletives fly. Evan did not stop him, but let him vent his frustration and then said, "Sorry for the damage Charley. I hit the windscreen with the boat hook and it shattered. All my fault."

"Damn right it is!" Charley practically yelled. Then he pulled out his notebook and began scribbling more notes without saying anything else. Once finished, he looked sternly at Evan and said, "I've got your address, I'll send you a bill for your portion of this mess." Charley then turned on his heels and headed back to his building, leaving Evan, Michael and Katie alone on the dock. The three of them looked at each other and let out a collective sigh of relief. Then Evan gathered his gear and set it on the dock next to the boat while Michael headed to the parking lot to bring the van closer for loading. Katie took the opportunity while alone with Evan to express her feelings about Deena leaving so abruptly and hoped that both Deena and Evan would be OK. Evan indicated that he would be fine and was more concerned about Deena and how she would recover from the recent adventure and trauma. Katie agreed that Deena had had the toughest time of it and then nothing more was said about it.

With the van now parked at the top of the ramp to the floating dock, Evan exited the boat, grabbed his gear bag and hauled it toward the van. Michael had been loading his gear and when Evan arrived, he loaded Evan's bag in the back of the van as well. Then both men headed back to the boat Michael had been using to retrieve Evan's Diver Propulsion Vehicle. Once all the equipment and gear was loaded in the van, Michael jumped in the driver's seat, Katie took the passenger seat, and Evan settled into the passenger side Captain's chair in the second row of seats. Michael started the van, shifted into Drive and slowly navigated around the building and through the small parking lot to the road that follows the shoreline around Gig Harbor. He stopped briefly to check for traffic and then turning left onto Harborview Drive, smoothly accelerated away from the scene of one of the strangest experiences of his life.

Chapter 41

Early Saturday morning, Evan was already up and out of bed and getting prepared to attend to some work for Dungeness Technologies when his mobile phone rang. He didn't recognize the displayed number, and was a little annoyed by the early time of the call, but decided to answer it anyway. He was surprised by a deep male voice getting right to the matter of yesterday's incident at the Tacoma Narrows Bridge. Before saying too much though, the caller wanted to verify who they were talking to and asked, "Whom am I speaking with please?"

Evan replied with, "This is Evan Mason," but asked his own question with, "and who are you?"

The caller immediately responded with, "My name is Patrick Tuttle, Sargent Tuttle actually, Intelligence Specialist with the U.S. Coast Guard."

That got Evan's attention and his demeanor became serious. The caller continued, "I've been briefed on the incident at the Tacoma Narrows Bridge yesterday and I am following up. In particular, I'm interested in the gold that was reported as being recovered from the bottom."

"That is apparently what got everything started, and I do still have it all. Total weight is roughly two pounds I would say and it appears to be gold nuggets in their unrefined form." Evan provided.

"That's quite a find Mr. Mason, and I understand it was all found together. Might I ask what you plan to do with it?" Sargent Tuttle inquired.

Evan had already formed a basic plan of action and told the Sargent as much, "I first plan to declare the find and claim any salvage rights to the site. I happen to have a contact at MOHAI in Seattle and so I plan to let them have a look at it. I'm hoping that they'll be able to provide some help about what else might be down there."

The Sargent had some advice and offered it, "That sounds like a reasonable way to proceed. Just be sure to declare everything that you've found and provide complete descriptions."

Evan thought about the log book that had so far not been mentioned at all during the whole time of Deena's kidnapping and subsequent rescue. Realizing he would be better off going the route of full disclosure with the treasure he had retrieved from the cold dark waters of Puget Sound, he mentioned the log book find to Sargent Tuttle.

"I had not heard that there was a log book recovered," the Sargent said with a slight bit of questioning in his voice. "I'm glad to know that such a valuable piece of history has been found, and I hope that the content is at least partially legible."

"So do I Sargent, so do I. It was not an easy piece to bring to the surface and the tale of the recovery is almost unbelievable. I don't think I'd believe it if I hadn't actually lived it," Evan said with some melancholy in his voice as he reflected back on the last two weeks.

Ending the call with the Coast Guard Sargent, Evan leaned back in his comfortable office chair and imagined what else might be down at the bottom of the Tacoma Narrows Strait. With a ship's log book uncovered, surely there's a ship that goes with it somewhere. Some far away alarm bells started going off in Evan's head when he thought about the possibilities of another encounter with the Giant Pacific Octopus, but he held tightly to the imaginary adventure. In his mind's eye he visualized himself safely recovering more treasure from the past and bringing it to light in the present.

Epilogue

There was only one survivor of the 1791 shipwreck of the Spanish Treasure Frigate Bonita Joya. When Harry Garcia had flipped over the rail, the fact the he was clear of the ship when it went under had saved his life, temporarily. He had drifted quickly south with the current and with very little strength left from the bone chilling water and struggling to stay afloat with his clothes weighing him down, he had fought his way east toward the closest shoreline. Nearly dead from the ordeal and coughing up seawater, Harry had managed to find piles of leaves all around him and used them to help dry himself off and considered that the leaves might provide some means of protection for the night that was coming fast. He knew his death was just hours away in the unknown land, but stumbled through the underbrush of the forest around him anyway. After collapsing near a river running toward the body of water he had just climbed out of, Harry welcomed the break from the grueling hike along the river bank. Finally succumbing to exhaustion and the cold, he laid his head back and closed his eyes. The darkness of the night was now upon him and he retreated as best he could into the hollow of an old tree trunk. There, he anticipated that the night's sleep might very well be his last.

Harry did not dream or die that night, but thought he might die when he opened his eyes in the morning and gazed upon four strange looking people. He had heard stories of the natives of the New World, and was fearful of actually running into them. Now it would seem that Harry needed help and he was possibly going to get it from them, or be dead as he had expected last night. Unable to really move with his stiff joints and with his muscles aching, Harry simply closed his eyes and let his head drop back down on the small pile of leaves he had fashioned into a pillow of sorts. The natives then engaged in an animated discussion amongst themselves using a language Harry did not understand. When they finished with the discussion, they turned on their heels and walked away from him, disappearing almost silently through the forest's edge.

Wondering what had just happened, Harry didn't know if he should be glad or sad that he was alone. That thought was interrupted by the sound of the forest opening up and the four natives walking through, each leading an impressive looking horse. Harry must have look bewildered as they attempted to communicate with him. Apparently frustrated with the situation, the native who appeared to be in charge advanced toward the horse he had been leading and with a quick jumping move, was atop the horse. He spoke some words and gestured in Harry's direction. Seconds later, Harry was lifted from the ground and carried to the mounted native's horse. He was unceremoniously lifted higher and positioned in front of the native with each leg astride of the horse. The native behind him reached down and grabbed the horse's mane and tugged a few times. He released the horse's mane and looked at Harry and nodded. Given the circumstances, Harry understood he was going for a ride and he better hold on. He grabbed the horse's mane as he was apparently instructed to do and with a slight kick by the native, the horse stepped forward and they traveled the edge of the river deeper into the forest with the other three natives falling in behind.

Harry had survived the shipwreck was able to integrate with the natives that had taken him in. He knew of the gold deposit at what is today the mouth of the Nisqually River, and he prospected and mined the gold in and around Puget Sound for almost sixty years before he died. Over those years, Harry had created a family owned business that was well managed and successfully survived his death. Shortly after Harry's death, a new company was formed and in honor of Harry, was founded as "HG Enterprises".

As for Davis Garcia, his interest in Deena's story about her first dive with Evan was based on his knowledge of a rumor, or more aptly a legend, about the origins of HG Enterprises. The legend involved the founder of the company years before the official incorporation date of 1848. The founder had supposedly come to America as a young man some two hundred years ago and a shipwreck in south Puget Sound had left him stranded in a strange land. The story hinted that the ship had carried gold that had simply been plucked from the shoreline by the ship's crew. Davis had been aware that the rivers emptying into Puget Sound had contained gold in the past, so there was some viability to the tale. After hearing Deena's story of a possible shipwreck in the Tacoma Narrows Strait with gold involved, Davis had taking up the hunt for treasure. In the end, his uncontrollable greed drove him to the bizarre behavior that ultimately cost him his life.

Visit www.jamesmaureen.com for more information about the author and for a sneak peek at upcoming books in the Evan Mason Adventure series.

Book 1 At Water's End   (2019)

Book 2 Beyond the Deep   (2020)

Book 3 The Gray Ghost   (2021)

Made in the USA
San Bernardino,
CA